THE WOMAN ON PLATFORM 8

M. A. HUNTER

B
Boldwood

First published in Great Britain in 2025 by Boldwood Books Ltd.

Copyright © M. A. Hunter, 2025

Cover Design by Lisa Horton

Cover Photography: Shutterstock and Alamy

The moral right of M. A. Hunter to be identified as the author of this work has been asserted in accordance with the Copyright, Designs and Patents Act 1988.

All rights reserved. No part of this book may be reproduced in any form or by any electronic or mechanical means, including information storage and retrieval systems, without written permission from the author, except for the use of brief quotations in a book review. This book is a work of fiction and, except in the case of historical fact, any resemblance to actual persons, living or dead, is purely coincidental.

Every effort has been made to obtain the necessary permissions with reference to copyright material, both illustrative and quoted. We apologise for any omissions in this respect and will be pleased to make the appropriate acknowledgements in any future edition.

A CIP catalogue record for this book is available from the British Library.

Paperback ISBN 978-1-83561-732-8

Large Print ISBN 978-1-83561-731-1

Hardback ISBN 978-1-83561-730-4

Ebook ISBN 978-1-83561-733-5

Kindle ISBN 978-1-83561-734-2

Audio CD ISBN 978-1-83561-725-0

MP3 CD ISBN 978-1-83561-726-7

Digital audio download ISBN 978-1-83561-727-4

This book is printed on certified sustainable paper. Boldwood Books is dedicated to putting sustainability at the heart of our business. For more information please visit https://www.boldwoodbooks.com/about-us/sustainability/

Boldwood Books Ltd, 23 Bowerdean Street, London, SW6 3TN

www.boldwoodbooks.com

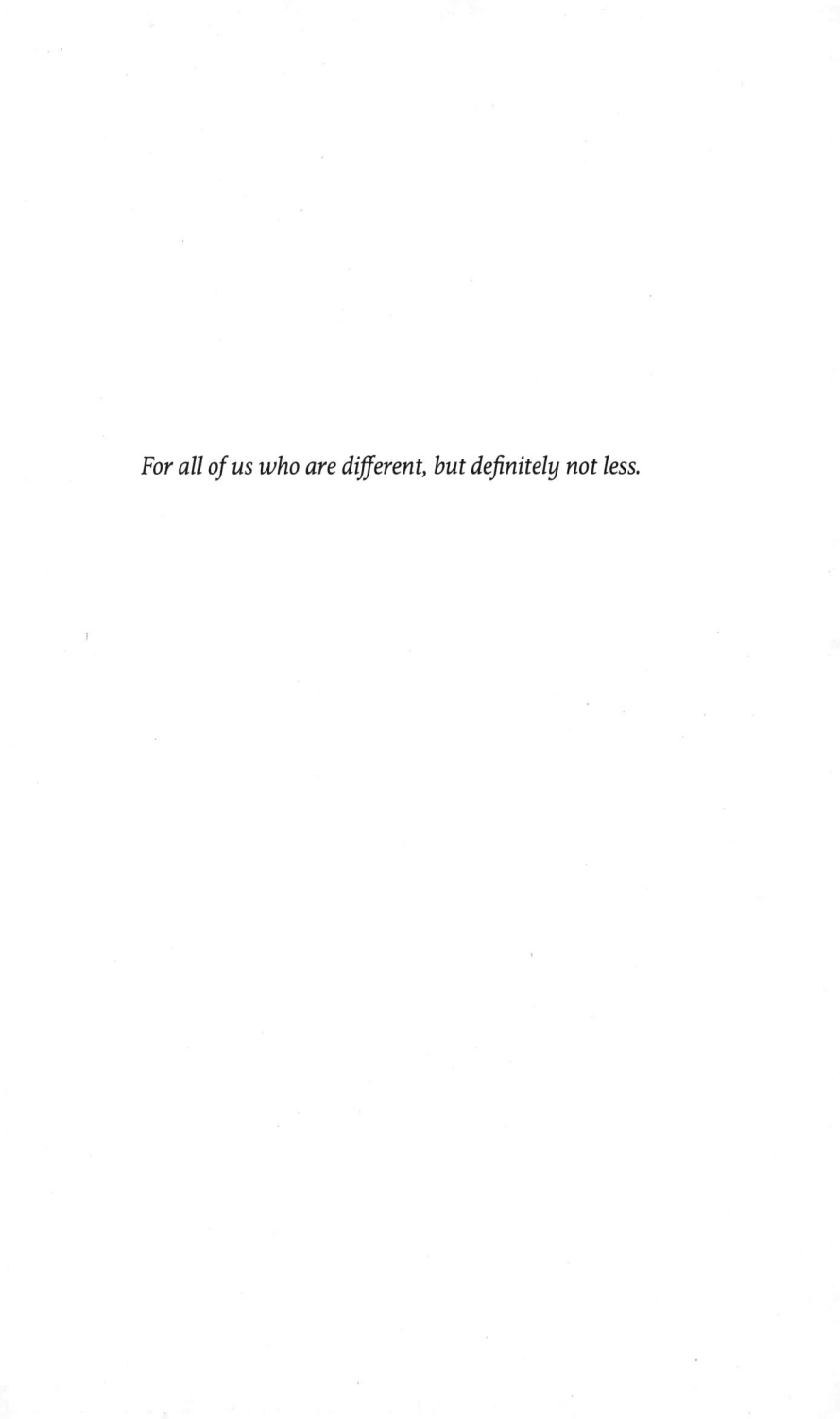

For all of us who are different, but definitely not less.

AUTHOR'S NOTE

Before you start reading *The Woman on Platform 8*, I want you to know that the story features an openly autistic character in Jenna Morgan. This was a conscious choice, and not just some effort to be on trend or because I think it will help boost book sales. It is because there are not enough openly autistic characters accurately portrayed in literature at present, and I not only want to raise awareness of divergent neurotypes, but also to encourage acceptance.

I was diagnosed as autistic in December 2023 and with ADHD in December 2024, and for me, it has been and is still a lot to come to terms with.

There are so many stereotypes of how autistic individuals look and behave, but there is no one way for an autistic character to be written, and so I want you to understand that how Jenna reacts to certain situations and describes her challenges are unique to her. She may not mirror your own experiences of autism (whether you yourself are autistic or you know/care for an autistic individual). And that's okay. She is a character unlike any

I have written before, and I hope you will accept her for who she is, and see the world through her eyes.

1

When did life become so bloody predictable? I remember a time when I actually believed I would spend my days making a positive difference to those around me. Naivety or simple ignorance? I'm no longer sure which to believe.

As the train doors whoosh closed and the carriage begins to shake again, I can't help but wallow in all the compromises I've made along the way and all the missed opportunities I failed to take because I didn't believe I could achieve them. I can't blame it on the cards I was dealt; I'm in this rut because I didn't play them tactically enough. I could blame my parents' separation and my mum's poor mental health, but none of that stopped me graduating college and securing admission to university. None of that stopped me falling in love with a man who excited me, and with whom I felt confident about starting a family of my own; one which I vowed would be stronger than the one I emerged from.

And who am I to complain? A loving marriage, two children, a job I'm good at, and a home – albeit mortgaged to the hilt – of our own. Compared to many, I am incredibly lucky. But at what cost has all of this come? Will my children remember all the privileges my long hours have afforded them, or will they simply recall how Mummy was never there when they woke in the morning? Will they only remember the nights when Daddy put them to bed because Mummy hadn't made it home in time? These are the thoughts that trouble me whenever I have to make this journey from Southampton to London. And the morning from hell certainly isn't helping my state of mind.

It's always the same when I know I need to wake up by a set time. I might as well not bother setting an alarm. As usual, my body clock had me awake almost an hour before the alarm was supposed to do the job. And as per every previous occasion, I then spent the next thirty minutes tossing and turning and trying to drift back off, before eventually caving and dragging myself from the comfort of the duvet and into the shower. But for some reason the hot water hadn't engaged and so I had to make do with a spray slightly warmer than freezing.

Then, when I was dressed and trying to fix some toast, I found the breadbin empty. Brett is responsible for keeping the fridge and cupboards stocked, but had failed on this occasion, so I had to make do with a bowl of the children's overly sweet cereal. Struggling to remain composed, I was already close to breaking point when I realised I'd forgotten to fill the car up after our weekend away. I didn't need a trip to the petrol station, and just about made it to the train station car park before the emergency light flashed on. At least that will serve as a reminder to fill up when I get back tonight. And hopefully Brett will have baked a loaf by the time I'm back.

I know the reason that everything has felt out of kilter this morning: I know that I really don't want to be going into the office today. Marcus has made no secret of how much the company is struggling, and that cuts need to be made if we're to keep everything in the black by tax year end. This morning is the deadline

The Woman on Platform 8

for providing him with the name of someone to make redundant. Despite my desperate pleas that we should be expanding, rather than cutting, he's said the choice is culling one now or two in the summer. But how does he expect me to offer the name of someone from my team? It's like he's asking me to choose my favourite child; something no parent could ever do. I had hoped he'd change his mind when he saw all the great work we'd been completing, but he's so obsessed by the upcoming audit that the quality of our output seems irrelevant to him now. It wasn't always that way. But I know he's right, and we have struggled to secure clients since the pandemic. Even with our hybrid operating model, costs remain high and income not high enough to match it.

I close my eyes and try to push these anxieties from my mind; I know fretting about such matters won't alleviate them. I will end up wasting so much energy on the worry that I'll have less to find a genuine solution to the problems.

The conductor announces our arrival at Winchester over the loudspeaker and that we'll be stationary for five minutes due to a signalling fault.

My eyes fall on the man sitting diagonally opposite me at the table across the carriage. He must be about my age, maybe a fraction older, considering the splashes of silver emerging above his ears. Like many of the others crammed in around me, I recognise him from the previous times I've made this journey. As usual he's wearing a suit jacket, trousers and a shirt. He never wears a tie, choosing to leave the top two buttons of his shirt unfastened. His laptop is open on the table before him as usual, and whatever he's doing, his eyes remain glued to the screen. He always opts to sit at a table and the speed with which his fingers navigate the keyboard leads me to wonder whether he may be a writer of some sort, or possibly a programmer. His glasses frequently slip down his nose, and he pushes them up with his thumb yet again, and looks over, maybe sensing that I'm watching him, so I quickly look away, willing the heat not to rush to my cheeks. He never seems to speak to any of the other passengers, but then neither do I.

I much prefer to imagine what their lives are like than to actually try and strike up a conversation. Small talk has never been a strength of mine, and I always panic I'll say the wrong thing or overshare, as I was warned about so many times growing up.

'Just act and speak like the others and you'll be fine,' my mum used to regularly say.

She never wanted to listen when I tried to share how much I was struggling to fit in at school. Her answer was always to tell me just to try harder. She never realised how I tried so hard that I ended up burning myself out. Things came to a head while I was at university, where a psychiatrist diagnosed my neurodivergence, and then so many things just made sense. He'll never know but he saved my life and helped me to realise that there was a reason I was struggling to pick up on so many social cues. I adapted and pursued my special interest in art, which is what led to my career as a graphic designer.

And that's the worst part about my situation, and why I spend countless hours reviewing where it all went so wrong: I love my job. I mean, I really love my job. How many people can say that? I love receiving a new project, with clear guidance on what the client is hoping to achieve, and then having the creative freedom to deliver that vision. I don't always get it right at the first attempt, but that's the fun of creative design. I wouldn't swap my job for anything, despite the unsociable hours required when the office moved from down the road in Southampton to a smaller building a short tube ride from London Waterloo station. Marcus thought we were missing out on too much business by not having a presence in the capital, but I'd argue we now have fewer clients as a result. I know there are other graphical design companies out there, but I am terrified about starting again.

One of the challenges of my autism is I struggle with interviews, never knowing exactly what the interviewer is trying to discover about me. Even if I wanted to leave Marcus and my team, there are too many unknowns about finding a job elsewhere. I've tried to explain it to Brett, but despite his best efforts, he doesn't understand why it's so much more difficult for me than him.

Being married to a bestselling debut author comes with challenges of its own, but I love my husband's creative force. I remember reading the first draft of his novel and being moved to tears by the ending. He deserves every plaudit that has come his way, and I am so proud of all he has achieved. And when he finally finishes his follow-up, maybe we'll be able to talk about making some changes to our future before it's too late.

I shouldn't complain about Brett's lack of progress with the new book. He's six months behind the delivery date, but he tells me his agent and publisher understand this is because he's had so much promotion to undertake for the first book. Signings in bookshops, appearances on podcasts, and the like. Plus, he manages the home, making sure the kids are taken to and collected from school, that we're all fed and watered and that the house doesn't resemble a bombsite despite the presence of a seven and nine-year-old. I love that my hard work allows him to flex his creative muscles. And I know he appreciates everything I do, albeit he'd prefer I didn't have so many late meetings with clients and my team.

The conductor warns all passengers to mind the closing doors, but just as the one at the end of the carriage is beginning to whoosh, a woman flies in through it, crashing into the glass pane of the opposite door. She is doubled over and panting, and as she begins to straighten, I recognise the blonde hair and slim figure. I first saw her on Platform 8 of London Waterloo station a few weeks ago. She is effortlessly pretty. In my head, her name is Lucia, and she's a glamorous model from Milan who now lives in Winchester and commutes to London where she owns every catwalk she walks down. She takes lunches with publicists and movie stars, quaffing champagne, and never having to pay for a thing. She's probably running late this morning as she's just dragged herself from the bed of some gorgeous hunk who put her pleasure above his own.

But as I continue to watch her, I see something isn't right. She's wearing a pencil skirt and matching jacket, but her blouse is only partially tucked in, and she appears to be visibly shaking. Is she crying? No, I don't think that's it, but this is not the cool and confident woman I'm used to seeing riding from here to London Waterloo.

She straightens, and looks around, but although our eyes meet it's only for the briefest of seconds, as her gaze continues to wander the carriage as if she's looking for someone. And I can't say why, but I am certain that glassy look in her eyes, and the way her lips hang slightly open, mean she is terrified.

Nobody else on the carriage appears to have noticed how distraught she is, and against my better judgement, I stand as the train begins to move forward, the carriage shaking and almost sending me back into my seat. I grip the headrest of the seat in front of me to steady myself, before moving one foot in front of the next.

'Is everything okay?' I ask when I make it to the end of the carriage.

Her eyes snap to mine, and it's only now that I see how pale she looks. She's wearing eyeliner, but her usually glossed lips are

The Woman on Platform 8

bare. Her eyes widen as she seems to recognise my face, and I attempt to smile to show her I just want to help.

I take her arm and lead her to the vacant priority seats near to us, and I put her in the seat by the window, sitting beside her. Her hands are trembling, and she looks as though she is in shock. Maybe I should alert the conductor, in case she's having a medical emergency. Could she be diabetic and suffering with low blood sugar? Or maybe this is a full-blown anxiety attack?

I look around me, wondering if any of the two dozen passengers around us might be a medical professional who can help, but then my eyes fall back on this terrified woman, and I see...

Wait, is that blood on her neck?

2

The speck of red disappears behind the mop of shoulder-length blonde curls as her head snaps around, and her watering eyes stare into my own. Instinctively, I know I won't leave this woman until I've helped her.

'My name is Jenna,' I say, maintaining eye contact, and offering what I hope is a reassuring smile.

I can't tell if she registers the name, as her face remains taut with anxiety. Up close, I can now see traces of lip gloss smeared at the corners of her mouth, as if she was previously wearing it, but somehow it has been violently wiped away. I continue to study her appearance, searching for clues as to what has happened to her this morning. I catch sight of the blood streak on her neck again, as she buries her face in her hands, but this time it looks like a scratch of some kind. It vanishes again beneath the hair, and when I hear her crying, each sob feels like a stab to my own heart as I sit here, uncertain what to do for the best.

An idea strikes between my eyes, and I rub at her shoulder, leaning in closer so she'll be able to hear me.

'I'm just going to go and collect my bag from the other seat. Okay? You wait here, and I'll be back in seconds.'

Again, it isn't clear whether she's heard me, but I stand and shuffle back along the carriage as the conductor's voice announces our next stop will be Basingstoke. There is now a man sitting in the aisle seat, my laptop bag and handbag lounging beside him. He is wearing a large set of noise-cancelling headphones, and his eyes are closed, but I'm going to have to wake him to get at my stuff. I gently press a hand against the forearm hidden beneath the black leather jacket, and he starts awake.

'I just need to collect my things,' I half-mouth, pointing at the two bags.

He gives me a curious look, but doesn't object as I lean across him and grab at the handles. But I feel his hot, arid breath on my neck as I do, and my skin crawls at the sensation. And that's when my mind connects the dots. The terror in the young woman's eyes, her inability to communicate whatever has happened, the smudged makeup, and the scratch on her neck: she's been attacked.

I straighten and hurry back to her just as the train arrives at the station and I see the platform beyond the window. I squat back in beside her before any newly arrived passengers pinch the seat. The train is fairly busy today, and will only get busier as we reach the next stop of Winchester. Nobody else appears to have heard the woman's gentle sobs, or if they have, they've chosen not to check on her welfare.

Opening my handbag, I rummage inside, pulling out the small bottle of juice and croissant I'd bought before boarding the train. It is supposed to be my midmorning treat for getting through the meeting with Marcus later, but this woman is in greater need. I open the bottle and wave it under her eyes.

'Something sweet is good for shock,' I say, wishing it was something stronger.

There's no beverage carriage on this train, and on some days it's standing room only, so my options are limited.

'Drink it,' I encourage, and she accepts the bottle, taking a sip.

Her cheeks are so pale, and I really don't know how to broach the subject of whether she was attacked on her journey to the station this morning.

'What's your name?' I try, hoping to establish a rapport first, though small talk remains a challenge.

'Allie Davis,' she replies, so quietly that I'm not sure if I've heard correctly at first.

'Allie? I'm Jenna.'

I offer a handshake, but quickly realise it's not appropriate and lower my hand. Picking up on social cues has never been easy, and I've never had to face a situation like this before. My natural response to stressful settings is to stim or get away from the overstimulation, and it's taking all my willpower to remain where I am.

'I'm a graphic designer,' I say, hoping that if I can at least get her talking, it will make her feel safer to open up and tell me what's happened. Once I know that, I'll be better placed to know how I can help her, or who I should put her in touch with.

She doesn't respond to tell me her profession, so I try again.

'And I live in Southampton, well, actually our house is in Rownhams, which officially is outside of the city boundaries, but I'm a Southampton girl, and because most people don't know where Rownhams is, I always say we live in Southampton.' I'm aware I'm waffling, but now that I've started it's difficult to stop. 'We is me, my husband Brett and our two children. Luke is our eldest, and he's nine, and then there's Caley and she's seven. Would you like to see a picture?'

I stop myself as my hand reaches for my mobile phone. I wish there was some kind of manual to explain what I should be doing in this situation. I open the bag containing the croissant instead, and break it into two, offering half to Allie. She takes it in her left hand, the open bottle of juice still in her right, but makes no effort to put either to her mouth. At least she's stopped crying now.

I break a piece of the croissant from the remaining half, and push the pastry between my lips, hoping she'll follow my lead and copy, but she doesn't.

'You live in Winchester, don't you?' I try again, keeping my voice upbeat as the train pulls away from the station. 'I've seen you on this train before. I always assumed you were a catwalk model.' I add a half-hearted chuckle at this, but can feel my cheeks blazing with embarrassment.

If she has been mugged or worse this morning, trying to get her to open up is key, but if the shoe was on the other foot, would I really want to reveal such a secret to a perfect stranger? I would want to rush home to Brett and have him hold me and tell me everything is going to be okay.

'Are you married?' The question is out of my mouth before I can stop it.

'No.'

The tension in my shoulders eases fractionally as she answers.

'And you live in Winchester?'

'Yes.'

This is definitely progress, and her monosyllabic answers are giving me encouragement to continue.

'And you work in London?'

'Yes.'

'Are you a catwalk model?'

'No.'

'Well, you certainly could be. You're very pretty.'

Oh no, what if she now thinks I'm trying to come on to her?

'I'm not gay,' I say quickly, in an effort to correct myself. 'I just meant, you have a pretty face and a figure I'd kill for.'

I add a passive smile, but I can visualise the hole I'm digging.

It's a relief when she bites into the croissant, and I break off a second chunk and place it between my lips, but it is drying out my mouth, and making me thirsty. If she isn't going to drink that orange juice, then I wish she'd hand it back.

'I went to university in Southampton,' I continue, realising that I'm oversharing with this poor woman – info-dumping is what Brett calls it – and it's something I do when I haven't had the chance to pre-script a conversation. I don't know if she can tell I'm trying to wing it.

'That's where I met Brett. At university, I mean. He was studying English Literature, and I was sure all the girls on my course fancied him. I used to watch him whenever I was at the Student Union bar. He always seemed to have at least one girl beside him, hanging on his every word. Out of my league, I was certain, so of course I never approached him. My autism is not the superpower some claim it to be. It can make talking to strangers more than a little complicated. But then he approached me at a party.'

I can visually see the moment he walked over and asked me if I'd like to dance. It was at the university's end-of-year ball. I'd only gone along because I was being presented with an award as part of the evening's celebrations. It was so loud inside the dance hall that I spent most of the night propped up against the bar, resembling an alcoholic, even though I was on orange juice all night.

'He asked me if I wanted to dance,' I tell Allie now, enjoying the fondness of the memory, and the butterflies in my stomach as if I'm experiencing that moment for the first time. 'I told him that I didn't like the noise, and he told me he had a better idea. I couldn't understand why he took my hand and led me out into the cool night air. I momentarily panicked that he had ill intentions and that I should notify someone that I was with him, but he stopped just outside the door, placing his tuxedo jacket over my bare shoulders, and then he took my hands and we danced to the quiet echo of the music beyond the windows behind us.'

I stop narrating as I get lost in the feelings of that memory. It felt like a dream that I didn't want to wake from. He told me he'd wanted to speak to me all year, but had assumed I wouldn't be interested in a writer. He'd felt more confident after a few drinks, and although he didn't attempt to kiss me that night, we did exchange numbers and went out together several times over the summer months between the second and third years.

I look down and see that Allie has finished her croissant, and has consumed half the orange juice. Despite my best efforts, I know I'm not the right person to help her. I have no way of finding the words to ask her about what may have transpired this morning, and the best thing I can probably do is take her to the train guard, and ask him to take over. I should be thinking about what I'm going to say to Marcus when he asks me about redundancies later.

'Thank you,' Allie says, and again I offer what I hope she sees as a reassuring smile.

'You're very welcome. I feel as though something bad may have happened to you this morning. Am I right?'

She looks at me for what feels like an age, as if trying to determine whether she can trust me or not, before eventually nodding.

'Would you like me to help you find the train guard so you can report... whatever it is?'

She slowly shakes her head, her jaw locking.

'Should I phone the police for you?'

Her eyes widen at the question, and she shakes her head more vehemently. But then her cheeks take on a different hue, and her breathing becomes heavier.

'I think I'm going to be sick,' she says, and I quickly stand, my eyes scanning both ends of the carriage, looking to see if either of the bathrooms are vacant.

'Come on,' I say, 'I'll take you to the toilet.'

But she drags me back down to the seat.

'You don't understand,' she whispers, sweat beading at her hairline.

But it's what she says next that makes my blood run cold.

'I think I killed my boyfriend.'

3

I don't immediately respond, assuming I've misheard, but then I repeat the words in my head.

I think I killed my boyfriend.

I stare at Allie, waiting for her face to break into a grin and reveal the poorly timed joke, but her face is as green as when she said she was going to be sick. I stand and glance back over my shoulder at the accessible toilet, and drag Allie with me, as the train buffets us against the rows of seats.

What am I supposed to do with this new information? She thinks she killed her boyfriend: how; why; when?

So many questions are racing through my mind that it's hard to focus on any single one. Has she told the police yet? If I help her does that mean I'm aiding and abetting a crime after the fact?

I nearly lose my footing, as I try to keep Allie upright, but everyone we pass appears to be either trying to avoid eye contact, or too lost in their phones and laptops. As we're nearing the door to the bathroom, I see a man in a suit about to press the button to enter.

'My friend is going to be sick,' I shout in his direction, and the noise is enough to make him take a step backwards, as I pull Allie into the room with me.

I mouth a thank you to the bewildered man, as I slam my elbow against the close button and then lock the door. I have no idea how soundproof these train bathrooms are, so we'll have to keep our voices down if we don't want to be overheard. I actually think I might be sick now too, so I close my eyes and try to focus on regulating my breathing. Emotional dysregulation is something else I've realised I struggle with, and I curse as I realise my fidget spinner is in my handbag in the seats we just vacated. I was so desperate to get her in here that I didn't even think about collecting our belongings. I should go and get them now, but as I'm about to unlock the door, I feel Allie's ice-cold fingers on my arm.

'I need your help.'

I turn back and catch her sincere and still terrified stare.

'I didn't mean to kill him,' she says, and I have a horrible feeling it's already too late to close this Pandora's box.

'I'm sure you didn't,' I say empathetically, hoping to draw a line under the conversation.

She grabs my hands and forces me down to the closed toilet seat. And it's only now I realise I've locked myself inside this toilet with a woman I don't know from Adam. All those imagined stories of her being a famous model who wined and dined with the glitterati were simply the musings of my imagination, but for some reason I allowed them to influence my decision to approach and offer support to this woman; this killer.

Is it too late for me to scream out? There's a chance that bewildered man is still standing outside the toilet, waiting to use it. If I shouted, would he be able to get help? He wouldn't be able to open the door whilst it's locked, but perhaps he could fetch the guard; that's assuming he hasn't already gone off in search of an alternative toilet.

'He came at me,' Allie says, her eyes darting in both directions as if she's reliving the moment in her head. 'This morning, I mean. Clark was so... so angry. I thought he was going to...'

I need to get a grip. If I can keep her calm, then there's no reason that she should harm me. If I show a little empathy and understanding then she's bound to unlock the door and let me go.

'I'm sure it wasn't your fault,' I say, nauseated by how trite I sound. 'The best thing we can do is contact the police and explain what happened, and then—'

'No,' she interrupts. 'No police. You don't understand.'

I gasp at the venom in her eyes in that moment, but it passes so quickly that I can't be certain I didn't imagine it.

'Okay, okay,' I say, raising both hands, palms out in what I hope is a pacifying manner. 'No police.'

She steps backwards, crashing into the closed door, and blocking any access I have to the unlock button.

'Clark was still asleep when I woke this morning,' she continues, 'and I was getting ready for work, when he came stomping into the kitchen. I've never seen his face so red. He was angry, and began shouting, throwing crockery from the table against the wall. I tried to get him to calm down, but it was like he was a man possessed. You know? There was no getting through to him. When I tried to leave the kitchen, he grabbed hold of my arms, and told me I wasn't going anywhere, and then he shoved me hard, backwards into the wall. He's not a violent man – at least, he's never been violent before – but as I say there was something different about him this morning.

'He closed the kitchen door, and told me he wasn't going to let me go. I was so scared that I don't think I was in control of what happened next. I tried to leave again, but this time, he put his hand around my neck, and forced me back against the wall again. I tried clawing at his hand, but nothing I did seemed to make a difference. I thought he was going to kill me there and then. His grip was so tight that I couldn't scream for help, and in desperation I lashed out. I think I caught him in the groin with my knee, and he let go. I tried to scramble away, but he grabbed my hair and dragged me to the floor, sitting across me, a knee either side so I was trapped.'

She is visibly shaking as she recounts her story, and I'm visualising every moment, even though I have no idea what her antagonist looks like. I know Brett would never hurt a hair on my head, and I've never been subjected to an abusive partner, but I've read stories; who hasn't? All my paranoid delusions about her vanish in an instant, and I find myself standing, and embracing her, gently stroking the back of her head, as I would do with my own children when they're scared or upset.

'There, there,' I say quietly, holding tight, even when she tries to break free of my hold.

'He kept saying he couldn't let me go,' she says, crying into my shoulder. 'And I was so scared that my hands scrabbled around for anything I might use to defend myself. My fingers brushed against something smooth and hard, and suddenly I was bringing the frying pan crashing into the side of his head. He toppled off me, and I wriggled until I could get to my feet, but he grabbed at my leg, and I hit him with the frying pan again, this time on the back of his head, and he dropped to the floor. I hurried out of the kitchen, but the front door was locked, so I had to go back into the house to find my keys. I grabbed my bag, but as I was passing the kitchen door again, he lurched out, and tried to grab at my neck again. I kicked out as hard as I could, and he dropped to his knees, and this time I used both hands to crack the pan over the back of his head. He fell unconscious to the floor, and this pool of blood started spreading out across the carpet behind his head. I think I cracked his skull.'

'But you got free, and that's the main thing,' I offer encouragingly. 'It sounds like he put you through an awful ordeal, and you did the right thing to fight back.'

I let go of her head, and look into her eyes.

'And from what you've told me, there's every chance you haven't killed him. Injured, yes, so the best thing we can do right now is phone the police and explain what happened.'

She opens her mouth to interrupt, but I talk over her.

'They can fetch an ambulance to deal with his injuries. No woman should ever have to deal with someone like that, and I'm happy to stay with you until the police arrive.'

She shakes her head at me.

'No, you don't understand. I know he's dead because I checked his pulse, and there was nothing there. I didn't know what to do, so I ran from my flat and ended up here. If we tell the police I fled the scene, they're going to say I killed him on purpose.'

'No, I'm sure that won't happen, Allie. I've listened to your story, and I don't think you've done anything wrong. You were terrified – as well you should have been. Your flight response kicked in, but you need to do the right thing here. I think you should get off the train at Basingstoke and catch a taxi back to your flat in Winchester. You can call the police from there and explain what happened.'

'But what if I'm wrong about him being dead and he's there waiting for me now? I can't do this on my own.'

I take a deep breath, uncertain whether my next words are a response to feeling compelled to help Allie or just an excuse to avoid *that* conversation with Marcus at work.

'Okay, well, what if I come with you? I'll get off the train too, and we can phone the police once we're there. I promise I won't leave your side until they've listened to you and we've got things resolved. How does that sound?'

Her eyes brighten for the first time since we met.

'You promise?'

'I promise,' I say, with a smile.

I wash my hands before nodding for Allie to unlock the door, and while she waits there, I return to our seats and collect my bags, relieved that they appear untouched. I stand there for a moment, gathering my thoughts. I'm going to have to message Marcus and let him know I won't be in the office today, but I don't know what excuse I'm going to provide. I can't tell him the truth, because he'll think I'm making it up. And I can't just tell him I've had a family emergency, as he'll still expect me to log on from home and dial in to our resource review meeting. I don't want to feign illness, but I've given Allie my word I'll help her, so my only choice is to say I'm too ill to work today. He'll probably see through it and assume I'm avoiding having to choose whose jobs I'm going to snatch away, but that's not a total lie. I can't run away from the decision forever, but at least I can buy myself some time. The train guard announces our arrival at Winchester, and I plaster on a confident smile as I approach the door and Allie catches my eye.

4

My stomach is in my throat as the taxicab traverses the narrow lane towards the tall block of flats. Allie's barely said a word since we left the train, so I can only assume she's equally nervous about what we are likely to find when we enter the flat. My gut is telling me that we should have phoned the police already. Whether her boyfriend is in a critical condition inside (or worse), from what she's said the relationship was toxic and she should be reporting his violent nature either way. I'm certain there's more she hasn't told me, but I don't want to push at this point. I sense Allie needs a friend right now, and I'm determined to be that for her, even if only for the interim.

The taxi pulls up at the kerbside, but Allie doesn't flinch. She's been staring out of the window for half the journey, and I hope for her sake she isn't reliving her nightmare over and over again. I know that I often replay incidents over in my mind, trying to better understand what I may have missed the first time around, but it is a dangerous spiral to get into.

I gently press a hand against her arm and advise her that we've arrived. She jars, deep crevices forming in her brow as she looks at me with uncertainty, as if I've woken her from a dream and she can't quite see through the blurred lines between the dreamworld and reality.

I pay the taxi driver without a second thought, and climb out, relieved when Allie slides across the seat and also disembarks.

'You need to come in with me,' she says, before the car has even pulled away. 'Please? I don't want to be on my own.'

I'm conscious that I don't want to interfere with what will inevitably become a crime scene, but my heart aches as I see the desperation in her eyes and find myself agreeing to the request. I will just have to make sure I keep my hands in my pockets and don't progress too far into the flat. Based on how she described the scene when we were on the train, I'm expecting to find him slumped over in the hallway, outside the kitchen door, and hopefully it will be obvious if he hasn't moved since she left. It must be less than an hour since she ran from the flat this morning, so if he isn't dead, there may yet be time to save his life. Even though she's described him as a violent monster, I certainly wouldn't want another person's death on my conscience, and I want to help Allie avoid such a sentence.

She unlocks the communal entrance and tells me her flat is on the fourth floor. There's an out of order sign on the lift, so we take the stairs, Allie leading the way, but taking slow and considered steps. I can't imagine what must be going through her mind right now.

We eventually make it to the front door, and I put an encouraging hand on the small of her back, telling her to be brave and that I won't leave her side. Her hands are trembling as they place the key in the lock and slowly turn. The door parts a fraction and I see her take a deep breath before slowly swinging it open. Both of us stop still as we peer into the hallway and see the large patch of deep crimson stained on the carpet. But there's no body.

I'm relieved, because it means that Allie's boyfriend didn't die at her hand, but Allie doesn't budge. If she shares in that relief, it isn't obvious as her feet remain planted to the spot.

'I don't understand,' she whispers quietly, her voice cracking under the strain.

'It's good news,' I say encouragingly. 'You didn't kill him.'

'But where is he?'

I'm assuming he must have come to after she left the flat and probably took himself off to hospital, but when Allie turns to face me and I see that the blood has drained from her face, I realise what's troubling her.

'You think he's still in the flat?'

She nods and tears escape her watering eyes.

Against my better judgement, I take her hand in mine and lead her into the flat. On tiptoes, we creep slowly towards the kitchen doorway, ears primed for any sound of movement within the flat, and it is a huge relief when I look into the kitchen and find the space empty. Allie knows Clark better than I do, so if she thinks he's lurking somewhere, waiting to extract his revenge, then I'm not willing to disagree. I pull Allie into the kitchen and close the door to, so we won't be overheard.

'How big is the flat? How many rooms?'

'There's a lounge-diner at the end of the hallway, and then a second corridor to the main bedroom and en suite, and a second door to the spare room.'

My eyes scan the kitchen for anything we might use to protect ourselves. I don't want to reach for the knives in the block beside the hob, but maybe a knife will deter Clark from lunging at us. Ultimately, he could equally have dragged himself to another of the rooms and collapsed, so we can't leave until we know for certain.

I spot the bloodied handle of the frying pan poking out

beneath the radiator but given that was the weapon that inflicted the initial damage, it's probably best to leave that where it is rather than disturb the scene any more. I reach for one of the knives, feeling the cold wooden handle in my palm. I have absolutely no intention of using it but feel immediately safer.

Pulling the door open, I feel Allie huddled behind me, but I think she's overestimating just how brave I am. I wish I'd phoned Brett to come and help us, but it feels too late for that now. It would take him at least half an hour to drive here in normal traffic, but longer as it's rush hour. The truth is we are on our own, and I'm freaking out that this Clark will be too strong even for two of us.

We make slow progress along the hallway, and the door to the lounge-diner at the end is ajar. I nudge it open with my foot, and the room is dim, as the curtains are still closed. I resist the urge to flick on the light switch, not wishing to draw attention to ourselves just in case. I take a moment to allow my eyes to adjust to the darkness, and then scan each corner, and across both sofas, searching for anything resembling a prone body, or a figure in the shadows waiting to pounce.

'He's not in here,' I whisper, and Allie joins me in the room.

Without putting on the light, I can't see if there are any splodges of blood to indicate if he came back in here or dragged himself to a phone.

'That's the way to the master bedroom,' she whispers, nodding at one of two doors on opposite sides of the room. 'Can you head that way, and I'll check out the guestroom?'

I don't understand why she now wants to split up but find myself nodding and creeping over to the door she indicated. There's no sign of any light beneath the door, but her terror must be infectious, because now I'm visualising him waiting for me in the bedroom beyond the second corridor. I pull my sweater sleeve over my hand, and depress the handle, tensing when the hinge creaks as the door slowly opens. I turn back to glance at Allie, but she's already inside the guestroom.

I squeeze between the small gap in the doorway, not wanting the hinges to squeak any more, and slowly make my way along the corridor. The door to the bathroom is open, and as I near, light from the window reveals a bloody handprint on the outside of the door. I presume this means he did come this way at some point, but the question remains whether he is still here now.

There's no sign of him in the bathroom, but I see splashes of blood around the inside of the basin, and can picture someone standing there, examining their head wound in the mirrored cabinet that hangs above it. Is that what he did? Are the bloody splashes where he tried to clean up his wound? There is a second door that must lead into the bedroom, but it's closed, and there's no obvious sign of blood on the handle.

I turn to leave the bathroom and start as I see a figure at the opposite end of the corridor, until I realise it is Allie, having completed her search of the guestroom.

All that stands between us now is the closed door to the master bedroom. It's the one remaining place Clark could be hiding and every bone in my body is urging us to halt our search and just get out of here. But Allie prises the knife from my hand, and moves towards the door, suddenly less afraid than she seemed when we arrived.

She pushes it open, and steps inside. This room is the brightest in the flat, sun pouring through the French windows, covering everything in a golden hue. But to my relief, there is no sign that Clark returned to this room after the attack. We both let out audible sighs, before giggling like excitable schoolgirls as the adrenaline slowly leaves our bodies.

Allie lifts and passes a photo frame to me. In it is a tall man, wearing a serious expression and a baseball cap.

'Where do you think he is?' Allie asks, no longer whispering.

'I presume the hospital,' I say, the most logical place I would go if I'd sustained a serious head injury. 'The good news is he's still alive, but I think it's now more important than ever that you phone the police and report what happened. He attacked you and you fought back. He needs to be prosecuted for what he's put you through.'

I'm not expecting her to argue this time, but she stands still, shaking her head.

'No, you don't understand, Jenna, I can't go to the police.'

'Why not?'

'Because Clark... Clark is a police officer. There's no way they'll believe my version of events over his. And you don't know what he's like. He's manipulative. He has a way with words that wins people over. He's like the devil in that way. He chooses his words very carefully and will twist what happened. He'll tell people that it was me who attacked him, and he was just an innocent party in what happened. And when you look at my lack of injuries compared to what I did to him, even I'd have trouble not believing his lies.'

'I still think we need to speak to the police.'

'No, Jenna, whomever we speak to will know him or they'll know a friend of his, and it wouldn't surprise me if he hasn't already started spreading his lies amongst his colleagues in case I do choose to come forward. Please, I just need to get out of here.'

Finally, something we agree on. She can't stay here and wait for him to return and inflict more damage. I won't let her stay here.

'Come home with me,' I say. 'You can stay in our spare room for a few days until you figure out your next steps.'

She takes two quick steps forward and throws her arms around me.

'Thank you so much, Jenna. I don't know what I would have done if you hadn't come to my rescue this morning.'

We part and I suggest Allie packs a few items, while I wait outside the flat, making sure Clark doesn't return and disturb us. I phone Marcus and tell him I'm unwell and won't be making it into the office today. He doesn't sound pleased, but doesn't question it, and as I hang up, I let out a huge sigh of relief. At least I won't have to stab one of my team in the back today.

5

We decide to walk from the flat in Winnall Close to Winchester train station as we are both craving fresh air. A dense blanket of cloud overhead adds to the feeling of pressure that I've been experiencing since Allie told me she thought she'd killed her boyfriend. The fact that we didn't find Clark in the flat suggests he's still out there, and I guess that's why Allie spends most of the walk checking back over her shoulder for any sign that we're being followed. This only serves to heighten my own paranoia, and it's a relief when we make it to the station without being intercepted. It's after ten by the time the train arrives and we board, but there is only a handful of people in the carriage when we enter, so I suggest we sit away from them and close to the door in case we need to make a sudden exit.

The colour has returned to Allie's cheeks at last, but she looks far from relaxed as the train buffers and pulls away from the platform. I want to help calm her down, and am curious to learn more about her situation, so we can plan the best strategy to help get her out of this abusive relationship.

'What brought you down this way originally? Your accent is Lancashire?'

She smiles.

'Manchester. I grew up there, but headed to Southampton for university.'

'Wait, you went to Southampton university as well?'

She nods, though I'm curious why she didn't share that pearl when I mentioned I went there back on the train, but then she was in shock so I shouldn't judge.

'Once I graduated, I figured I'd have a better chance of finding a job in London than heading home, but couldn't afford to live in London, so commuting became an acceptable compromise. When Clark said I could move in with him I thought it was fate's way of pushing me towards a happy future together. At first, everything was wonderful. He worked shifts, but was so careful not to wake me when he was coming and going. And he was so attentive, buying me little gifts and letting me know how much he cared. I even started to believe that he would propose one day. But then things started to change.'

Her expression hardens, the look behind her eyes no longer one of love, replaced by regret.

'I don't know what happened but something seemed to change inside him. I initially put it down to the stress of his job – when you deal with as much shit as the police have to, it's bound to have an effect – but we stopped going out places. I'd try and arrange to meet up with our friends, but then something would crop up last minute and we'd have to cancel. My own close friends were all starting to settle down as well, and though I tried to maintain those friendships... I don't know, Clark was influencing me to cut off most of them. He'd say things like, "Why do you need them when you have me?" and "Aren't I enough for you?" It was like the relationship meant I had to turn my back on my old life. And the more time I spent with him, the more I became reliant on him. For everything.'

My rage is boiling on the inside, as I can see exactly how he was gaslighting her, but I force myself to remain quiet and allow her to speak.

'I should have seen the red flags sooner, but I kept thinking I was reading too much into his actions, and that if I just tried harder, I could make him change back. I just had to keep trying. I thought I was starting to succeed until this morning. He's never been violent before today, but his voice has been more aggressive these last couple of weeks. It's been like walking on eggshells, never knowing what mood he would be in when I got home.'

It suddenly strikes me how little I know about her. From the first moment I saw her on the platform at Waterloo, I've been picturing her as this beautiful model who has others eating out of the palm of her hand, but all this time she was struggling with far more than I realised. I've been judging her unfairly. It makes me even more certain I'm doing the right thing in helping her get away from him. And whilst I understand why she's afraid of reporting him to the police, I'm sure part of that is shock at what happened this morning. She needs to report his behaviour or he'll never stop.

The train reaches Southampton Central and we alight, heading to my car, before I remember I need to top up with petrol on the way home. I'm hopeful that today is one of the days when Brett has decided to go and do some book research at the library or has gone off to town to write in one of the many cafés. I don't know how I'm going to explain to him why I've brought this stranger into our house. I don't want to betray her confidence and reveal the full extent of our interaction this morning, so I will have to come up with a script for what I will tell him.

My heart sinks when I pull on to the driveway and see Brett's car there, and I don't know what I'm going to say to him. At least Allie should feel safer having Brett here. He's not the biggest or strongest, but I know he'd do anything to protect me and the kids. And it's not like Clark will have any clue that Allie is staying here with us. She should be safe for now, and then I'll see what I can do to help her put as much distance between herself and Clark as possible.

I hear Brett talking to someone in the lounge as we enter the house, and I swiftly take Allie upstairs to show her the spare room. Fetching a towel from the airing cupboard, I encourage her to take a shower, promising I'll fix us both a cup of tea. I'd offer her something stronger, but it's only just gone eleven. When she seems settled, I head back downstairs and enter the lounge, seeing the back of Brett's head on the sofa. He's wearing a headset and gassing away to someone through it. On the large-screen television is some kind of role-play game. He must catch sight of my reflection in the screen, as he suddenly starts and pauses the game, turning to face me.

'What are you doing home?' he asks, his cheeks flushing with embarrassment.

'I'm not feeling too well. How's the writing going?'

My question is loaded because he's months behind his deadline for book two and has been telling me how he's spending hours every day working through his writer's block, but I've had my suspicions that he's been elaborating.

'I'm just having a break,' he says, and I don't challenge him on it. 'Are you okay? Do you want me to draw you a bath?'

I'm about to answer when we both hear the shower start up.

'Who's upstairs?' he asks, lowering his control and rising from the sofa.

'Don't be mad, but I've invited a friend to stay for a few days.'

'What friend?'

'Allie. You don't know her. She's going through a rough patch at home. I said she could crash in our spare room until she gets herself back on her feet.'

His face is a veil of confusion.

'You've never mentioned anyone called Allie before. Why have I never met her?'

'Because we met this morning, but she needs our help.'

His eyes widen in disbelief.

'You met her this morning? And you've invited her to come and live with us?'

I raise my hands in a passive gesture, but I already know I should have taken the time to prepare what I wanted to say.

'It's only for a few days, and you won't even know she's here.'

'And what about our children? Who is this woman? Where did you meet her?'

Now definitely isn't the time to explain the exact nature of how we met, so I try to change the subject.

'She's not a threat, and I just need you to trust me on this. I'll make us a cup of tea. Why don't you get back to your game?'

6

It's almost an hour since we returned home, and Allie is yet to reappear from upstairs. I haven't gone up to check on her, as I want to give her space to process, space I've also required, but I don't feel any closer to contriving a solution to her problems, short of reporting Clark's behaviour to the police. Could I do it anonymously, so I leave Allie out of it? But what would I tell them: that I'm aware of him being violent towards his girlfriend but can't provide any evidence or state my name? I don't even know his surname. Any mention of Allie will put her on their radar, and that will tip him off.

Brett is still in the living room, but the television and games console are now off. He has his laptop open, but I haven't heard the usual rumble of keys being tapped, so I've no idea what he's doing. Research, hopefully. He's made no secret of the fact that he's annoyed at me for inviting Allie to stay without consulting him first. But I'm sure if he was in my position, he'd have done the same thing. I couldn't have left her on the train trying to piece her life back together.

I haven't eaten anything since the half a croissant and am

looking through the cupboards for inspiration when my mobile rings, and I see Rose's name on the screen. The last thing I need is one of my team members asking questions about why I've phoned in sick, but not answering will only lead to more questions, so I quickly answer it, trying to recall the exact words I used with Marcus, to avoid fabricating more deceit.

'Hi, Rose.'

'Oh my God, Jenna, thank God. I'm so sorry for phoning – what with you being off sick and all – but I desperately need your help.'

Rose hails from Bristol originally and despite living in London for several years, she's lost none of her West Country accent, which can make it difficult to understand her, especially when she talks as fast as she is now.

'That's fine, Rose,' I say, deliberately drawing my words out, in the hope that she mirrors my intonation. 'What is it I can help with?'

'Well, you're not going to believe what's happened,' she continues, somehow even quicker than before. 'You know we were working on that file for the boutique bakery client yesterday – do you remember? We were eating some of their bao buns – how delicious were they by the way? – anyway, the thing is Marcus said he wants to see it for a final review, and I can't find it. The file isn't in the client folder.'

I can hear the panic in her voice, and I can picture her biting on her fingernails; a stim I've noticed whenever she's feeling overwhelmed.

'Don't panic, Rose, there will be a back-up copy of the file in the online archive. You just need to download it.'

'No, I've checked there and there's nothing. All traces of the presentation have vanished.'

If I was in the office, it would be a lot easier to show Rose how to recover the file, but it will take longer to explain over the phone than just to log on remotely and find it myself.

'And what's worse is, there's a rumour that Marcus is planning to fire someone.'

I start at Rose's final statement.

'Where have you heard that, Rose?' I ask, neither confirming nor denying the validity of the rumour.

'Well, Trudy overheard Marcus and his secretary discussing packages and they've had everyone's personnel files out of the cupboard this morning. It's all everyone is talking about. And now I've lost the presentation for the boutique bakery. I don't want to get fired, Jenna.'

'Calm down, Rose. Nobody is getting fired. You work for me, not Marcus, which means nobody's job is at risk unless I say it is.'

I feel guilty about lying, but it's what I would tell my whole team if I was with them now. I need to quash the rumour, at least until Marcus and I have had that conversation. There's still a part of me – albeit a slim one – that hopes to convince him we can survive without culling. The guilt of avoiding today's meeting is overwhelming, but first things first, I need to find the file for Rose.

'Leave it with me, Rose, and I'll call you when I've located it.'

'Oh my God, babes, thank you so much.'

I end the call, and move to the bottom of the staircase, looking up, listening for any sound of movement. It's possible that Allie is taking a nap, as I've heard no creaking floorboards since she left the shower. But I have no choice, I need to go up to my office and log on. If I close the door, and talk quietly when I phone Rose back, hopefully I won't wake Allie.

Brett appears at the door to the lounge as my foot hits the first step, his dark, neck-length mane pushed back over his head, but in dire need of a wash.

'Where's your friend?' he asks.

'Resting. I need to log on to work quickly, and then I'm going to fix some lunch. Are you eating?'

'I had a late breakfast,' he replies casually. 'We need to talk later.'

I know that means he wants to vent – presumably about my bringing Allie here – so I nod passively, and continue upstairs.

The door to the guestroom is ajar, but I resist the temptation to poke my head through and check on her. If there's no movement once I've spoken to Rose, then I'll check on Allie.

I close the door to my office and fire up my work laptop, before opening the client file on the server. Rose is correct about there being no trace of the presentation, which is odd. I can't think why anyone in the team would have removed it, but this is precisely the reason why we pay for online storage. The server is set to back up periodically throughout the day to keep our data safe, but when I log into the online archive, there's no sign of the file there either.

This is really bad. We've been working on this pitch for weeks; virtually all of the team have contributed to what should be exactly what the client is looking for, and it isn't something we can quickly replicate. Marcus and I are supposed to be presenting it to them tomorrow morning, and they won't react well if we ask for an extension.

I can feel the overwhelm already starting to fog my mind. I close my eyes, and focus on my breathing, forcing the voice inside my head to share only positive, reaffirming thoughts instead of the usual naysaying. The file must have been moved for some reason, and all I need to do is find it. I slowly open my eyes, and allow my imagination to think of alternative locations, but I check every other client folder in the online archive, and there's no trace of it.

I can almost hear Marcus's anger when I tell him we've

screwed up. He'll want someone's head on a platter for this. Why did this have to happen today?

I sigh audibly, and then start as I hear Allie clear her throat over my shoulder. I was so engrossed in what I was doing that I didn't hear the door opening.

'Are you okay?' she asks.

I turn to look at her, my face betraying my anxiety. Her hair is still damp, but now in jogging pants and a sweater, she looks less catwalk model, and more normal human being.

'I think I'm losing my mind,' I admit, aware that I have a tendency to overshare information when I'm in a sense of overwhelm. 'My team have been working on an advertising pitch for a new client and it's gone missing. We're meeting the client first thing, and I don't know what to do.'

Allie steps further into the room, her eyes darting across the laptop screen.

'Ah, we use that company for our cloud storage as well,' she says, moving closer, until she's standing beside my desk. 'May I?' she says, taking control of the mouse.

I wheel my chair back to give her more room, but my eyes don't leave the screen. I shouldn't be allowing a perfect stranger to access my work laptop, but I need all the help I can get.

'Did you know they have a secondary back-up hidden within their servers? Where I work, we had an issue last year where an employee who was facing redundancy deleted a load of our presentations from the online back-up server, and we thought we'd lost over half of our files. But then I spent two hours speaking to one of their tech-sperts and they showed me how to access the secondary recovery point.'

The mouse flits around the screen as she speaks, opening menus I didn't know existed, until she's sitting in a duplicate window of our client folders. I give her the name of the client, and when she opens the folder I'm expecting to see it empty again, but there is the file. My heart leaps into my mouth.

'Oh my God, you found it?'

She downloads the file to my desktop, before taking a step backwards, a warm smile breaking out across her face.

'I'm glad I could help,' she says.

The relief is palpable, and I quickly back up the file to the online server again, before sending a copy of the file to Rose via email.

'I could use someone like you on my team,' I tell Allie.

'Well, if you're hiring, I can provide you with a copy of my CV and references,' she says, but it's only when I see the sincere look on her face that I realise she isn't joking.

'Oh, I'm sorry, we only hire qualified graphic designers,' I quickly explain.

'That's precisely what I am. I work at Acorns. Actually, I think your company and mine are officially rivals for a lot of the same clients.'

Did I know she was a graphic designer as well? I remember telling her what I did as a profession on the train, but I don't recall what she said she did.

'What a small world,' I say.

'And kudos to you for having more than just a junior role in a design firm. For an industry that has so many women, the number in senior roles is disproportionate.'

I catch myself involuntarily touching my hair as she says this, and quickly return my hands to my lap.

'I wish my CEO shared your view,' I say. 'He wants me to cut my team to save costs, but I think if we increased the team, we could go after larger contracts and the finances would look after themselves.'

She nods knowingly.

'It's all about the bottom dollar, right? But you must have earned some credibility to be able to voice an opinion. If you feel strongly enough about it, why not give him an ultimatum?'

I quickly shake my head at this suggestion, knowing Marcus doesn't respond well to challenge, and not wanting to give him a reason to sacrifice my career to fix his accounts. Plus, I don't think I should be taking advice from someone I barely know.

7

There's no sign of Brett when Allie and I head down to the kitchen, so I assume he's gone out for some air. He always tells me that he gets his best ideas whilst walking, and I can't criticise anything that might help him get over his writer's block. I wish he could just see how brilliant a writer he is and believe in his own ability. I understand the feeling of imposter syndrome better than most, so I know the advice I'm giving him is valid, even if I don't always follow it myself.

The kitchen smells incredible, a freshly baked sourdough loaf sitting on the breadboard, waiting to be torn into. As much as I sometimes wish Brett had a more traditional job, he's become a dab hand at baking bread, and he wouldn't keep us in fresh loaves if he was working in an office somewhere.

When the sandwiches are made, I catch sight of Allie staring out of the window at the grey landscape that is our neighbourhood.

'How are you doing?' I ask her to break the silence.

She doesn't immediately respond, until she must pick up on the fact that I'm watching her.

The Woman on Platform 8

'Oh sorry,' she offers, 'I was just...'

I don't want to push her. I can't begin to imagine what she must be going through. From fearing for her life, to panicking that she'd killed Clark, to then discover he's still out there somewhere, it's certainly been an emotional rollercoaster for her.

'Why don't you come and sit, and have some lunch?' I suggest, pulling out one of the chairs at the antique wooden table.

Allie sits, and I slide the plated sandwich in front of her, before sitting and tucking in to my own. I watch as Allie picks at the crust, tearing off crumbs, and placing them between her lips, but a blank stare remains on her face. Given the trauma she's suffered this morning, maybe I should be putting her in touch with a medical professional. She insisted she didn't need to have the bruises on her neck checked at the hospital, but maybe I should be booking her an emergency appointment with a psychologist or counsellor of some kind. If Clark was gaslighting her for as long as she said, there must be years of abuse that needs unpacking.

And I'm not the best person to help her process it.

'Were you always artistic? As a child, I mean?'

This time she breaks off a larger chunk of the bread and chews it while nodding.

'Oh, yeah, art was always my favourite subject at school. I loved experimenting with different textures and design, not just traditional pen and paper. My art teachers always said I had an eye for art, and so when it came to choosing subjects for college, it was a no-brainer.'

It flashes up memories of my own childhood. Whenever Mum and Dad were arguing, I'd hide in my bedroom with a pad of paper and my felt tip pens. When Dad eventually left home – when he could no longer stomach Mum's paranoia and temper – I remember him giving me an expensive set of pencils he'd bought from a fancy stationer in London. He told me if I was going to pursue a dream, I should start off with the best tools. The pencils came in a tin case, and each had its own place in the tin. All the colours of the spectrum, and in hindsight, I now wonder whether he suspected my difference. My struggles didn't really present until university – I was always described as such a gifted child at school, so nobody knew how tough I was finding things.

Mum wasn't well enough to attend his funeral, so it was just me and Tom, and a few random stragglers whose faces looked vaguely familiar. They said he passed away peacefully in his sleep after a battle with pancreatic cancer that he never mentioned to me or Tom. Whether Mum knew remains a mystery.

I bite into my sandwich, not wanting that trip down memory lane right now; my university experience was one of the darkest times in my life. I offer a sincere smile at Allie. I've no doubt that if she was in my position, she wouldn't hesitate to offer Marcus an ultimatum regarding the redundancy conversation, but I don't know what I'd do if he called my bluff and sent me packing. There are other graphic design companies out there, but I've helped Marcus build that company into what it is today, and the thought of having to start over – and lose all that routine and structure – terrifies me.

'Do you miss Manchester?' I ask next, keen to learn more about Allie's background.

'Of course, you can take the girl out of the north, but you can't take the north out of the girl.' She smiles to herself.

'Maybe this is a sign that you should start your own agency,' I suggest, trying to shed some optimism on her situation.

'Oh, no, I'd be an awful boss,' she says. 'We'd be bankrupt in no time as I don't have a head for numbers. And I wouldn't want to step back from the design side of things.'

Conversation dries up after that, and I can't help feeling I've said something to offend her in some way, but I can't figure what. It bugs me for the rest of the afternoon, and when Brett returns, I tell him I'll go and collect the children from school as it will give him a chance to focus on his writing. The truth is, I need some fresh air and to better process my thoughts. Allie has taken herself off for a nap, so I don't ask whether she wants to accompany me.

I spend the fifteen-minute walk to the school replaying the lunchtime conversation with Allie over in my mind. Did she think my questions about her returning to Manchester were an attempt to get rid of her? I've never been good at reading social cues, and I'd hate her to think that I was implying something, when I was just trying to show a genuine interest in her life. I continue playing the other snippets of conversation through my mind, trying to paint a picture of who Allie is, and whether she's given any previous clues as to her mindset that I might have missed.

I know Brett would say – as he always does – that I'm reading too much into her silence, but my mind is good at spotting patterns, especially in other people's behaviour. My issue is that whilst I can notice when someone changes, I can't necessarily understand why.

I was trying to take Allie's mind off what happened with Clark, but maybe that was the wrong thing for me to do. Maybe what she actually wanted was to attack that head on. I don't know enough about trauma therapy to know what to do for the best. So, I spend the final minutes of the walk searching online forums on my phone, but a lot of the information appears contradictory, and by the time I make it to the school gates, I'm no wiser than when I began searching. I guess my only option is to ask Allie directly. If I explain how I struggle with communication at times, and offer an apology for whatever I've done wrong, then maybe she'll be able to enlighten me.

There are only a handful of other parents inside the school gates when I put my phone away, and when I check the time, realise I must have walked faster than I was expecting, as I'm five minutes early. I hang back near the gate, not wanting to get too close to where Luke and Caley will emerge into the playground. The last time I was here, it was so loud and busy with adults crossing the playground in all manner of directions that I became overwhelmed and couldn't spot my children when they appeared. They don't know that I'm collecting them today, so they'll be looking for Brett. I wish I'd asked him where he usually waits for them.

I don't recognise any of the other parents and start to worry that I'm standing in the wrong playground. This was definitely the playground I collected them from last time, but what if the rules have changed and I'm not aware? Surely Brett would have told me if the routine had changed before I left home.

My fingers are starting to twitch as the plethora of panicked questions race through my mind, and I'm feeling hot in my coat. I only brought it as the forecast said there was a 20 per cent chance of showers, and I hate getting caught out in the rain.

I slip the coat off, folding it, and tucking it over my arm, feeling instant relief as my senses reset. As the seconds tick by, the playground begins to fill with more faces I don't recognise. I bet if Brett was here right now, he'd be over there chatting with the groups of mums and dads. But I don't know where I'd begin.

If I walked over to the one woman who looks vaguely familiar and said, 'Hi, I'm Jenna, Luke and Caley's mum,' she's going to think I'm an oddball. And although I'm sure I've probably met her at some point in the past, I have no recollection of her name, or whether it's her son or daughter who shares a class with Caley.

I wish I'd suggested Brett come with me now. He could have introduced me to some people, so then I wouldn't be feeling as isolated as I do right now. It's just like being back at halls of residence. The other people on my floor just seemed to congregate and build friendships with minimal effort, whereas I was soon overlooked and avoided.

I force the memories of my rejection away, and widen my eyes expectantly as the first group of children emerge into the playground. I've only met Caley's teacher once, at last term's parents' evening, but I can't recall exactly what she looks like. I think she had dark hair, but I can't say for certain that I'm not mixing her up with last year's teacher.

I can't spot Caley amongst this group of children, but then two other classes are led out, and then I spot Caley's bright yellow coat bringing up the rear of the group. Frustratingly, as I try to wave and get her attention so that she knows to tell the teacher that I'm here instead of Brett, another group of parents sidestep and block my view. At the far side of the playground, there's no way the teacher is going to be able to see me over the mass of parents now convened.

I have no choice but to move closer, shuffling my way through, until I can see Caley again. She's standing with the teacher, and they both have blank faces as they search the crowd for Brett. I wave furiously, and eventually have to call out her name, until Caley spots me and whispers something to the teacher, who scrutinises me, before nodding and releasing my daughter.

'What are you doing here, Mummy?' she asks, as I pull her into an enormous hug, planting a kiss on the top of her head.

'I wanted to surprise you,' I tell her, straightening and leading her back to the safety of my spot near the gate. 'Where does Dad stand for Luke?'

'It's Tuesday, Luke's got football practice.'

She must catch sight of my frown.

'Dylan's dad takes him and then drops him home afterwards.'

I do my best to hide my embarrassment at forgetting this salient detail. I know she's right, and I remember now that the calendar hanging in the kitchen states that today is Luke's football day. I take Caley's hand in mine, but as we step towards the gate, I feel a hand on my arm.

'Hi, it's Jenna, right?'

I turn and come face to face with a petite blonde woman whom I don't recognise. She's so pretty that I instantly feel like an ogre not worthy of being in her company. Memories of university try to penetrate my mind again, but I chase them away.

'Um, yes,' I say, tripping over my own words.

'You're Brett's partner, right?'

'Wife,' I correct, before quickly offering an apologetic smile.

She smiles back, but I sense she's having to force it. She reaches into her designer clutch purse and extracts a piece of folded paper, passing it to me.

'Brett was on at me to give him my recipe for the macadamia and cranberry cookies that he loved so much. I was going to hand it to him today, but as you're here, would you mind?'

It takes all my effort to ignore the voice of negative reasoning in the back of my head. I have no reason not to trust Brett. This woman probably has absolutely no romantic interest in my husband and has given me no real reason to question this innocent exchange.

I accept the piece of paper, and thank her, promising to pass it to him. She thanks me and disappears off into the crowd before I even have a chance to ask her name.

On the walk home, Caley entertains me with stories about her day, and how the teacher was really pleased with a poem she'd written. I don't know how she can have this much energy after a day of learning, but it doesn't escape me that my daughter seems as gifted as I was at that age.

The sound of laughter greets us as we walk in through the door. Not just polite chuckling, but uproarious belly laughs. Caley heads to her room to change, and I cross to the kitchen to find out what the joke is, but as I poke my head through the gap, spot Brett wearing an apron, and miming into a metal whisk, while Allie is playfully slapping his arm and twerking.

They both stop the moment they see me, and I see the heat rush to my husband's face, like he's been caught red-handed, but Allie just smiles, and asks if I also want a glass of wine. And in that instant, I feel like a stranger in my own home.

8
___

I can see the cogs turning in Brett's head as he quickly wipes his hands on the bottom of the apron, and rushes across the room, kissing my forehead.

'Oh, hey, we didn't see you there,' he says, his cheeks still ablaze. 'Allie asked whether she could cook for us by way of saying thank you for letting her stay, so I was just showing her where everything is and how the air fryer works.'

Allie is busying herself at the counter next to the hob, chopping onions and carrots. She is no longer looking at me, and I can't help thinking she's deliberately avoiding eye contact.

'I'll fetch you that glass of wine,' Brett offers, heading for the fridge.

'No, I, um, I have a work call I need to make,' I lie, suddenly desperate to be out of the room, as I feel heat building where the collar of my coat is pressing against my neck.

It's my flight response, and I know if I don't remove myself from this overstimulating environment, it will lead to a meltdown, and I'm not ready for Allie to see that side of me. I turn instead, and head back out of the room, and hurry upstairs without even removing my shoes and coat. I hear Brett calling after me, telling me the call can wait until later, but am grateful when he doesn't follow me up the stairs.

Once in the room, I close the door, tear off my coat, kick off my trainers, and then fall back into the door, and slowly slide down it until I'm sitting on the carpet.

Brett has always had a way with words, and that was one of the things that first attracted me to him. I never really understood the subtlety of flirting, my approach much more direct. But I've watched enough television shows to recognise the signs, and whilst I've never had reason to question Brett's loyalty before now, I can see how some people would take his playful charm to be flirtatious. And maybe Allie is unwittingly falling under that spell in the same way the school mum with the macadamia and cranberry cookies recipe has.

Seeing Brett and Allie laughing together, their bodies brushing against one another in an effortless and natural way, set my paranoia to ten. It was like I'd walked into *their* house, and I was the cuckoo. I feel ashamed that these are the thoughts rushing through my mind right now. There are too many unknown variables about Allie. If I knew she was the sort of person who would never dream of instigating an affair with a married man, then I'd probably be able to accept the downstairs scene as the perfectly innocent exchange that Brett described.

I stand, suddenly realising what it is I need to do. Crossing to my desk, I pull out my phone and unlock the screen, opening the Facebook app and searching for Allie Davis. Over fifty profiles appear, some with no information or profile pictures. I ignore the ones that clearly flag the individual as US based, as well as those with images that don't belong to the woman in my kitchen. And it's impossible to tell if the accounts without images or information belong to her, as I don't know any of her friends. For all I know, she doesn't have a Facebook profile. Given she's almost a decade younger than me, maybe she missed the boom when everyone was downloading and searching for friends on Facebook.

X and Instagram are also busts in terms of locating anyone that resembles Allie, but by chance I do locate a profile for Allie on TikTok. There is limited information about her on the profile, and the dozen or so videos she's posted are makeup tutorials. She only has thirty followers and hasn't shared anything in several months, but it's definitely her. I guess I was expecting her posts to be linked to graphic design in some way, rather than just following a trend. But then, I've never posted a video of myself – why would anyone want to hear from me? I wouldn't know where to begin in recording and posting content, and I don't have the time or energy to learn.

I think back through all the things she told me on the train journey back to Southampton Central, searching for any clues as to her real identity. I was so willing to believe that fate or some unseen force had placed us on the same trajectory, but maybe that was just naïve.

I kill this thought in an instant, terrified by how much it sounded like my own mother when her delusions were at their worst. I don't want to suffer the same mental health breakdown she did.

I begin to search for her boyfriend Clark, but all I know about him is that he lives in Winchester and works for the police. I don't even know if serving officers are allowed social media profiles. I would assume they're not prohibited, but that doesn't necessarily mean he would choose to engage with social media. I try to think of anything else Allie has told me about him, but my mind is blank. Maybe I should ask her for more information about him. My search is even more fruitless, because I don't know his surname or age. I don't want to come across as intrusive, so I'm reluctant to ask her about him, especially as I don't want to force her to relive her trauma.

I work at Acorns. Actually, I think your company and mine are officially rivals for a lot of the same clients.

The memory of Allie telling me about her employer cuts through the fog in my mind. Of course! If she works for Acorns Graphic Design as she claims, then she should be listed on their website. I open a fresh search window, and locate the company, skimming the landing page, and searching the menu for more information. It takes several minutes of sifting through client reviews and affirmations, but I can't find a list of staff names. But why would she lie about working for them?

I should probably tell Marcus that I allowed her to see our list of clients on the server when she was helping me recover the file, but then I'd have to explain that one of my team misplaced the original, and I don't want to give him ammunition to target anyone specific. Allie has given me no real reason to question her integrity, and there's not a lot she can do with knowledge of our client base, apart from approaching those individuals and trying to steal the business, but too many things would need to align for that to happen, so it's probably safer not to tell Marcus. I was watching Allie the whole time and she didn't make any notes, and she probably wouldn't be able to recall the whole list she saw.

I can hear my mother's voice in my head again, and force myself to lock my phone. I have always been overly analytical, and that's all this is, I tell myself.

I slide the chair beneath my desk, taking several deep breaths and cross to the closed door, but as I reach for the handle, I hear the rumble of laughter coming from downstairs. I can see now I'm jealous that she's making Brett laugh so hard. I used to be the only one who could tickle his funny bone, and it's been too long since I heard him laugh that way. Hearing his laughter stirs so many fond memories, and warm feelings cascade through my body, but all of that is tainted by the fact that I'm not the instigator of it.

One thing's for sure: I'm going to have to keep my eye on Allie, and the sooner she's back on her feet and out of this house, the better.

9

The scent of garlic and onions greets me as I descend when I'm called down for dinner. Brett has put out the good dinner set: the cutlery his parents gave us as a wedding gift that we usually reserve for dinner parties, and the gilt-edged plates I inherited from a distant aunt. I feel under-dressed in my jeans and hoodie, even though nobody else has made any effort to change.

Brett is no longer wearing the apron but is dishing up whatever he and Allie have created, and I'm drooling as I take my usual seat. There's no sign of Allie, and as Luke and Caley enter the room and sit, my heart fills with warmth, seeing my family all together. Most nights we don't get to sit and eat together as Luke is out at football training or Caley is at swimming or taekwondo. And of course, on the days I'm trekking back from London, the kids are already in bed by the time I get through the door. I like that Brett's delayed dinner so that Luke can join us too.

'Smells delicious,' I say when Brett catches my eye.

He stops what he is doing, comes across and hugs me from behind, planting a kiss on my cheek.

'Can I pour you a glass of wine?'

'Please.'

He straightens and pours a large measure of the chilled white into my glass, before raising his own, and clinking it to mine.

'I love you,' he says, and although my senses are telling me that this overt show of affection is probably driven by his guilt at what I oversaw when I returned from the school run, I remind him that I love him too.

'We are in for a treat tonight,' he declares to the room as he returns to the hob and continues dishing up.

'What are we having?'

'Risotto-stuffed peppers, with dauphinoise potatoes, and steamed vegetables,' Allie says from somewhere behind me, before moving into the room and sitting between Caley and Brett's chair.

'Sounds wonderful,' I tell her, offering a sincere smile, 'and it smells heavenly.'

'It's the only decent thing I know how to cook,' she says, placing a napkin across her lap. 'The risotto is made with onions, white wine, parmesan, and lots of garlic. Brett said the kids aren't fans of garlic, so their peppers are stuffed with plain rice.'

Caley is beaming at Allie like they're new best friends.

'What do you usually cook for dinner?' my daughter asks, and before I can apologise for the bluntness of the question, Allie laughs disarmingly.

'Honestly, I can do a mean beans on toast. I travel a lot for work, so I often get to eat out, which is a bonus.'

I feel my brow furrowing at this statement, based on what she told me about her role with Acorns, would a Concept Artist travel much? Marcus certainly wouldn't authorise overnight stays for any of our Concept Artists. It's hard enough to get him to stump up for a round of drinks when we have a new deal to celebrate. But then maybe Acorns is a more progressive company. Maybe it should be me pitching my CV to Allie rather than the other way around.

'I hate beans on toast,' Luke declares.

'That's because you've never tasted *my* beans on toast,' Allie says, fixing him with a playful look. 'Have you ever melted cheese in the beans?'

He shakes his head, even though we tried that trick last year and he told us it made the beans taste even worse.

'There you go,' Allie says. 'Maybe tomorrow night I should make you all Allie's beans, and you'll see what I mean.'

Luke doesn't look convinced, but none of them seem to have picked up on her assertion that she'll still be with us tomorrow. When I invited her to stay, we never agreed on a set period of time. I'd figured tonight, and possibly tomorrow, but would have anticipated her speaking to the police by then and getting Clark out of her life. I don't want to spoil the mood right now, but I'll raise the subject with her later.

Allie looks the most relaxed I've seen her all day, and my stomach grumbles with impatience as Brett begins to place plates of food before us all. She really has pulled out all the stops, and it is a nice gesture she's made, although I hope she doesn't feel like she has to repay me for the kindness I've shown today.

'What position do you play in the team?' I overhear her asking Luke.

'We take it in turns to play different positions,' he says, making no effort to hide his frustration at this requirement. 'I'm best up front where I can run with the ball and score goals. I scored a hattrick last month, but the coach then put me in defence the week after and we lost the match.'

'That's so you all get to try out different roles,' Brett reminds him. 'Everyone loves playing up front and scoring goals, so he's just trying to give everyone a chance to have some fun.'

'Yeah, but none of them are as good at scoring as me,' Luke protests, as he always does when talking about his team. 'We'd be top of the league if he let me play where I'm best. Coach doesn't know what he's doing.'

I like that Luke is passionate about his football – his walls are covered with images of players from his favourite team, and if he's not physically playing football, he's playing it on his Xbox, or watching it on television – but I also want him to understand that there's more to being a team than just scoring goals. Their team is currently third, and they beat most of the other teams, so there is an argument that they're ready to step up a league, but the coach was the only parent willing to coach them, so it's not fair to criticise. I did suggest Brett could volunteer to help, but with my erratic office hours, it isn't feasible.

'And who do you support?' Allie asks.

'Arsenal,' Luke says, patting the badge of the football shirt he's wearing. 'We're going to win the league this year, I reckon.'

'Yes, we are,' Brett echoes, as he joins us at the table, and we all tuck in to the food.

'I hope you don't mind me taking over the kitchen,' Allie says, and it takes a moment for me to realise she's talking to me.

'Why would I mind?' I say, swallowing the first mouthful of the dauphinoise potatoes and savouring the taste.

'I wanted to thank you for all your help today. I hope you enjoy it.'

I take a sip of my wine as I feel my face warming.

'And thank you, Brett, for showing me where everything was. You have such an incredible kitchen. You are a good sous-chef.'

'It's nice to have a night off cooking,' he says, laughing, but then catches himself, realising I will take that statement as a criticism.

Brett does most of the cooking because he enjoys doing it, and

I'm not always around to help out. I am responsible for washing up or emptying the dishwasher, as well as weekly vacuuming. Like any marriage, we have our roles and responsibilities and it's what works for us. But I don't want him to think I take him for granted. And ultimately, I would be home more if I wasn't the main breadwinner in the house. Brett's royalty payments will help once he's earned out his advance, but we'd be doing even better if he could just finish his second book.

'And are you a football fan as well, Caley?' Allie asks next.

Caley pulls a face.

'Eurgh, no. I hate football.'

'More of a rugby girl then?' Allie chortles.

'No, I like watching basketball, and Dad is going to take me to New York one day to watch the New York Knicks play in Madison Square Garden.'

Brett's mouth drops.

'Am I?'

'Yes, you promised.'

He fires me a questioning look, and I simply shrug.

'I'll have to sell a few more books before I can do that.'

'You should definitely go to New York,' Allie says. 'It's one of my favourite places in the whole world. The food, the sights, and the shopping. I reckon you'll love it, Caley.'

Caley is beaming again, and I can't help smiling, seeing how at ease Allie is managing to put both my children. On the few occasions when we do all sit down as a family like this, we're usually greeted with bickering between the two of them. But they're both happily eating and talking.

'And what sort of a brother is Luke?' Allie continues, leaning closer to Caley like they're conspiring.

'Smelly,' Caley whispers back with laughter, and promptly receives a punch on the arm from her brother.

'No hitting, Luke,' Brett chastises.

'She started it,' Luke fires back, without missing a beat.

'And I'm ending it.'

'You're very lucky to have a brother,' Allie tells her. 'I don't have any brothers or sisters, and it was quite lonely for me growing up. I always wanted an older brother or sister, someone I could talk to when things were tough, and someone who could show me what to do and how to react to certain situations.'

'Mum has an older brother too,' Caley says, 'but Uncle Tom lives in France, and he comes to visit whenever he can.'

'Uncle Tom lives in Geneva, sweetie. That's in Switzerland. Besides, you can always videocall Uncle Tom if you want to chat. You know that.'

Brett has finished eating and carries his plate to the counter by the sink.

'I've already loaded all the pans into the dishwasher, but can you add the plates and bowls when you're done?' he asks me.

'Of course,' I reply, confused. 'Are you going somewhere?'

'Writing Club.'

My eyes snap to the calendar hanging on the wall, but there's nothing written in the box for today.

'It's not on the calendar.'

'Isn't it? Shoot, I must have forgotten to put it on there. Sorry.'

I grind my teeth together, not wanting to show my annoyance in front of our guest and the children, but Brett knows how important routine is in my life. It doesn't bother me that he still attends this so-called Writing Club, nor that it's just an excuse for five middle-aged men to get together and put the world to rights while getting drunk. How much writing they actually discuss is beyond me, but they met online during the pandemic, and I don't think Brett would have submitted his manuscript to agents without the encouragement of the group.

'Sorry about the calendar,' he says as he moves closer. 'We were supposed to be meeting next week originally, but then the day got moved last minute, and I must have forgotten to update it. But you're here for the kids, and you've got Allie for company, so it's all good, right?'

It isn't good, but I don't tell him that, instead just nodding.

He leans in and kisses my cheek before heading out.

'Too bad for your dad,' Allie tells the kids, in an effort to lighten the mood, 'he's going to miss out on pudding.'

Caley's eyes widen with excitement.

'What's for pudding?'

'Well, I went up to the local shop looking for ideas, and they had some Ben & Jerry's on offer, so I bought a couple of tubs, and some chocolate sauce and marshmallows, so I thought we could have homemade sundaes.'

Caley actually whoops at this news, and even Luke appears to be smiling. Allie stands and tops up my glass.

'And I also bought a bottle of wine for Mummy and me to enjoy once everything is tidied up.'

I toast to that, as it will be good to speak to Allie alone and plan how to get her back on her feet.

10

Getting the kids to bed isn't as plain sailing as I'd hoped. Loaded up on sugar from their ice cream sundaes, Caley in particular is like a firework trapped inside a house. She's a ball of energy, dragging Allie up to her bedroom to show her all her stuffed toys, then back down to the living room to show all the board games we have stacked up in the unit beneath the television.

'What's your favourite game?' I hear Caley's voice carry through to the kitchen. 'I like Monopoly, but Luke always cheats.'

'I do not,' Luke shouts back, temporarily raising his eyes from the tablet on the kitchen table.

Usually, I would make them help me load the dishwasher, but I don't want to make a scene in front of Allie. I feel like she'll judge me if I play the strict mum. It's after eight and Caley should already be tucked up in bed, but I know it will be a battle to get her to comply with anything because we have a guest, so I'm choosing my battles carefully.

'Can you go up and start getting ready for bed?' I ask Luke, while I rinse the plates before stacking them into the dishwasher.

'In a minute,' he replies dismissively.

I was hoping he'd be less of a challenge than Caley.

'Um, no, I've asked you to go and start getting ready for bed, Luke.'

'I'm just in the middle of a level.'

He didn't always answer back, but since he started Year 5, I've noticed the troubling development of this attitude. It's not that he's being rude per se, and yet this stubborn streak reminds me so much of Brett.

I stop what I'm doing and glare at him in silence, until he senses my growing impatience, and finally locks the screen.

'Fine,' he says tersely, but I don't pick him up on his passive aggressive tone. 'Are you going to tell Caley to get ready too?'

'I will deal with Caley separately, and I'd appreciate it if you watched your tone.'

He stares back at me, his face a mixture of disappointment and guilt. Or maybe I'm just reading too much into it.

'Once you're changed and have brushed your teeth, I will let you continue playing on your tablet until Caley is in bed.'

He considers the proposal, before hurrying out of the room and upstairs, maybe already sensing just how long it's going to take me to get Caley into her room. The bottle of wine that Allie bought glistens on the table. The earlier bottle is already empty, and I don't hesitate in opening it, and pouring myself a small top-up, downing it like a shot.

Just to take the edge off, I tell myself.

I finish loading the dishwasher, absentmindedly listening as Caley lists all her favourite movies, in alphabetical order, to Allie. I'm aware that my autism means there is a greater chance that both Luke and Caley may also be neurodivergent, and I often notice small things that they say or do that remind me a lot of myself at that age. Books were one of my special interests. One of my earliest memories is Mum taking me to the local library, and my mind almost exploding when I saw all of the coloured covers and her telling me I could borrow them for free, so long as I looked after and returned each book I read.

By the time I was ten, going to the library was part of my weekend routine. I'd either drag Mum, or if she was busy, beg Tom to walk me there. That was one of the benefits of having a brother a few years older; he was almost like a second parent after Dad walked out. At my wedding, Tom reminded me that I'd once told him I would one day marry a writer because then I'd always have something new to read. I don't specifically remember telling him that, but it absolutely sounds like something I would have said. I don't think I consciously chose to fall in love with Brett because he was a writer, but who's to say I didn't on some subconscious level?

I pour myself another glass of wine, and also pour a measure into Allie's glass as well, but leave both on the table, while I head through to begin the Caley extraction process.

'But I don't want to go to bed yet. It's still early,' she complains, crossing her arms and scowling.

'And I don't want to argue with you, Caley. It's time for you to get ready for bed.'

'Can Allie read to me?'

The question is like a punch to the gut, as I'd been looking forward to watching her drift off while I read.

'I can do that,' Allie says, 'but only if you can get your pyjamas on before me.'

And with that Caley races out of the room, with Allie in feigned pursuit, and I'm left standing in the living room alone, while those I hold nearest and dearest get on with their lives without me.

I shouldn't be jealous of Caley's desperation to impress Allie, and I am sure her willingness to read to my daughter is just another attempt to be helpful, but I wish she'd given me the space to deal with my daughter myself. Trying to push the feelings of rejection from my mind, I head upstairs, finding Luke already in bed, the tablet between his hands. I enter his room and kiss the top of his head, and as I'm leaving, I hear him say, 'I love you, Mum,' and my heart feels like it will burst.

'I love you too,' I say, my vision blurring slightly as I close his bedroom door.

Caley is in the bathroom brushing her teeth with Allie watching on.

'Thank you for the offer of help, but I can finish getting Caley ready for bed, and read to her,' I say quietly, hoping Caley won't hear over the sound of the electric toothbrush in her mouth.

'No, it's fine,' Allie says, brushing my arm with her hand. 'You've had a tough day, and it's the least I can do. Why don't you go downstairs and put your feet up for five minutes? You look exhausted.'

And I *feel* exhausted, I don't tell her, as Caley pushes past me and charges off in the direction of her bedroom, with Allie hurrying after her. I catch sight of my reflection in the mirrored doors of the medicine cabinet. She's right: I do look tired, but then that's to be expected with all of the changes to my usual routine I've had to process today. The day certainly hasn't played out how I'd mapped it in my head last night.

I can hear Allie reading from Caley's favourite book, *The Velveteen Rabbit*, as I pass the bedroom door, and I make myself a promise to come up and kiss both kids good night once they're settled. It's something I do every evening, and I'm not going to miss out tonight.

Allie joins me in the living room ten or so minutes later, and I already have my laptop open on a page for the Southampton City Council domestic abuse support page. I wait until she's seated and has had a sip of her wine, before I turn the screen so she can see it.

'There are phone numbers you can ring to get help,' I explain, having skim-read the page.

'I told you before: I can't report him because he's in the police.'

'I understand that,' I say calmly, 'but you can't let him get away with what he's been doing. The people on the helpline will listen to your story and be able to suggest routes you can go down.'

'But what if he finds out and comes looking for me?'

I remind myself that there is no way he can know she is here with us, but I don't want that to change. I won't put my family's lives in danger for anyone.

'I think the initial conversations are confidential, so you don't have to name him, or give your own name. I don't know about you, but I always prefer to be fully armed with as much information as possible before I make decisions.'

Her cool demeanour has evaporated and now all I can see is a frightened girl on my sofa. And despite the small age gap between us, I feel my maternal instinct kicking in. I desperately want to help her, but I am in no way qualified or experienced enough to be able to help her make the best decisions for her future. The best I can offer is a place to sleep until she can set the right wheels in motion. She needs more than that.

'I don't know for certain, but I think there are safe houses and temporary accommodation for victims of domestic abuse, so you won't have to go back to your flat and confront him.'

'But all it would take is one person's careless slip and he'll know that I've reported him and where I'm hiding, and I think next time he will actually kill me. You don't know what he's like, Jenna. He manipulates people to his way of thinking. He's probably reported me to his superiors as some kind of nutcase who attacked him, and if it's my word against his, I know who they're going to believe.'

I take a sip of my wine, trying to choose my words carefully.

'I know you're scared, and I can't imagine how difficult this is for you, but I'm here to help. Okay? I'm happy to speak to this team on your behalf if you want, or we can do it together.'

'No, I can't risk him finding me again. There has to be another way.'

'And what happens if you don't report him and he meets someone else and continues his campaign of terror against them? Could you really live with knowing your inaction allowed him to harm someone else?'

Her mouth hangs slightly, and I sense maybe I've said the wrong thing, or the right thing in the wrong way. I try to replay my words in my head to see how they could have been misinterpreted, but I think I've had too much wine to make sense of the conversation.

'I know you're trying to help me,' Allie says evenly, 'but right now, I just need to put as much distance between him and me as physically possible. I'd rather find a new place to live, collect all of my stuff when he's not there and once I'm settled, *then* take action. Will you help me to do that?'

I recall her words from dinner: *I always wanted an older brother or sister, someone I could talk to when things were tough, and someone who could show me what to do and how to react to certain situations.*

I find myself nodding.

'I can help you do that,' I say. 'We can have a look at flats available to rent online. Do you have money for a deposit?'

'Some, but not a lot.'

'Good. Well, I'll help you find a flat,' I tell her, opening a fresh search window. 'And you can stay here for as long as it takes until we find you somewhere.'

11

My phone's alarm starts me awake, and I do my best to snooze it before it disturbs Brett. His bearlike snore rumbles on as I push the duvet back and shuffle my half-asleep brain to the en suite bathroom, where I leave the light off and brush my teeth in an effort to wake myself. There is part of me tempted to message Marcus and tell him I'm going to work from home today, but I don't want him to accuse me of shirking my responsibilities.

I can't escape the feeling of déjà vu: me standing in this very bathroom yesterday morning, anxiety riding high at the thought of the redundancy conversation Marcus is going to force me to have.

But I also know I can't run away from it forever. I wish I had Allie's confidence to give him an ultimatum. He's too focused on the bottom-line figure and seems to have forgotten the need to take some risks in business. With a larger team, we'd be able to pitch for bigger contracts, and whilst that would mean short-term pain to the profit and loss accounts, the long-term effects could be exponential.

I try to picture myself saying these words to Marcus, and I hear his voice in my head dismissing each and every argument. I continue scripting the conversation while I shower and dress, preparing alternate arguments for each of his challenges. I sense it would be far easier having someone like Allie by my side, pushing me onwards, but it's easy for her to suggest giving Marcus an ultimatum; she doesn't know him.

Makeup applied, and hair brushed, I take one final glance in the mirror, and tell my reflection that she's got this and can achieve anything she puts her mind to. Exiting the bathroom, I kiss Brett's forehead, before heading out to the landing, but stop as I hear what sounds like crying. Instinct drives me to Caley's room, but when I open the door, she's still fast asleep, her favourite rabbit toy snuggled beneath her chin. My next thought is Luke, but when I open his door, he's the one who jumps. He is sitting up in bed, headphones on, and eyes glued to the television where he has a football game paused.

'What are you doing awake?' I whisper.

He slips off the headphones and tells me he was woken by my alarm and thought he'd get in a quick game before breakfast. I don't want to waste my energy arguing with him, and blow him a kiss instead, closing the door behind me.

But there's that sound of crying again. And I realise now it's coming from the spare room. I don't want to pry, but I don't want the sound to wake Caley and Brett prematurely, so I gently knock on the door, and open it, finding Allie sitting with her back to the wall, her legs dangling over the side of the bed.

'What's wrong?' I ask, closing the door behind me, and joining her on the bed.

She's clutching her phone close to her chest.

'Clark's been sending me messages all night long, telling me he's going to find me, and he won't stop until he does.'

'He doesn't know where you are, Allie. Nothing bad is going to happen to you while you're here.'

'No, you don't understand,' Allie whimpers. '*This* is what he's like. He won't stop until he finds me. He's going to kill me.'

Feelings of guilt flood through my body for doubting any part of the gravity of the situation. I don't usually instigate bodily touch with people who aren't family, and hugs from non-family members make me cringe, but I find myself draping an arm around her shoulders, and allowing her to bury her head in my neck.

'I know you don't want to report him, but if you don't think he'll stop, it may be your only option.'

She breaks free of the embrace immediately, and fixes me with a hard, tearful stare.

'He'll find me and that will be it. That isn't an option. If I can keep away for long enough, he'll lose interest in me; that's my only choice.'

'But what if that doesn't—'

'Oh, God,' she interrupts. 'He knows where I work. What if he's there waiting for me this morning?'

Based on the messages I've just read, there's nothing I can think to say to allay her fears. He doesn't know she's staying here, and he knows she hasn't returned to their flat. If I was in his shoes, I'd absolutely go to her place of work and wait for her to show up.

'He'll make a scene in front of my co-workers, and make out like I'm the crazy one. He threatened to do that the last time I told him I'd had enough and was going to leave him. He phoned my manager and told him I was too ill to come in to work, so then when I got to the office, my boss thought I was trying to prank him. And then Clark showed up outside the building, telling everyone who entered that I'm an alcoholic who needs to enter rehab. He only stopped when I promised that I'd come home after work. And then when I got home, he'd filled the flat with flowers, telling me how sorry he was, and how he loves me so much that it sometimes makes him do crazy things.'

'And you stayed?'

I don't mean the question to sound so blunt, but her facial expression changes.

'He said he would seek professional help for his feelings of jealousy, and I believed him when he said he was receiving counselling at work, even though I later learned he was lying.'

Maybe I'm just being naïve, but I don't understand why she would put up with someone who is so cruel and frightens her, but then I've never been in a toxic relationship. I did, however, witness my mum's slow journey into paranoia and jealousy. Sometimes in the dead of night I still dream about the arguments Tom and I would overhear at night. There were occasions where the shouting and banging were so loud that Tom would come into my room and cover my ears with his hands, staying with me until I drifted back to sleep.

I glance at my watch. If I don't leave soon, I'll miss my train.

'Okay, here's what you're going to do,' I say. 'Let your boss know you're planning to work from home for a few days. It's up to you whether you explain the real reason why, but it might be an idea to warn your boss or supervisor that Clark might show up unannounced and cause a scene. I have to go in, but when I'm home later, the two of us are going to go and speak to someone at the police station in Southampton city centre.'

She opens her mouth to argue, but I speak again before she has the chance to formulate the words.

'I can't in good conscience allow his behaviour to go unpunished, but I will be beside you every step of the way. We can show them some of his messages to support your version of events.'

'And you'll be able to tell them what kind of state I was in yesterday. You saw the marks where he throttled me. You're a witness.'

I don't like the thought of her placing any reliance on me as a witness, as I can only testify to how she appeared emotionally raw, but this feels like the start of her coming round to the idea of taking more formal steps against him, and I don't want to slam the door.

'Exactly,' I say instead, hoping to leave it open to interpretation.

'And it's okay for me to work from here? I don't mind using my laptop on this bed if you can give me access to the Wi-Fi.'

'Don't be silly, you can make use of my office. I don't want you injuring your back hunched over your legs in here. And Brett can give you the code for the Wi-Fi.'

Suddenly her arms are around my neck and she's pulling me into her. I don't break the embrace despite my own inner turmoil at the contact. And in that moment, I see a flash of what I observed when Caley and I returned from school yesterday afternoon: Allie and Brett laughing together.

In an ideal world, I wouldn't want to leave them alone in this house, but then isn't that my mum's voice in my head? Given everything Allie has going on in her own life with Clark, there's no rational reason why she'd be interested in trying to seduce Brett. And I trust my husband, so there is absolutely no justification for the nagging voice gnawing away.

'I'll go let Brett know the plan,' I say, standing, while Allie reclines back on the bed.

'Thank you, Jenna. I don't know what would have happened if I hadn't met you yesterday.'

I try to smile in acknowledgement, uncertain what to say, and make my way back to my room. It takes several shoves to wake Brett, and he is still half-asleep when I do manage it.

'W-what's happening?' he stammers.

'Sorry to wake you, but I need to go into the office and I'm going to be late if I don't get moving. I've told Allie to work from here today and that she can use my desk and chair in the office. Is that okay? What are your plans for today?'

He rubs at his eyes, trying to focus.

'Um, I was planning to go to the café to write today, away from the usual distractions.'

I assume he's talking about the PlayStation.

'And then, of course, I have my talk at the library this afternoon.'

My eyes widen as I try to recall what day of the week it is.

'Is it Wednesday already?'

'You are still going to come, aren't you?'

When he'd first told me about the library asking him to come and talk to fans of his book, I was thrilled for him, and when we wrote it on the calendar, I had every intention of working from home, and blocking the time out in my calendar so I could attend. But I must have forgotten to put the note in my calendar or I would have remembered the talk was today. I have to go in to the office now, but maybe if I tell Marcus what he wants to hear, he'll be okay with me finishing early to get back for the talk.

'I doubt anybody will show up,' Brett continues, his voice downcast. 'I mean, who is going to want to hear from me?'

I'm sure half the cause of his writer's block is his belief that he doesn't deserve all the acclaim coming his way. If only he could see himself through my eyes, he'd realise how brilliant he is.

'What time does the talk begin?'

'Two o'clock.'

'I'll do my best to be there, and I'm sure it will be standing room only. The library staff have been advertising it for weeks, so I have no doubt there will be loads of interested readers.'

He doesn't look convinced, but a glance at my watch tells me I don't have time to keep fluffing his ego. I will have to make sure I'm back in time, even if it means telling Marcus that I'll log on from home this evening and catch up on anything I miss.

12

The journey to the office feels so odd this morning. It's like I'm a puppet, with some mysterious force controlling my actions. The car is parked and I'm heading in through the doors with tea and a pastry in my hands without even realising I've left home. And then the train arrives, and I board and find my usual seat in my usual carriage, but sit with a sense of dread. It's as if my body is still in shock over what happened yesterday, and as the train arrives at Winchester, there's a growing sense of unease.

The events of the past twenty-four hours are draped in the same mind fog as a dream, and I'm half-expecting to see Allie diving through the door just as it's about to close. It's like déjà vu, only not.

But while I'm picturing her ghost-like shape bursting into the carriage, I can't help considering how I'd act if the day was played over again. Would I still offer Allie my support, knowing what I now do? I certainly didn't spend any time considering the consequences of my good deed before leaping into action, but maybe I should have. I've always been impulsive. Whilst I crave structure and routine – there's a reason I always sit in the same seat in the same carriage on the same train every day – my mind is often at odds with itself. Maybe if I was better able to control those impulses, I would have kept my head buried when Allie rocked up.

And I hate myself for even thinking this. I know, deep down, I did the right thing in offering support to a fellow woman in need. God knows, if we don't stick up for one another, nobody else will.

My mind is still exploring all the other ways yesterday could have gone when the train guard announces our arrival at London Waterloo. My work laptop sits unopened on the tray table before me; my tea not drunk and my pain au chocolat still in its brown bag. I return my laptop and the pastry to my satchel, down the now lukewarm tea, and head off the train. I need to focus on the day to come. Marcus is going to force me to give him a name, and I still haven't managed to think of a single member of my team who deserves to be let go.

The rest of the team are already in the open-plan office when I arrive, and I hear excited chatter, as I hang my bag and coat from the pegs in the small breakout area. The hot drink vending machine is still out of order, so I pour myself a mug of water from the kitchen sink, hopeful one of the team is about to take an order for takeout drinks.

There's no sign of any light in Marcus's closed door at the far side of the room, but then it's rare we ever see him in here before ten most days.

Brett suggested I should use logic to determine whose name to give Marcus.

'Last one in, first one out,' he suggested.

But that would mean releasing Rose, and she has so much potential. I've taken her somewhat under my wing, because she has an eye for lines like nobody else in the team. She has the uncanny ability of looking at two lines and being able to guess the angle between them within a one-to-two-degree deficit. It's uncanny. We've tested her so many times and more often than not she's spot on. You can't train that kind of attention to detail. She joined the team six months ago, and I know she's saving for a deposit to finally leave her parents' bungalow, whilst still trying to pay off her student loan. If anyone ever needed a helping hand, it's her.

But then how would other, more seasoned team members feel if they were sacrificed? Sebastian is the only male in the team, and I don't want to be accused of sexism if I put his head on the block. Besides, he has a brilliant way with people, and we'd miss the way he can charm even the most reclusive of clients.

This is my dilemma. Out of a team of six, I can make arguments for keeping each of them. I hired them precisely because they all bring something different to the table, and it isn't fair that I now have to lop one of them off.

'Why not just leave it to Marcus to pick a name?' was the last solution Brett had offered when we discussed the subject at the weekend, but I know Marcus won't consider anyone's personal circumstances or what they offer. He'll probably pick a name at random, or allow the Magic 8 ball toy on his desk to make the decision. And my team deserve so much more.

'Penny for them?' Rose asks as I find myself pulling the chair out from beneath my desk.

'Just trying to remember what I've got on this morning,' I lie, conscious that I don't want to add to the already swirling rumour mill.

'And how are you feeling now?'

'I'm fine,' I say absentmindedly, connecting my laptop to the box of cables and flicking on the external monitor.

'Just a twenty-four-hour thing then, was it?'

At first, I have no idea what she's talking about, but then I remember I phoned in sick yesterday.

'Yeah, something like that,' I say forcing a thin smile in an effort to cover my own deceit.

If she suspects my fib, she doesn't make a show of it.

'Did you read that Gliders is now seeking new representation?' she says next, her eyes bulging with giddy excitement.

My own eyes widen to mirror hers.

'Hot off the press,' she adds, and I now know exactly why there is excited chatter around the small office space.

Gliders is the fastest-growing sustainability tech company in the UK, and last year allegedly recorded profits of over fifty million, only eighteen months after it was founded. They're essentially a think-tank of some of the brightest global minds where thinking outside the box is a prerequisite. They are a white whale, and the design agency that lands their business will be pretty much set up for life.

'Imagine if we pitched and won the contract,' Rose muses, allowing her imagination to get way ahead of herself.

Not wanting to spoil her ambition, I don't want to offer unrealistic hope either.

'Gliders could hire any creative design agency across the globe,' I temper. 'Just because their team is based in London doesn't mean they will only be looking in our pond. And given their size and potential future growth, I would imagine their ambitions would be higher than a bespoke team like ours.'

'Yeah, but if we scaled up as well, then why not?'

'Marcus would never sign off on us pitching to them.'

'He would if you persuaded him. Come on, Jenna, you're the one who's always saying that if we shoot for the moon and miss, we'll still land amongst the stars.'

I'm not sure I've ever uttered those words, but don't correct her on this occasion.

'Gliders started from humble beginnings, just like us,' Rose continues while I log in to my laptop, 'and we can offer them something no other agency probably will.'

'Which is?'

'Exclusivity. A contract with them would mean we wouldn't need any other clients.'

I frown at this suggestion.

'And what do you suggest we do with our existing client base? Just walk away? Hardly fair on them.'

'No, not walk away necessarily, but it would probably only take three or four to keep our existing business ticking over, while the rest and your new, expanded team focus on the Gliders account.'

She's waggling her eyebrows suggestively, but Marcus will be a lot more of a challenge to convince. My mind is already buzzing with ways we could demonstrate our capability to Gliders, but we're a tiny fish compared to most of our rivals, and it is pointless dreaming about snaring the big whale when every other major design agency will be the competition. And yet, now that Rose has planted the idea, I can think of nothing else; the moment that Marcus arrives, I follow him into his office, a pad of sketched ideas gripped firmly in my hands.

'Morning. Are you feeling better?'

'Oh, yeah, it was just one of those twenty-four-hour things,' I say, hearing Rose's words in my voice.

'And does this eager arrival in my office mean you've come to a decision about you know what?'

I close the door to his office so that nobody will overhear what follows.

'No, not exactly, but I do have something urgent to discuss with you.'

'You're not handing in your resignation, are you?'

I can't tell if he's joking when he says this, or genuinely concerned, but my mind is so busy with images of blueprints and three-dimensional designs that I don't have the energy to process what's going on in the room. I decide to launch into the speech I've spent the last hour rehearsing in my head, though now that the moment has arrived, I wish I'd jotted some physical notes. My body feels as though it's on fire, and although I'd carefully honed my speech, I can't remember how it began.

'You are worried about profitability this year—'

'The next few years, as it goes,' he interrupts, throwing me further off course.

'Right... anyway... um... what if there was a way we could guarantee financing for the next few years, without cutting the team?'

'You find the winning lottery ticket on your way in this morning, did you?'

'No, not exactly. Gliders are open to submissions.'

His face remains blank, and it's impossible to see if there's even a hint of excitement.

'Your idea is to hook Moby Dick?'

For the briefest moment I picture my secondary school English teacher reading Herman Melville's novel to us during a wet break time.

'Sure, why not?'

'Um, gee, let me see. Maybe because they're an international conglomerate, and we're a tiny boutique agency?'

'Exactly! They're a company who specialises in discovering and developing the unique. That's our USP.'

Heavy creases form in his forehead.

'This is your big idea? Are you sure you're over your illness, because you sound pretty delirious to me.'

'You're right that we're smaller than a lot of the other agencies, but that doesn't mean we're any less worthy. I think we have a lot to offer, and we could easily scale up if we won the contract.'

'You're dreaming, Jenna.'

'Come on, Marcus, you're the one who's always saying that if we shoot for the moon and miss, we'll still land amongst the stars.'

Again, Rose's words in my voice sound so odd, but he nods at the statement.

'That definitely sounds like the kind of thing I'd say, but we don't have time to pull together a pitch before Friday's deadline.'

Wait, he already knew about Gliders before I raised the subject?

And if he read the news this morning and made a mental note of the deadline, then that means he must also have already considered the prospect. Despite the wall he's building here, I think deep down he wants me to force the issue.

'Yes, we can. We have today and tomorrow to pull it together, and we're up for it. With your permission, I want to try.'

'And when you're not ready by Friday, you'll give me the name of someone I can release?'

I don't want to agree to this demand, but I know he won't let me progress if I don't.

'Fine.'

'Very well, then do what you need to do, but Jenna, don't embarrass us.'

It's hardly the vote of confidence I was looking for, but I try to ignore the nagging voice of doubt at the back of my mind as I leave, and relay the news to the team, and give each specific tasks to complete before the day ends.

I'm excited as I return to my desk, but that quickly evaporates when I see the text message from my brother, asking me to call him urgently to discuss Mum.

13

I pretend like I haven't seen Tom's message, and try to focus on explaining my vision to the team. Submissions for the Gliders account close on Friday, and there are no guarantees that they'll even invite us to formally present to them, so Marcus could be right and everything we're going to spend the next forty-eight hours preparing could be an absolute waste of time. But I'm excited, and I can't remember the last time I felt truly electrified by a design project at work.

We are a small team and have always focused our efforts on winning smaller, bespoke clients. The largest chain we ever worked with was a series of four beauty parlours. The owner, a former nail technician, had a dream of franchising her business across the south coast, but overextended, and ended up in administration with our contract not paid. It took months before we even received a modicum of what we were owed, and deep down I think that experience has scarred Marcus.

But Gliders is different. The company has made real waves in sustainable technology in the last eighteen months, and their presence at 2024's G7 summit in Italy was no fluke. When the seven largest developed economies in the world invite you to attend their annual meeting to discuss international economic and monetary issues, you know you're more than a flash in the pan.

Are we mad to even be considering pitching for their business?

Gliders is massive and we really are a pin dot by comparison. Yes, we could probably scale up to meet their needs, but I don't want to waste my team's creative energy on something we're destined to fail at from the outset; especially when one of their futures literally hangs in the balance.

I try to quieten the voices in my head by plugging in my noise-cancelling headphones and allowing the playlist of my favourite songs to play on a loop. Sometimes that's all I need to bring me back from the edge of a shutdown, but sometimes it takes a lot more. I know my mind is feeling overwhelmed by the prospect that my team won't meet the Gliders submission deadline – I'm asking them to produce a lot in such a short space of time – but it isn't just that which is causing me to pick at the skin of my fingers more than usual.

Every time I catch sight of my phone on the corner of my desk, I am picturing Tom's message. Why does he want to speak about Mum now? I have too many other things to focus on, and opening that particular Pandora's box is not what I need right now.

I haven't been to visit her at the private hospital in over two years, and whilst at first the guilt of shutting her out of my life was difficult to handle, there's a lot to be said for the old adage of 'out of sight, out of mind'. The last few times I made the journey to Graveside to visit, she was so heavily drugged up to control her paranoia and violent outbursts that she didn't even speak. I'm not sure she even knew I was there. It's no life for her, but it's safest that she remain in there and under twenty-four-hour care; and not just safest for her.

And I know that the cost of keeping her there doesn't come cheap, and Tom has been shouldering that responsibility single-handedly. I guess, deep down, I'm worried that he's going to ask me to share some of the financial burden, but unless Brett delivers his next book and signs on for more, there's no physical way I can support the cost.

My ringing phone cuts through the latest song on the playlist, and I cringe when I see my brother's name in the display. My instinct is to decline the call, but I can't run away from the conversation forever. Grabbing the phone, I dart to the breakout room and answer.

'Morning, Tom, I'm at work, so it's a bit difficult to talk right now.'

'Good morning, Jenna, and I won't be long, I promise. Did you see my message?' he asks next, which is moot, given he will have seen two blue ticks to confirm I have.

'Yeah, you said you want to talk about Mum, but I'm going to be stuck here for the next few hours. Maybe we could talk at the weekend when—'

'She'll be sixty-five soon,' he interrupts, 'and I was thinking maybe we should do something nice for her. Y'know, to celebrate? It's a big milestone.'

Is this what he wants to discuss, or is he just lulling me into a false sense of security? I wish I was better at reading between the lines.

'As I said, Tom, I'm at work at the moment, and—'

'I've been in discussions with Dr Yates, and she says Mum is making real progress. They've reduced her dosage, and they think they've found a good balance.'

Suddenly I'm transported back to secondary school, hearing all the other girls laughing when Mum turned up for parents' evening wearing odd shoes – a trainer and a pump – a green skirt, red turtle-neck, and a lurid pink scarf. She'd literally put on the first things she'd managed to grab from the tumble dryer. And she was slurring her words so badly that the school made a report to social services.

Secondary school was hard enough to navigate as an undiagnosed autistic girl. I excelled in most of my subjects, and was able to play the part of social butterfly during the day, but I cried myself to sleep every night, physically and mentally drained from all the effort to be this other person. But none of it was conscious. I didn't tell Mum – or Tom for that matter – how much I was struggling to keep up appearances, because I just assumed everyone suffered in the same way; they were all just better able to hide how tough it was.

I remember growing to despise Mum's breakdowns. I was trying so hard to fit in, and she seemed to be countering all my effort, to the point when I started walking myself to and from school, so nobody else would be able to see what a shitshow I'd emerged from. She eventually got the message and allowed me to be more independent, which briefly made things easier, but I was on a one-way road to implosion, and so it shouldn't have been such a surprise when I had a breakdown at university. And thank God for those who were able to recognise why I was struggling so much.

'Jenna, are you still there? Did you hear what I said?'

I'd forgotten I was still on the phone to Tom.

'No, sorry, the line broke up,' I say. 'Can you repeat that last bit?'

'Dr Yates says Mum is the most coherent she's been in years, and this new drug they have her on is helping keep her mind in better balance. She wants to see us. Both of us.'

I want doesn't get, I want to fire back at him, Mum's voice loud in my head.

'I don't know, Tom. Now isn't a good time. Things with work are hectic, and Brett is knee-deep in his new novel, so I need to be there for the kids more than usual.'

Can he hear the tremor in my voice, and will he connect it with the fact that I'm lying to avoid agreeing to his demands?

'Dr Yates says that if she remains stable on this new drug, then there's a prospect she can leave the facility.'

'No,' I shout down the phone, my pulse accelerating. 'It's not safe for her in the real world. Besides, there's nowhere for her to stay.'

'Listen, sis, I didn't want to say this over the phone, but the thing is...' The line crackles as he sighs loudly. 'The thing is, the hospital fees have increased again, and I don't know how much longer I can afford to pay them.'

He pauses, and I remain silent, because I don't want to make promises I can't keep.

'Listen,' he starts again, 'I'm thinking about flying back for a few days so we can talk properly, and I thought maybe if we went to visit Mum at Graveside, we could have an honest conversation with Dr Yates and see what our options are. Maybe she could become an out-patient – so they can continue to monitor her – but we'd need to find her a place nearby she could stay. Or one of us could...'

He leaves the line hanging, but I'm not prepared to get into an argument with him over the phone.

'Yeah, well, as I said before, Tom, things are pretty hectic for me here right now, and I don't really have the time or mental capacity to be making those kinds of decisions. Why don't we leave it a few weeks, allow things to settle a bit, and then we can speak again.'

'Her birthday is *this* weekend, Jenna, or had you forgotten?'

There is a single red dot marked on the calendar hanging in my kitchen. I don't want Brett to suggest sending a card or the children asking awkward questions about the grandmother they've never met, but it's there to remind me about the added emotional stress I'm going to feel on that day. That's the problem with trauma: you can try to squash it down for as long as possible, but it *always* has a way of clawing back to the surface.

'My flight arrives at Gatwick on Sunday morning.'

So, this call wasn't about him suggesting we do something to celebrate Mum's birthday, he already had the intention of flying back, and the call was to try and guilt-trip me into acquiescing to his plan.

'I'll be back for a week or so, and I'd really love it if we managed to find a long-term solution to Mum's care. Try not to worry about it, Jenna. We'll talk more when we're face to face. There's more going on than I've alluded to, but you're busy now, and I'd rather not share everything over the phone.'

Try not to worry about it, like it's that easy. I already know I won't get to sleep tonight because the prospect of seeing Mum again after all these years is going to play over and over in my mind. And with it will come the ghosts of all those memories I've tried to keep from Brett and our children. It feels as though an enormous weight has just been added to the already full plate I'm carrying.

14

I'm still reeling from Tom's news because I'm not ready for Mum to bulldoze her way back into my structured and well-organised life. And how do I suddenly tell Luke and Caley that they have another grandmother after all these years of keeping them in the dark? A grandmother who is locked away day and night for the good of everyone.

Brett knew how strained things were when we first met, and although he questioned my decision to keep her out of the children's lives, he understands it was as much for their sake as mine. And just because this Dr Yates now says Mum is better medicated and under control, she doesn't know how bad things got before Mum was sectioned. I'm not ready to replay those events and bring that kind of havoc into our lives.

She became so paranoid that she started to think the whole world was out to get her, including those who loved her the most. Dad leaving was the straw that broke the camel's back, but rather than things becoming easier for her – no longer questioning where he was or who he was with – it sent her over the edge. At one point she insisted on knowing where I was every second of the day, phoning and messaging my mobile during lessons, and when I turned it off, phoning the school demanding proof that I hadn't bunked off to visit Dad. I know for a fact there were some days when she was parked outside the school to watch me go in, and remained in the same spot all day to check that I hadn't snuck out.

I know I should feel sorry for her, and that the chemical imbalance in her brain wasn't her fault, but that doesn't mean the challenges I faced were easier to handle. I wrongly assumed that Mum's behaviour was perfectly normal for some, and that I too would one day inherit that level of paranoia and overreaction to things. It's why I'm so desperate not to replay that scene in the kitchen yesterday when Brett and Allie seemed to be so in tune with one another. I guess that was the sort of thing that Mum's mind obsessed over, but because I know the harm it brought, I'm going to force myself to see it as what it was: my hilarious husband being his usual empathetic self, and trying to put Allie at ease in a stranger's house.

It's a good thing I have the ability to hyperfocus on tasks I'm passionate about, and pulling the pitch together for Gliders keeps my mind focused for the rest of the morning. In fact, it's only when Rose asks if I want her to collect me a sandwich while she's out that I even realise how late in the day it is. With the news about the Gliders account and then Tom's call I'd totally forgotten about Brett's talk at the library.

It's nearly midday, and the journey back to Southampton is going to take at least two hours by tube and train if I leave now, and probably even longer if I could afford to pay a taxi to take me all the way.

And what's worse is Marcus and I haven't even discussed the prospect of me leaving early today. His door is shut and the blinds are drawn, which suggests he's either on a call, or is fast asleep beyond the door, and both mean he doesn't want to be disturbed. I know that, given I promised we'd be ready to pitch by Friday, I should just stay and make sure the team advances the pitch as much as possible. I should probably pull an all-nighter to ensure readiness. But then I picture Brett's face this morning when he realised I'd forgotten all about his talk. I don't want to see that pained expression again. And what if he's right and nobody turns up for the talk, how much worse will it be if I'm missing as well?

Snapping my laptop shut and throwing it into my bag, I tell Rose that something has come up at home, and I will log on once I'm back. She doesn't question it, and tells me she'll keep the team on point until I'm able to reclaim the reins. We've made good progress this morning, but there are still so many tiny pieces of the puzzle we need to put together. I'm now starting to understand why Marcus was so convinced we wouldn't be ready. Of course, if we had a larger team this would be less of a challenge, but it's too late in the day to start hiring. It would take at least a week to get a job advert live. Then there'd be another couple of weeks to sift through applications and another week to organise interviews. Throw in another week for checking references, and then up to six weeks for the successful candidates to serve notice in their current roles. And then a few days more to bring them up to speed with our work ethos and the project itself, we're talking over two months just to get bums on seats.

I hustle down to the Jubilee Line platform and my luck is in as a tube arrives and I'm able to jump in through the doors. No matter what I do, I'm never going to make it by two, but by hook or by crook, I'm going to do my best to limit how much of the talk I'm going to miss. From memory, he said he's going to be starting with a reading from his bestselling debut, and that will probably last twenty or so minutes, and in my defence I have read the book several times, so it's not the end of the world to miss that part.

Then I think the librarian who is compering the talk will ask him some questions about his inspiration behind the book and inevitably what his next book is about. And then I think the final twenty minutes will be opened up for audience questions.

Racing up both escalators at London Waterloo, I scan the screens above the platforms for the next available train to Southampton, and again I'm in luck as there is a train due to depart in the next three minutes. I hurry to the platform and board, darting through the carriage until I find a vacant seat and collapse into it. I'm panting and my hairline is dripping with sweat, and I feel so uncomfortable that I end up slipping off my shoes in an effort to regulate my temperature.

If a room is too hot or too cold, I find it more challenging to regulate my emotions and process what's going on around me. Or if a room is too bright or too noisy, I end up becoming overwhelmed, and unless I can break free of the situation it ultimately ends in a verbal meltdown. I unfasten several buttons of my blouse, and hitch my skirt up so it is over my knees in a desperate attempt to cool my body temperature. I slip in my noise-cancelling headphones and flick on my playlist, focusing on the beats and melodies of the songs, allowing my fingers to tap and click as much as they need to help self-stim.

And then, before I know it, the train guard is announcing our arrival at Southampton Central station. I must have fallen asleep, as I have no recollection of passing through Basingstoke or Winchester, and as I look at my watch am relieved that I've only missed ten minutes of Brett's talk so far. I hustle off the train, through the barrier and into my car, accelerating away with only one thing in my mind: being there for my husband.

It takes twenty minutes of running amber lights to reach Station Road in Romsey, and although the library has its own car park, there are no spaces. As I pass, there are several people standing just inside the library, the door wide open, which must mean the talk is better attended than Brett was fearing. I continue driving for another five minutes until I reach one of the town's many public car parks, and then I hurry back to the library. I have to squeeze my way in through the entrance, and am amazed by just how many people have come out to hear Brett speak, and I've never been prouder, nor more pleased for him. I can just about make him out sitting in the small alcove, the crowd hanging on his every word. I wish he could see himself through my eyes, or the eyes of all these readers who are listening so intently.

'When is your next book out?' someone calls from the crowd, and I cringe, as I know how much Brett hates answering this particular question.

It sends him down a rabbit hole of self-recrimination; a reminder of just how far behind deadline he is.

'I wouldn't be much of a writer if I didn't keep you in suspense, would I?' Brett fires back without missing a breath and the whole room explodes in laughter and applause. 'On a serious note, you're not the only person desperate to get their hands on my next book – just ask my agent and she'll corroborate – but the good news is, the book is due to be released just in time for Christmas, and promises to be even better than the first.'

This is followed by whoops and cheers, and I've never heard Brett sound so calm about the difficult second book; I can only assume he's had a good day of writing, or his agent Becky has coached him in how to answer the question.

'We have time for one more question,' the compere calls out, and a flurry of hands shoot into the air.

By the time Brett has finished answering and the crowd begins to part, I feel high as a kite; he got the turnout he wanted – the turnout he deserves – and he shone. I just want to run over to him and tell him how proud I am, but as those in front of me pass, I see him in the arms of another woman, and my heart skips a beat.

What is Allie doing here when she should be at home working? And why is she standing where I should be: beside my husband?

And suddenly I hear my mother's voice in my head, the night of my dad's office Christmas party when she caused a scene, accusing him of sleeping with virtually every woman at the party. But I know Brett isn't my father, and I am certainly not my mother. But what if I've been lying to myself for all these years and the apple didn't fall as far from the tree as I hoped?

15

The crowd dissipates further and I can see now a man with a long grey ponytail and a large camera is posing him for photographs. I recognise the photographer from when he came to the house to take pictures for the local newspaper, though for the life of me I can't remember his name.

He's asking Brett and Allie to move closer together – does he think she's me? – and I can't hear what Brett is saying in reply, but he doesn't seem to be correcting the mistake.

My mind is racing with my mother's paranoid voice, and I realise now I don't want to be here. I spy the door, and shirk away. I don't want Brett to know I've seen his intimacy with Allie; certainly not until I can figure out what it really means. If this was a friend leaping to such irrational conclusions, I'd be telling them that they're being paranoid, that Brett is a loyal husband, and that they're blowing things out of all proportion. I hope with enough time to properly process this information in an environment that isn't as hot as this one, I'll be able to draw the same conclusion. But right now, I can feel the overwhelm coming, and that is then a slippery slide down to full-on meltdown, and I don't want to embarrass Brett, or myself for that matter.

I just need to get back to my car, so I can replay everything and hopefully prove to my brain that it is spiralling. I'll tell Brett that I got stuck at work, and missed the event, that way he won't have to make up excuses for why he's hugging the woman he only met yesterday.

But I hear Brett calling my name just as I reach the door. At first, I don't turn back, hoping there's still a chance I can escape and he'll just assume it's a case of mistaken identity, but then I feel his warm, strong hand on my upper arm, and I have no choice but to spin around.

'You made it,' he beams, pulling me into his arms, his face a pure picture of surprise.

'Yes, you were brilliant,' I say in return, hoping he didn't see my escape attempt for what it really was.

'I didn't think you were going to be here,' he says, kissing me, 'but I'm so glad you are. Come on, let me introduce you to Donna who organised today.'

I pull back as he takes my hand and tries to pull me over to where his agent and Allie are in conversation with the woman with auburn hair and bright spectacles who was quizzing him moments earlier.

'I'm getting a bit overwhelmed by the room temperature,' I say quickly. 'That's why I was trying to get some air. If it's okay with you, I'd prefer to wait outside until you're done.'

He kisses me again, but nods his head with understanding, knowing how the last overwhelming situation ended, and I watch on as he returns to the small group, relieved that he doesn't reclaim his position beside Allie.

Stepping outside, the cooler air on my face brings welcome relief. In a cooler environment, where the light is now more natural, and the background rumble of voices has stopped, I'm better able to compose myself. Brett is by my side a minute or so later, with Allie following him out, her face beaming as much as his.

'You never told me what a brilliant writer your husband is,' she says. 'I will absolutely be reading his books going forwards.'

'I wish he could see how brilliant he is,' I echo, though I'm not sure why I feel the need to compete to be his number one cheerleader. 'And did I hear you say you've made some progress on book two?'

His smile widens. 'Thanks to Allie here, yes. Earlier today we were chatting about the premise, and I was struggling to explain the corner I seem to have painted myself into, and while she was asking me questions about it, there was this light bulb moment, and suddenly I could see a way out. I've sketched the rest of the plot and I can now see how to reach the ending.'

His rejection is like a blow to my gut. I used to be his muse, the one he'd spend hours chatting to about his plotting issues, but in less than a day Allie has usurped me.

'I didn't really do anything,' she quickly counters, maybe sensing how low I'm feeling, or reading my face.

'But that's really great news,' I say, masking my own feelings. 'We should go out and celebrate, particularly after the success of today's talk.'

'I don't mind watching the children for you, so the two of you can have some alone time,' Allie volunteers.

'Would you? Oh, that would be great,' Brett replies.

But I don't agree, and I don't know why but there is something in the back of my head warning me not to leave my loved ones in the care of a woman who twenty-four hours ago thought she'd killed her boyfriend.

'That's kind of you to offer,' I cut in, 'but we shouldn't exclude Luke and Caley; after all, it is a family celebration.'

'Well then, Allie, you should join us as well,' Brett says without checking with me first and my heart sinks.

How has this woman made such an impact on him in such a short period of time? Is it something I've done? Have I been so busy with work and the children that I've left him seeking solace elsewhere? When I first brought Allie home, he was against the idea, but now he's inviting her to his talk and out for dinner; how long will it be before she's his first choice for everything?

I hate how intrusive my mother's thoughts are being inside my head. I trust Brett, and I'm seeing patterns that simply aren't there. But having Allie join us for a meal is only going to reinforce her presence in our lives, when really she needs to be putting steps in place to rebuild her own life. I want to say I don't want her to join us, but I don't want her to feel the rejection I am feeling right now.

'Actually, I have a bit of a headache, and I'm worried it might be the start of a migraine,' Allie says, with a pained expression, and I could almost hug her for giving me a way out.

She didn't look ill when I saw her hugging Brett inside, and I can't escape the possibility that she's either reading my mind, or that my face is doing a lousy job covering my own thoughts.

'You two should go and collect the kids, and I'll go back to the house and rest for a bit.'

And with that, she turns and heads away from us, and I'm relieved when Brett doesn't make a beeline to try and change her mind.

* * *

The Italian restaurant – my favourite – is able to accommodate our arrival, and I feel so lucky having my family around me. I know I should be at home helping my team prepare the pitch for Gliders, rather than ordering the spaghetti carbonara, but I need Brett and my children to know that they are my priority, even if it means I'll be logged on for the rest of the night.

The restaurant is dimly lit and otherwise empty, and although the waiters are busying themselves with setting up for the dinner rush later, they fade into the background and all I see is my family, and my heart feels as though it could burst. Luke and Caley talk us through their respective days at school, and although none of them ask how my day went, I wouldn't really want to bore them with the truth anyway; I also don't want to think about what will happen on Monday if we fail to impress Gliders. Marcus will force me to make the decision I'm dreading, but for now we have a stay of execution. Right now, I just want to soak up the perfection of this moment.

'Oh, hey,' Brett says, leaning closer to me, 'Tom called earlier to speak to you, but I said you were at work so he should try you on your mobile. Did he get through to you?'

I'd actually forgotten all about Tom's call and his wish for us to go and visit Mum, but given the children know nothing about their maternal grandmother, now is not the time or place to discuss it.

'Yeah, he did,' I say smiling, and hoping we can leave it there for now.

'He said he's flying back for a few days,' Brett continues, and before I can decide whether the children are eavesdropping, Caley cheers.

'Uncle Tom's coming to visit? When?'

Tom always makes a huge fuss of the children when he comes

to visit. With no children of his own, he spoils them rotten at birthdays and Christmas as well.

'In a couple of days,' Brett jumps in. 'Won't that be good?'

Tom never mentioned that he'd spoken to Brett before me, and if I'd known I'd have specifically asked Brett not to mention it to the children yet. I know they'll spend the next two days badgering us both, asking when he's going to be over, but I have too much to sort with work and Allie before he arrives, and I can sense the feelings of overwhelm starting to creep in around my vision again. I need to get control of this conversation before it strays into unwanted territory.

'He said he wants the two of you to go and see your mum,' Brett says, without thinking about what he's saying.

My head snaps round to Luke and Caley to see if they've picked up on his slip.

'I think he's right,' Brett continues, while my mind is desperately trying to process all the implications of his words, 'you should go and see her.'

'We should talk about this at home later,' I say under my breath, but I can already see the confusion crossing Luke's brow.

Brett's eyes widen, as he realises his slip, but that doesn't stop him adding, 'I think there would be real benefit in you going to see her.'

'Wait, Mum's mum is coming too?' Luke says, and in that moment I wish a hole would open in the ground and swallow me up.

'Mum's mum? You mean Grannie?' Caley says, her face creasing in confusion.

Oh, Brett, what have you done?

'Don't be silly, Grannie is Dad's mum,' Luke corrects, and as if a sudden gust of wind has breached the room, my own house of cards comes tumbling down.

'So, we have another grandma?' Caley asks, looking at the two of us for reassurance that I can't provide in that moment.

Brett looks as though he is about to say yes, so I quickly jump in.

'You did, but she died, remember?' I say quickly. 'Dad just meant Uncle Tom wants to visit her grave.'

I look at my children, trying to read whether they believe me, but it's impossible to tell. I've spent so long building these barriers to protect myself, but I can see now just how flimsy they are.

16

The sound of the alarm feels like a blessing after what I can only describe as a difficult night's sleep. I didn't come to bed until after one, having returned from the restaurant to log in to work and review the pieces of the pitch the team had put together after I'd left the office. And despite my big hope that they'd understood my vision and my revisions would be few, it took hours to write up my notes to each member of the team. We're not a million miles away, but today is going to be busy to fix what's not working, and to polish the whole thing. I don't usually go into the office more than a couple of times a week, but I feel like I need to be in with the team today as it will be easier to provide direct feedback in person than via videocall.

And maybe there was too much on my mind when my head hit the pillow, as I didn't drift off into a gentle sleep, rather I kept seeing Allie and Brett huddled together for that photographer's picture at the library, and then hearing Brett tell me that it might be time to build bridges with Mum. I suppose it was inevitable that my bursts of sleep would see my mind focus on her and the memories that I've long since tried to keep buried.

I'm also very conscious of the fact that things seemed to go quickly downhill after her fortieth birthday. And with my own milestone birthday hurtling towards me, what if these feelings towards Allie are a precursor of what's to follow?

Mum must have trusted my dad at some point. I don't remember her fits of rage and paranoid accusations when I was very young. We were happy once, I think, but maybe I'm just looking back at certain episodes with rose-tinted spectacles. I have flashes of holidays to Blackpool, standing on the beach, eating fish and chips, and watching fireworks. There's no hint of anger or anguish in those flashes.

But then I also remember the days when I wouldn't see Dad at all because he'd leave for the office before I woke, and wouldn't be home until after I'd gone to bed. I can see now how hard he was working to provide for us, especially after Mum was made redundant and couldn't find a new job. Tom once told me that they'd agreed that she would look after us and the house, while Dad was made the breadwinner, but that only seemed to add more pressure to their already shaky marriage.

The irony that Brett and I now find ourselves in a similar – albeit reversed – situation isn't lost on me: I've spent so many years trying not to turn into my mum that now I'm more like my dad. But unlike him, I won't ever cheat on my spouse. I am 100 per cent monogamous, so at least Brett won't drive himself crazy wondering where I am and who I'm sleeping with.

My dreams last night were dominated by Mum's voice in my head, accusing Dad of trying to escape their marriage. It got so bad that when he did eventually leave and I later learned that he'd moved in with a woman he was working with, I didn't blame him. Tom and I saw him less and less after he moved out, not because he didn't want to see us, but Mum would always manage to find ways to keep us from seeing him. She won custody and he had to pick up the tab. On days when we were due to see him, Mum would feign serious illness, or would claim she'd simply got her dates mixed up and had booked things – a trip to the theatre, a dental appointment, etc., etc. – and we'd be forced to stay home.

Ironically, she was so worried about losing us that she drove a wedge between us. I don't ever want to make Luke or Caley feel that way about me. So, I have worked hard to provide them with everything they need even if I'm not always around to watch them enjoying it.

I drag myself from the bed, knowing I only have a few minutes to get my shit together before I need to race across town to the train station. I don't shower this morning, granting myself a few extra minutes to savour my cup of tea and to eat some toast, before returning to our bedroom to dress. Brett is already up, and I can hear him tapping away at the computer in my office. I know better than to disturb him when he's hyper-focused and in the zone with his writing. Despite my feelings of envy that Allie is the one who's managed to get him over his slump, it really is a relief that he seems to have overcome whatever obstacle has been causing his procrastination. We could certainly do with the extra income if only to keep Mum at Graveside, rather than out to wreak havoc on our lives.

Once dressed, I cross to my dressing table to apply my makeup, and once I look vaguely human again, I reach for the antique perfume bottle, but it doesn't feel right when I lift it from its place beside the bathroom basin. Scrutinising it closer, I see now that the bottle is empty, but I'm more than certain it was half full when I used it yesterday. The bottle itself was a gift from Mum on my eighteenth birthday, and I've used it every day since, refilling it with my favourite floral scent. I don't understand how it could have emptied so quickly. Turning it over in my hands, I actually gasp when I spot the small crack in the base of the bottle.

When did that happen?

I try to replay the events of yesterday morning through my mind; I don't recall dropping the bottle or returning it to the basin's edge with too much force, but I can't explain how else it would have cracked in this way. The perfume must have been draining ever since, as when I lean closer to the basin, I can smell traces of it emanating from the plug hole.

I picture Caley now; she's always been obsessed with the bottle because it's shaped like a rose-coloured glass bauble with a gold lid. I've caught her reaching for it many times in the past and have reminded her to be careful every time. I'm disappointed that she hasn't come to tell me that she broke it. We've always had good, open communication, and I would expect her to find me and apologise for any accidental damage. I thought we'd raised her so much better than to keep it hidden.

I return the bottle to its stand, frustrated that my morning routine has now been disrupted, and go in search of more perfume in my underwear drawer where I keep the refills. But as soon as I pull open the drawer, I instantly know that something isn't right. I deliberately keep my bras and pants colour coordinated, so that it's easier for me to find a matching set when needed, but instead, the pants are on one side, with the bras piled together beside them. It's as if someone has rearranged the drawer, but I cannot think of any reason Brett or Caley would do that.

My hand shoots to my mouth as I think of a third potential culprit. Allie was here all day yesterday while I was in London, but I'm sure Brett would have noticed had she been poking around in the room. My eyes widen as I hear an echo of her voice telling us she couldn't join us for dinner last night due to a headache. It had been a relief at the time because I didn't want her gatecrashing our celebration, but what if it was a means for her to be in our house alone so she could rifle through our belongings?

I almost burst into laughter at the ridiculousness of the question in my head. Again, it's the exact conclusion Mum would have jumped to back in the day.

There is no reason that Allie would be rifling through my drawers, nor for her to have broken the perfume bottle. And yet now I can't picture anyone else doing those things. My mum would confront her immediately and kick her out of the house, but I don't want to follow in Mum's footsteps. I can't go leaping to conclusions without more information. For all I know, Caley could have accidentally dropped the bottle and gone in search of a replacement and if she'd pulled everything out of the drawer, it's possible she replaced everything in the wrong order. I need to ask her first before I accuse Allie.

I swear when I see the time on my watch. Closing the drawer, I finish my tea and hurry out of the door. I haven't asked Allie if she is planning to go to work today and given what she told me yesterday about Clark potentially stalking her office building, I can't see that she'd want to brave it today.

I get my regular parking spot at the station, and am actually on the platform when the train pulls in. I claim a forward-facing seat, and the journey begins. I try to push all thoughts of Mum, the perfume bottle and Allie from my mind. I need to be on my best game today, because the consequences of failing to deliver the Gliders pitch by the deadline is too much for me to think about. If everyone is in and firing on all cylinders, we can do it.

My imagination is racing with what life could be like if we somehow managed to secure the Gliders account; visiting their offices across the globe; hiring a new team of staff to scale up our business; Marcus agreeing to move us to a larger office space, maybe one closer to home so I'd see more of Brett and the children. My skin is prickling with so much excitement that I don't even realise we've arrived in Winchester until the train guard announces it.

I know I'm silly to be getting carried away, because Marcus is right and we are too small to land an account that size, but if we do a good enough job, it might be enough to convince Marcus to expand the team and allow us to push for other bigger contracts. I've not had a lot to look forward to in recent months, and I just want to enjoy the dopamine hit in my head.

Before I know it, we've arrived at Winchester, but then my gaze falls on the platform, and the breath catches in my throat when my eyes fall on a tall figure I instantly recognise from the photograph I saw in his flat. Unless my eyes are deceiving me, that is Clark on the platform. He's not dressed in police uniform, so his presence here can't be anything related to his job.

I duck lower down in my seat, but my eyes don't leave him. It looks as though he is searching for something. He is stalking along the platform, studying the faces of queuing passengers as he moves. When he reaches the end, he turns and stalks back, even stopping to check on certain passengers for a second time. But what is now obvious to me is that he's only looking at female passengers.

Instinct tells me he's looking for Allie. If he knows this is the train she usually catches to London, it makes sense that he would come here in an effort to intercept her. He stops near the ticket barrier, checking for those who are late and racing to get through and onto the train before it pulls away. I want to take a picture of him to show Allie to check that it is definitely him, but as I slowly raise my phone to the window, our eyes meet, and he stares at me for what feels like an eternity.

Oh, God, does he know?

I force my eyes to look away, squishing my back as far into the chair as I can, so that the frame of the window partially blocks his view of me. I'm at the exact midpoint of the carriage, so any attempt to head for the toilets for cover will be seen. I keep my gaze focused on the opposite side of the train, though I can still feel his gaze burning into me. My eyes fall on the reflection in the window across from me, but I cannot see the outline of his figure, and so I dare myself to look back out of my own window, but Clark is gone. I lean forward, fixing my eyes where he was definitely standing before.

Was he ever really there? Or did I imagine it?

I scan the faces of the few passengers who remain on the platform, evidently awaiting the next train. He was wearing a navy suit and tie, but nobody out there is wearing anything similar, so he can't just have been a figment of my imagination.

Right?

The silence is broken by the beeping of the doors as the closing mechanism is engaged by the guard, and that's when I see a splash of navy disappearing inside the door at the far end of the carriage, and instinct tells me he's now on board.

17

I duck down as far as I can, staring out through the gap between the seats directly in front of my face, scanning the end of the carriage, looking for Clark. There are so many passengers still to take their seats that it's impossible to make out exactly where he is, but I'm not prepared to wait for him to come and find me. Peeling myself out of the seat, I keep myself bowed as I plough through the half dozen or so passengers standing between me and the opposite end of the carriage.

The sign above the toilet cubicle indicates that it's occupied. I dare to glance back over my shoulder to gauge how close Clark is, but I can't see him through the throng of people. I shouldn't have made eye contact with him. The moment I saw him watching me through the window, I should have alerted the train guard, or hovered near the exit so I could make my escape when he tried to board.

The curved door of the cubicle begins to slide open as I near, and I don't hesitate, diving inside, almost knocking into the guy in cycle shorts and helmet who is exiting. I offer a quick apology as I slam my hand against the close button and then lock the door.

I have no doubt that the man in the navy suit was indeed the monster Allie left for dead in her flat two days ago. He's definitely over six feet, and despite his narrow waist, there is something domineering about the way his shoulders lurch over. And that venom in his eyes made my blood run cold.

I know how paranoid my internal monologue is sounding, but I can't forget the way he looked at me: recognition twinged with fury.

I should phone Brett and tell him what's happening, but there's not a lot he'd be able to do. Even if he left home now, he'd never get to me before the train arrives in London, and every passing second puts more distance between us.

The next station is Basingstoke, but we won't arrive for another fifteen minutes, so I'm stuck here until then. The platform there is usually pretty busy, so maybe I can sneak off the train without Clark noticing, and then I can just wait for the next train to London. It will totally blow my regular routine out of the water, but hiding in a toilet cubicle is already off track.

What would Brett do if he was in this situation?

It's a stupid question, because Brett wouldn't allow himself to get into a mess like this. And if he was here now, he'd go and confront Clark and tell him to back off. Brett isn't so terrified of confrontation in the same way I am. And given what Allie did to Clark when they were last together, I'm pretty sure she wouldn't be cowering in a toilet cubicle if she was here now.

My head is spinning as the train buffets me about, and I crash into the door. It feels so hot inside this cubicle, and this is the moment when I look down and realise I've left my laptop bag in the hold above my seat. I didn't even think about grabbing it when I saw Clark boarding. Marcus would go ballistic if he knew I'd left my laptop unattended. Although the data is encrypted and password protected, I can't afford to leave it where it is, which means I am going to have to go and collect it.

I remain where I am until I hear the train guard announce our arrival at Basingstoke, and then I unlock the door. My hope is that I'll be able to get back to my seat, grab my bag, and then exit, mingled with the other passengers so that Clark doesn't see me.

'About time,' a bespectacled woman huffs as the door slides open, and she pushes past to get inside.

I don't have a chance to apologise before the door is closing. There is already a queue of people on their feet, waiting to exit the train, and I offer apologies as I squeeze past them, my eyes darting from one face to the next, desperately searching for Clark, my pulse quickening with each passing face. I get pushed back as the line moves towards the exit, and then I'm through them, and find my seat has been taken by two teens in black school blazers who are watching something on one of their phones.

I reach up, relieved to find my laptop bag exactly where I left it, and pull it down. But when I look up, where there was previously a queue of people exiting the train, there is now a line of new passengers boarding, blocking my exit. I look back over my shoulder and the far exit is also blocked.

And there's still no sign of Clark. But what does that mean? Is it possible he scoured the carriage whilst I was in the toilet and, not finding me, he has left the train? I squint out of the window, searching the platform for any sign of a navy suit, but I can't see him amongst the sea of grey faces; men in suits and ties, some huddled beneath umbrellas as heavy rainfall washes the platform.

Or maybe he is standing by one of the doors, watching to see if I disembark.

'Are you going to sit there?' a woman's voice says behind me, and I see I am standing by a vacant seat.

I quickly slip into it, and she heads off towards the next carriage. It isn't my regular seat, but it will do for now whilst I consider my options. There is still time to get off the train, but that means I'll have to wait for the next one, and then I'll be late into the office. I can't see Clark, but even if he was here, what can he do in front of all these potential witnesses? All it would take is for me to scream out and I'm sure somebody would quickly start filming the unfolding scene.

There is beeping again as the doors begin to close, and the decision is taken out of my hands. I lean out and scan the aisle leading to the door at the front of the carriage, but there's still no sign of Clark. But that doesn't mean he isn't looking for me. What I need to do is locate the train guard and tell him I'm being stalked. Maybe he can have Clark ejected when we get to Winchester.

Grabbing my bag, I stand, and shuffle towards the front of the carriage. There are seven other carriages ahead of me, so I move into the next, my legs unsteady as I pass between the seats until I make it to the carriage two away from my original. There are no vacant seats, so I stand in the corridor, pressed up against the wall of the toilet cubicle.

There's no sign of the train guard, nor any sign of Clark, so I press on again, apologising when the train bumps me into seated passengers, until I make it to the end of carriage seven. I cross through to the next carriage, and stop when I see the guard at the opposite end, checking tickets. I'm about to move forwards when I spot a navy-suited arm sticking out about halfway along the carriage. I follow the arm up to the back of the thick head of dark hair, and my knees go weak.

There's no way I can get to the guard without passing Clark, so I remain where I am, not wanting to draw undue attention to myself. With his back to me, he doesn't know I'm here, but if he's seated, does that mean he's stopped looking for me? Or is he just biding his time until we arrive at Waterloo, and then he's planning to intercept me on the platform?

The woman in the seat beside me lifts her bag off the chair and asks if I want to sit down. I practically fall into the seat, keeping my gaze on the back of Clark's head. The train guard continues his slow passage through the carriage and when he reaches me, I'm tempted to take him to one side, and explain what's going on, but as I think through the conversation in my head, I realise how ludicrous it sounds.

That man in the navy suit stared at me in Winchester, and now I think he's stalking me because I'm harbouring his ex-girlfriend. No, he's not threatened me, and I appreciate it looks like he's more interested in his phone than me, but I swear he's an evil man.

The train guard is as likely to have me ejected as he is Clark.

I show the guard my tickets and allow him to go free, but at least I know where he is should Clark make a move. But the more I watch him, waiting for him to leap up and continue his hunt, it dawns on me that this may not even be Clark. Whilst my mind convinced me the man in the suit was Clark, logically it makes no sense.

Allie said Clark is in the police, so why would he be in a suit on a train to London? And how would he know who I am and what I look like? When Allie boarded the train on Tuesday, he was unconscious in their flat. So, he couldn't have seen the two of us talking, nor the fact that we both disembarked at Winchester. I'd never met Allie before that day, so there is nothing linking us prior to Tuesday morning.

Can I really be certain that my mind didn't superimpose Clark's face on this man's body because there was a slight resemblance? It wouldn't be the first time I've seen things that aren't there.

I continue to watch the man in the navy suit, until the guard announces our imminent arrival onto Platform 8 at London Waterloo. I usually find the familiar announcement comforting, as it's all part of my normal routine, but not today. Right now the words induce panic. I leave my seat and duck out through the electric doors behind me, where I can continue to watch. As the train arrives at the station, I watch the figure stand and move to the far end of the carriage, but at no point does he turn around, so when the doors open, I exit, and hang back, waiting to see him alight, and then I follow him. There is a crowd at the ticket barrier, so I keep myself hidden behind a couple of guys in baseball caps until I know that Clark has gone through.

I scan my ticket and the barrier opens, but I can't immediately see where Clark has gone amongst the throng of people crossing in all directions. He was by the Hotel Chocolat stand a moment ago.

Did he realise I was behind him and now he's waiting to leap out?

And then I spot the navy suit exiting the chocolate shop and his arms are wide as he greets a tall woman in a tan-coloured raincoat, and the two of them share a long and passionate kiss. And then they link arms and head for the main exit. And curiosity gets the better of me, and I follow them.

18

There are so many people milling about inside the station that it's difficult to keep track of Clark and the mystery woman. I don't want to get so close that they spot me and realise I'm tailing them, but I can't stay so far back that I miss a sudden turn and lose sight of them. A woman in a tabard, carrying a clipboard and a sympathetic frown, appears before me, asking whether I have a few minutes to sample a new drink and offer my opinion. I have to hold my hand up and interrupt her, apologising and saying I'm in a hurry. She nods with understanding.

When I look back over towards the exit, they're gone, and my eyes widen in panic. I can't have looked away for more than a few seconds, but they're not where I'd expect them to be. Maybe I was mistaken to assume they were heading for the exit, and that now they've darted to another platform to board a connecting train onto somewhere else. I do my best to scan the faces and clothing of those in the immediate vicinity, but there are too many people for my attention to settle on anyone for too long.

This is impossible, and underlines the reason this was such a bad idea to begin with. I mean, what am I really hoping is going to happen here? They could be going anywhere, and I can't tail them all day.

What was I thinking?

I'm about to give up my search, when I suddenly spot Clark's tall frame. They've stopped beside a stall selling pastries, and are actually only a few metres ahead of me. If I'd kept walking I would have shot straight past them. I turn back to the woman in the tabard, hoping I can talk to her while I wait for them to select and pay, but she's now happily chatting with a woman in a beanie hat and shorts. I remain where I am, hoping I blend sufficiently into the background, and will the seconds to pass. I still have time to revert to my routine and continue to the office. Nobody would know I've deviated if I turn and head for the Jubilee Line instead, but my feet don't move. Against my better instincts, my body doesn't want to alter the current course of action.

Pastries bagged, Clark and the woman are on the move again, back in the direction of the main exit, and this time I keep my eyes glued to them as I dodge passersby moving in all directions around me. They head down the stairs and out into the grey smog of the city, with me having to up my pace just to keep up. It's raining, but none of us have had the foresight to pack an umbrella today, and so I pull the hood of my anorak up and over my head.

Outside is as bad as inside in terms of the sheer volume of people milling about, but with the added danger of traffic now also thrown into the mix. I know I'm overstimulated, and that if I'm not careful, a meltdown could swiftly follow. I know better than to put myself into environments like this, but I need to know more about this man and why he did what he did to Allie.

They cross over the main road and move beneath the overhead bridge, heading in the direction of the Southbank Centre. I vaguely remember Brett bringing me this way last year when we had to go and meet his agent before his launch party. Although I commute to London several times a week, I never leave Waterloo station on foot, so I don't know the area at all.

We pass a bar with a blue and red neon sign on the door and benches outside, but they don't stop. Then we're on a narrower strip of road, a fleet of bicycles for hire to my right, and electric scooters to my left. They ignore these, and then we're climbing the rainbow-coloured steps up towards the Southbank Centre. There are bars and restaurants to my left, and I haven't thought about what I'm going to do if they suddenly stop for a reservation. But they continue onwards, climbing the steps to the Golden Jubilee Bridge, and all I can think is how much farther away from work and my own life I'm drifting.

To my right, the heavy cloud is hiding the London skyline, and to my left, a green rail bridge is covered in graffiti. The footbridge is so busy and it feels like we're going against the tide of people in suits and dresses, wielding umbrellas like they're battle-axes. One woman makes no effort to avoid crashing into my arm as she attempts to nip around someone in front of her, but she has noise-cancelling headphones on and makes no attempt to apologise.

It's a relief when we make it off the bridge and then head through Embankment tube station, and back out into a less narrow thoroughfare. I'm not close enough to hear what they're discussing, but every now and then I see Clark raise his hand and point at something and I imagine him giving this woman a guided tour, sharing a little anecdote about particular places he may have visited, and her enthralled by it all.

The lane narrows again with terraced shops and cafés to the right and office buildings to the left. I have to keep stopping myself from getting too close and then having to hurry to catch up. And then before I realise it we're on The Strand and Charing Cross station is to our left. They cross the road, and I'm so close to them that I can smell Clark's cologne, but I can't decide if I recognise the scent from when Allie and I were inside the flat. We cross the road and head towards Trafalgar Square, passing Nelson's Column and the National Gallery, before continuing along St Martin's Lane, passing several theatres until they finally stop outside an Italian restaurant, study the menu and head inside.

I look around me to try and get my bearings. I'm sure Covent Garden is only a stone's throw from here, which is where I thought they were heading, but now they've stopped and I don't know what to do. If I follow them inside the restaurant and Clark recognises me again, then I'll have no way of escaping.

The smell of fresh coffee hits my senses and I spot a café to my left and dart inside, ordering an Americano and sitting at a small table near the front door. From here I can see Clark and the mystery woman in the window of the Italian. But I've no idea what they're talking about. I stare hard, trying to read their lips, but they're too far away, so all I can pick up on is hand gestures and body language.

What is obvious is just how relaxed they seem in each other's company, and given the passionate kiss when they met at the turnstiles, I sense they're a lot more intimate than just friends. But how does that fit with what Allie told me about their relationship? She told me he was controlling and had kept her isolated from her friends, but how could he exert that much control and maintain a relationship with this woman as well? And why did she meet him in London, when his flat is in Winchester? A long-distance relationship, perhaps. Or I suppose it could be possible that their hookups are less frequent, allowing him to live out two separate lives. Or maybe she's also from Winchester and they just arranged to meet in London for a day out.

I don't know, and it's killing me that my mind is asking all these questions I cannot answer without more information. And I can't ignore the voice in the back of my head reminding me that this man may not actually be Clark and I'm creating all this backstory out of my overstimulated and overactive imagination.

My phone pings with a message from Rose, asking whether I'm coming into the office today or working from home. I unlock my phone and see half a dozen emails in my work inbox since I checked it before boarding the train at Southampton Central this morning. Both serve as a reminder that I shouldn't be here right now.

A waiter places two flutes of something sparkling – I assume prosecco – on the table before them, and they share a toast, while I drain my coffee. I can't afford to sit here watching two perfect strangers share breakfast when my presence in the office could be the difference between us landing the Gliders account and not.

I pay my bill at the counter and then head to the single toilet before pulling my anorak back over my shoulders and grabbing the strap of my laptop bag. But I freeze as soon as I hit the street and see the two of them emerging from the Italian restaurant. I'd assumed they would be in there for much longer, but now here they are, only a few metres from me, and now the woman is staring.

Is that recognition? Has she spotted me previously and is now certain I'm stalking them?

I look away, staring down at the ground while I fiddle with the uncooperative zip, and then I move forwards but I can hear her calling after me. I should just ignore her, and pretend I haven't heard, but now she's shouting louder.

'Excuse me?'

I stop when I feel her hand on my shoulder.

The game is up. I'm going to have to come clean.

'I'm sorry to disturb you. I was just wondering whether you'd be able to take a photograph of my husband and I?'

They're married? Does Allie know he's married?

I should just apologise and say I'm in a hurry, but my need to people please gets the better of me, and I accept the phone she's handing over, and move closer to the two of them.

'This is the restaurant where Charles and I first met,' she continues, pointing at the Italian behind them. 'Eight years ago today.'

I can't look at him directly because I don't want him to realise who I am, so I hold the phone out to obscure my face. I study the man on the screen, trying to compare it to the picture in my mind; the one Allie showed me the other day.

It looks like Clark, but this man is married and called Charles. Either I've made a huge mistake in following him today or Allie has been lying to me.

'Say cheese,' I tell them as I take the photograph.

'Can you do a couple more, and a couple in portrait mode as well?' the woman calls out, and I dutifully oblige.

Part of me wishes I had the courage to send myself one of the pictures so I can show Allie later, but I don't want to draw unnecessary attention to myself with this man watching on. Instead I hand back the phone, and congratulate them on their anniversary, before looking away and hurrying back the way we came. I'm sure there's probably a quicker way to get to Canary Wharf but I don't have time to waste looking at the tube map. So, I cross The Strand and make my way back along the Golden Jubilee Bridge, hoping I don't get lost on my way back to Waterloo.

Thankfully, my autopilot must kick in because I cannot stop questioning how much of what Allie has told me is true, and what she would gain from lying to me.

19

I drop into the chair behind my desk, and strip out of my coat, my mind still racing over whether the man I've been following is the same man Allie left for dead in her flat.

'Morning,' Rose says. 'Was it a bad journey in?'

I frown at the question.

'Not particularly. Why?'

'Oh, I just wondered if that's why you're late in, and you look a bit harassed is all. You don't need to worry, we'll get the pitch up to standard today.'

I don't tell her the real reason I seem out of sorts, connecting my laptop to the local network.

'There was an issue on the line,' I say now, even though it contradicts my previous statement. 'Just one of the downsides with travelling in.'

I skim-read the emails in my inbox, but quickly find my mind wandering back to Clark or Charles. Men who have affairs will go to all sorts of lengths to cover their tracks, so it isn't unreasonable to assume that he might have given Allie a false name, particularly if he didn't want her finding out about his wife. I'll just have to tell Allie what I saw and see if she comes clean.

'Oh, I just remembered, Marcus said he'll be in by ten,' Rose tells me, 'and wants to meet with you immediately.'

It's hardly a surprise he'll want an update on the Gliders pitch given we have to submit by close today. I will show him the notes I sent to the team last night, as I'm not ready to show him the draft of the pitch just yet; I'm worried that he won't be able to see beyond how rough it currently looks. And whilst I feel less confident than I did this time yesterday, I know I always have cold feet before a new pitch. And ultimately, even if we do fail with Gliders, I want him to see the potential of this team and the advantages to growing and not shrinking the number of heads.

Marcus strides in, shades on, his face a pale shade of green. Another heavy night on the alcohol if I was forced to guess, but my earlier jitters now feel better controlled, and so I march to his office, my head held high.

'Can you close the door?' he says as soon as I'm inside, and instantly my bubble of confidence deflates.

'You don't need to panic about the pitch,' I say as I take my seat. 'I know it looks a little rough around the edges right now, but I—'

'I want you to focus on our existing client base,' he interrupts.

'But what about the Gliders—'

He raises his hand to cut me off.

'I looked at the estimated numbers last night, and it just isn't feasible. You'd need to double your team in the next six months, and then again next year. We just don't have the money.'

I don't understand why he's bowling out with this now. We discussed this yesterday and I thought I'd won him over to at least try.

'Securing a client like Gliders would give us greater capital, and we could borrow what we need until we receive our first commission. You know all this.'

I can't read from his face whether he's angry at me for arguing or pleased that I'm so passionate about the company. He is so difficult to read behind those sunglasses.

'Gliders is pie in the sky, Jenna, and we both know it. I don't think you appreciate just how close we are to going into the red. The speed at which a firm like Gliders would expect us to upscale is unrealistic, and they'll see that no matter what you pitch to them. We've already wasted enough time chasing this pipe dream, and your time – your whole team's time – would be better spent on ensuring we don't lose our existing client base.'

I feel my cheeks flush with frustration, and for the briefest moment, I hear Allie's voice in my head: *If you feel strongly enough about it, why not give him an ultimatum?*

And before I can stop myself, the words are tumbling from my mouth.

'If you're not willing to put your money where your mouth is, then I'm afraid I can no longer continue to work for you, Marcus.'

I instantly regret the words, and want to retract them, but his mobile starts ringing, and having glanced at the screen he asks me to step outside so he can answer it. I willingly obey, desperate for air, and as I wait outside the door, I feel my legs go weak.

What have I done? We can't afford for me to be out of work while I search for a new job.

I will just have to apologise for my outburst, and ask for his forgiveness. I can't believe I allowed Allie to influence me in that way. I've worked for Marcus for such a long time, and whilst my specialism is on the design side of the company, nobody knows the numbers as well as him, and if he's really that worried, I should be supporting, not challenging him.

I can see Rose and the others busy at their screens, still

working on the notes I sent them, but maybe if I tell them to stop before I return to Marcus's office then he'll see that I'm ready to toe the line.

Time seems to be moving so slowly, and I desperately want to burst into his office and offer my apology, but I can still hear the rumble of his voice, meaning he is still on his call. I could tell him that things have been stressful outside of work, with Brett's writer's block, and then what happened on the train this morning.

The door to his office suddenly bursts open and he calls me back in, closing it behind us. I take my seat, certain he is going to shout at me, but he sits down, and removes his sunglasses.

'I don't want to lose you, Jenna, but I've checked the numbers and I don't see the Gliders pitch working out.'

I'm about to apologise, but he holds up his hand to cut me off once more.

'Despite all that, I can see how passionate you are about our business, and the potential opportunities expansion could bring, and so, I have just spoken to a friend of mine who happens to work at Gliders. CEO Chip Martin and I went to the same sixth form college; that was him just now returning my call. He has agreed to hear our pitch tomorrow morning ahead of anyone else. You no longer need to submit anything tonight, but promise me we will be ready to go first thing.'

I don't know what to say; my mind is racing with so many thoughts I can't string a sentence together. Is this a joke that I'm just failing to understand? Is he being sarcastic and I'm just not getting it?

All I can manage is, 'You know Chip Martin?'

'We used to play pool together at college, but I haven't spoken to him in years. I put a call in to his secretary last night, but when he didn't return my call I figured he didn't remember me. Turns out he does, and despite our small size, he's happy to listen to our ideas. But whatever you do, don't embarrass me.'

'When and where is the call?'

'Tomorrow morning at ten. It will have to be via Zoom as he's overseas this week. It will be you and me, Chip and a couple of his team. Tell me you'll be ready.'

I want to hug him, but dig my nails into my palms beneath the desk instead.

'We'll be ready.'

'You're sure? If it's not going to happen I'd rather phone him and cancel than be embarrassed.'

'We're going to be ready, Marcus. I promise.'

'Well then, you'd better get back to it. You don't have long.'

I practically float out of his office, and gather the team together. This next twenty-four hours is key to all of our futures.

20

The team ploughs on through lunch, and by half past one we've sent a final version of the presentation over to Marcus and he is pleased with the output, although still has questions regarding the scalability of our business. I leave him debating the finer details, barely able to contain my excitement and nerves about the morning. I decide I'm going to head home early so I can share the news with Brett and the children. But I still can't stop thinking about the man I followed this morning. There's a chance – albeit slim – that I could end up on the same train as him this afternoon, and it's making me extremely anxious.

This must be how Allie feels about him, and I think I now better understand why she was so shaken on Tuesday morning. That day started with me full of anxiety about the future of my team, but now I'm daring myself to believe that Marcus's previous friendship with Chip Martin might just be enough to give us an advantage in the race.

I don't spot Clark on the Jubilee Line, nor as I hustle through London Waterloo, just making it onto the 14.05 train. I walk the length of the train searching for him until I'm satisfied that he isn't on board, and then I sit, and play tomorrow morning's presentation over in my mind, carefully selecting the words I want to use, predicting Chip's responses and polishing little punchlines to keep the audience engaged. By the time the train guard announces our imminent arrival at Winchester, I've pre-scripted all of tomorrow's presentation, and so long as Chip doesn't ask me any direct questions about our profit and loss accounts – that's why Marcus will be there – then I should be okay. That doesn't mean I won't review the slides again after dinner, but for now, I feel as prepared as I'm ever going to be.

I am sitting on the right side of the carriage as far from the platform-facing window as possible, just in case Clark – or Charles or whoever he really is – is out there waiting for me right now. I realise as I think this just how ridiculous a notion it is, and yet I can't totally dismiss the possibility out of hand. If he is as controlling as Allie has said then I imagine he's capable of anything to get her back. I do consider hiding in a locked toilet cubicle again, but deep down I want to know if he is there, one way or another.

I can't see a lot from where I'm sitting, and end up standing and moving closer to the window, but still can't see the whole platform. Finally, I move to the train exit, and lean out of the door, my eyes scanning the handful of passengers standing on the platform, but there's no sign of him. The relief is palpable.

Retaking my seat, I push all thoughts of Clark from my mind, and don't even check the platform as we arrive in Southampton. I hurry to my car, keen to get home and see Brett and the children. Only, as I pull onto our driveway, there's no sign of Brett's car, which must mean he's still out with them. Both should have been out of the gate by half past three, and as far as I can remember there are no after-school clubs tonight, so I don't understand why they're not home.

Entering the house, I'm greeted by a deathly silence that only confirms nobody else is home. Removing my shoes, I head upstairs to check whether they've been here and headed back out again, but there's no sign of school bags in either Luke's or Caley's rooms. The school is only fifteen minutes' walk away, so it's also odd that Brett would have used the car to collect them, given the sky is clear following this morning's downpour.

But what's troubling me more is that there's no obvious sign of Allie either. My office looks untouched, and the door to the guestroom is ajar, but she's definitely not here.

Just because Brett is also out, it doesn't mean they're together.

And yet I can't get the image of the two of them huddled together and laughing from my mind.

Curiosity finally gets the better of me, and I call Brett's phone, keen to share that I'm home earlier than expected and desperate to see them all, but his phone goes unanswered before his voicemail cuts in. I know he never checks it, so type out a message instead, asking what their ETA is. I suppose if he assumed I would be working late he might have taken Luke and Caley out for something to eat, but I don't understand why he would have taken Allie too.

You sound just like Mum, the voice in my head says, and I'm ashamed that my first thought is that they're out together. For all I know, Allie has just popped out for some fresh air, or to the shop for snacks. It is a huge leap to assume she is off cavorting with my husband, trying to push me out.

And yet...

I inwardly curse at this voice in my head, and busy myself with changing out of my work clothes, but suddenly find myself inside the guestroom. I didn't consciously come in here, and I know I should immediately leave, and yet I picture the broken antique perfume bottle I found in my bathroom this morning, and I remain where I am.

I invited Allie to stay here because I felt sorry for her, and what she'd been through, but I don't really know anything about our houseguest, other than the measly titbits she's shared. That we both work for graphic design agencies in London, and catch the same train each morning could be purely coincidental, but my mind can also conjure a hundred other more sinister possibilities too.

The rucksack she filled with a few belongings on Tuesday lies open on the floor beside the bed, daring me to pick it up and rummage. And I know I shouldn't. I know it's wrong to invade someone else's privacy, and I know how annoyed I was this morning to find the items in my underwear drawer rearranged. I have no right to go through her things, but if I'm correct and she was going through my stuff while we were at dinner last night, doesn't that give me the right to carry out my own checks?

I don't wait for the voice in my head to answer, snatching up the rucksack and resting it gently on the unmade bed.

It's not like I'm planning to steal anything, I just want to know exactly who is living with us.

I part the flaps and peer inside. I find a couple of light-coloured tops screwed into balls, along with a pair of trainers, and the pair of jeans she was wearing when I saw her cuddling up to Brett. There's no sign of a purse or other means of identification inside the bag, so I carefully squash down the clothes and return the rucksack to the floor. The bag wasn't exactly full when we arrived back here on Tuesday, and if the two screwed-up tops are anything to go by, she may already be on her last clean outfit. I have no issue with her using the washing machine and tumble dryer here, but she can't live in just three outfits forever. At some point she is going to need to return to her flat and collect clean clothes.

I move to the en suite, and scan the few items she's removed from her wash bag and placed on the windowsill: deodorant, lash curlers, mascara, lip gloss, toothbrush and toothpaste. We really did leave her flat in a hurry on Tuesday, so it's a wonder she remembered half this stuff given how frazzled we both were. In that state, I'm not sure I'd have even remembered to pack spare underwear.

I try to replay the few conversations we've had since we met, searching for any clues I've previously overlooked. I can't find her phone, but I would imagine that if she's popped out for air she would have that and her purse with her. Maybe I'm just going to have to wait until she's back and preoccupied to come checking up again.

I feel awful for even thinking that, given what this poor woman has been through, but I can't ignore the irritating voice of doubt that persists in the back of my head; the same voice that drove my own mother to the point of incarceration.

I freeze as a fresh thought strikes me.

Yesterday morning when I found her crying in here and she showed me the threatening messages Clark had been sending, I suggested she work from here, using my office as I was going to be in London. She said she would, but if she did, where on earth is her laptop now? It wasn't in my office when I checked just now, and it isn't here in the guestroom, so where is it? If she has popped out for air or to the shops, I can't see that she would have carried that with her as well, so where is it now?

I step back to the doorway, allowing my eyes to take in the whole room: the flock curtains; the dressing table with framed pictures of Luke and Caley on either corner; the built-in wardrobe, which contains most of my summer outfits that I have yet to swap with the winter outfits currently hanging in my own wardrobe; the bed; and the chest of drawers.

I check the drawers initially, but they are as empty as they always are. I cross back to my office to check I didn't miss the presence of her laptop, but it's definitely not in here.

I return to the guestroom for one final look, and realise that the rucksack doesn't look quite right, so crouch down and try to make it look undisturbed, which is when I spy the shiny grey object poking out from beneath the mattress. Lifting the edge slightly, I pull out a laptop that doesn't belong to me or Brett, and with a feeling of satisfaction turn it over in my hands, but stop when I read the label on the back of it, which reads 'Property of Allie Boland'. Who is Allie Boland? She told me her surname was Davis.

I freeze when I hear the sound of the front door opening, and Allie calling out my name.

21

I try to shove the laptop back beneath the mattress, but it won't go in. Panicked, I look for anywhere else I could hide the laptop, but if it isn't where Allie left it, she's going to realise I was in her room, and I can't have that. I can hear the echo of Caley's laughter downstairs, and if Luke is there too, I have seconds at best before the two of them are up here dumping their school bags and changing. And if Allie comes up with them, I'll be caught red-handed.

Standing, I press my fingers beneath the weight of the memory foam, and lift with all my might. A small gap appears, and I force the corner of the laptop into it, pushing as hard as I can, relieved when it begins to slide out of sight. I have no idea whether I've put it back in the same way she'd left it, but I don't have time to worry about it.

Slipping off my shoes, I hurry to the door on tiptoes to avoid the creaky floorboard, and press my ear to the door. Being caught exiting Allie's room will be as bad as being found inside. If any of them are on the stairs, I'll have no way of explaining where I am, but I can't hear any sounds. I take a deep breath, and lower the handle, carefully prising the door open. I can hear their voices downstairs, and quickly sneak out, but it's too late to dart to my office as I can hear Caley telling Allie she's just going upstairs to change. With no other choice I dive towards the bathroom, and make an audible effort to press the flush, straightening to wash my hands at the basin as my daughter walks past.

'Oh, hey, Mum, you're home early,' she says casually, not stopping for a reply before continuing on to her own room.

My heart is pumping so quickly that it might just explode out of my chest. I grip the edges of the basin, and stare at my reflection in the mirrored doors of the medicine cabinet.

How many times was Mum almost caught sneaking about where she shouldn't have been?

Caley reappears outside the door, her school bag now gone, and pulling a hoodie over her vest top.

'Allie said she'd fix us a snack and then we're going to watch *Friends* until Dad is back.'

I stop myself from reminding her that watching *Friends* after school used to be our thing, until I had to start commuting to London. It was my favourite show growing up, and like me, Caley watches every episode back to back, before starting from the first series all over again.

Heading downstairs, I find Allie in the kitchen, floating from one cupboard to the next with the air of a woman who has lived here all her life. She stops chopping banana slices as I enter.

'Oh, I wasn't expecting you to be home yet. I'm just fixing the kids chocolate spread and banana sandwiches. Is that okay? Caley said they always have an afternoon snack after school.'

I nod, grateful that Allie is so switched on to my children's needs, but equally envious that she is the one they've turned to even though I'm here. It also troubles me that I feel more like a guest in her house.

'I'll give you a hand,' I say, filling the kettle at the sink. 'So you collected Luke and Caley from school today?'

'As a favour to Brett.' She pauses and her hand shoots up to her mouth. 'Oh, God, I'm sorry, am I treading on your toes here? Please tell me if I am. I don't mean to be getting in the way. It's just... you've been so good to me, and so when the radio station phoned, and Brett asked me, I...'

Her words trail off at my blank expression.

'Radio station?' I say.

'For the interview.'

I have no idea what she's talking about. I don't remember Brett mentioning he had a radio interview today. If he had I would have made a point of listening to it. Have I been so caught up in work that I wasn't properly listening again?

'Brett's being interviewed on the radio?'

'Yeah, they heard about his talk at the library and invited him in for an interview about the book and his writing process. Didn't he tell you? It was all very last minute, and he initially said he couldn't make it because he had to collect the kids, but I had nothing else to do, so I said I could collect them if it would help. He phoned the school to let them know, and he should be back in a few minutes, I guess.'

Well, at least I'm not at fault, but it would have been nice for him to message and let me know.

'Thank you for collecting Luke and Caley,' I say, squashing down the negative voices in my head.

She finishes slicing the banana and lays the pieces across two slices of bread, before smothering chocolate spread on two other slices, squashing the alternating halves together and then cutting the sandwiches in half. I pass her two plates, and she carries the sandwiches out of the kitchen.

I know I should be grateful that Allie was here and able to do the school run so that Brett could go to the radio station, but if he'd phoned and let me know, I probably could have been home an hour earlier to play my part. Or would he not have phoned because he knows how busy I am at the moment and wouldn't want to force me to make a difficult decision? How many other opportunities has Brett passed up because I've been too busy to support him?

Allie returns a moment later, but I insist on making tea, while she stands and waits. At my core, I want to prove I still belong in this house and that I'm not a redundant mother.

'Luke said he has one sugar in his tea now,' Allie says, as I'm about to pass her the mug with his name on.

'Of course,' I say, though have no memory if I knew this or not. It's been so long since I made the after-school snacks that my knowledge of the routine is rusty.

'I can disappear upstairs, if you want some time with Luke and Caley,' Allie says, as if reading my mind once again. 'I really don't mind.'

'No, that's fine,' I tell her, forcing a thin smile. 'I have an important presentation to review before the morning.'

She nods, taking the mugs and carrying them out of the kitchen, leaving me alone with my thoughts.

* * *

I'm halfway through my third or fourth walkthrough of the presentation, when there's a knock at the door. I open it and find Allie standing there with a tray of food in her hands. The room immediately fills with the smell of spaghetti Bolognaise and garlic bread, and my stomach grumbles as my brain considers whether to accept the gift or not.

'Sorry to disturb, but I thought you might be peckish. How's your presentation prep going?'

I accept the tray and move backwards, returning to my chair, and placing the tray on the pile of papers beside the laptop. I've been scribbling notes on small postcards, every time I've thought of something clever to say about my team and how we're a better fit for Gliders. They look a mess, and I probably won't need them, but figure it will be good to have them beside the computer tomorrow should my mind go blank at any point.

'I think I'm just about ready.' I pause, knowing I probably shouldn't admit I'm going to be speaking to Chip Martin tomorrow, but Allie is probably the only person in this house who will appreciate what a big deal it is, and why I'm polishing so hard. 'I'm going to be pitching for the Gliders account tomorrow.'

Allie raises her eyebrows, and I know I've impressed her.

'Oh my God, that's amazing!'

'I know,' I say, unable to keep the proud smile from spreading across my face. 'You can't tell anyone though.'

She shrugs nonchalantly.

'Who would I tell? I quit my job this morning.'

I can feel my mouth hanging open.

'What? Why?'

She leans back against the bookcase.

'Because Clark turned up there this morning and caused a scene. My manager phoned to ask what was going on, and I told her, and then I said I can't cope with him knowing where I work, and I handed in my notice there and then.'

In that instant I picture the man and his wife at the Italian restaurant, but he can't have been the same person if Clark was at Allie's office causing trouble.

'It's funny, you know,' I say, 'but I was convinced I saw your Clark on the train this morning.'

'Oh, God, he was on your train?'

'Yes, well, no... what I mean is I thought I saw him on my train, and followed him out of Waterloo, but it turned out the person I was following was called Charles and married.'

I leave the line hanging, trying to read her reaction, but her expression gives away nothing.

'The guy I saw could have been his double. Does he have a brother called Charles?'

'Do you mind if we talk about something else? I don't really want to relive those memories.' She pauses. 'Hey, great news about Gliders though. Have you met Chip Martin before?'

I shake my head, but choose not to mention Marcus's relationship to him.

'I haven't either, but I've heard he's a really great guy to work with. A real out-of-the-box thinker. How exciting!'

I lift the tray onto my lap, and begin to tuck in.

'Would you...' I start to say, but then don't know how to finish the sentence.

'I don't mind if you want to deliver the presentation to me for feedback,' she says, once again seemingly reading my every thought.

I restart the presentation video, which introduces our company in a two-minute clip. Allie watches, and I try but fail to read her expression again, while shovelling strands of pasta into my eager mouth. When it ends, I hold my breath, uncertain why I'm so desperate for her approval.

'Good start,' she says, eyes still glued to the screen.

I click to the first slide of the presentation, but she grimaces in an instant.

'Wait, you're planning to use PowerPoint? You do know Chip Martin *hates* slide presentations, right?'

I frown at the comment.

'I thought everyone knew that,' she continues. 'I read it in a magazine interview he did last year. He's fed up of slideshows with writing firing across the screen, and won't work with any companies that aren't as forward-thinking as Gliders.'

Now that she's said this, I vaguely remember reading something similar last year. Oh, God, our entire pitch is a series of slides showing our vision. I feel my cheeks burning and it isn't from the heat of the meal I've suddenly lost the appetite for.

She looks over to me, and her brow ruffles empathetically.

'Sorry. Listen, it might be okay. If *your* vision is unique enough, then maybe he'll make an exception.'

Despite her best efforts, I can see she doesn't mean what she's saying. I can't believe I didn't remember that magazine interview sooner. I've had my team pulling this presentation deck together for two straight days, and it's the worst thing I could have done. I've screwed everything up, and there is no time to fix it. Chip Martin is going to hate the pitch, Marcus is going to be embarrassed, and at least one of my team is going to be laid off.

My hands ball into fists as I try to steady the emotional dysregulation now taking control of my mind.

'Hey, it might be okay,' Allie tries again. 'Why don't you run me through the slides, there might be something we can salvage. Some of the images, for example: these were probably copied into the deck, so you could still use them, just in the software used to create them.'

The room swims before my eyes, and I can't move; I'm frozen to my chair, as my mind plays out scenario after scenario, each one worse than the previous.

I see Chip cutting me off at the very start, accusing me of showing him disrespect for daring to use a slideshow; I see Marcus erupting with rage and firing me; I see Brett shouting because I've lost my job and now we'll have to put the house up for sale; I see Luke and Caley sobbing as they accuse me of ruining everything.

'Jenna? Jenna? Can you hear me?'

My brain screams out at the sting from Allie slapping me across the face. My hand shoots up to my cheek.

'I'm sorry,' she quickly says. 'It was like you were in a trance. Are you okay?'

I don't know how to begin answering the question.

Allie lifts the tray from my lap, and places it back on the pile of papers on my desk.

'Let me help you fix this,' she says. 'If there's one thing I'm good at, it's problem-solving. Talk me through your vision verbally, and we'll take it from there. We have all night. It's going to be fine.'

And in that second something snaps in my mind, and the tears come.

22

I wake on Friday morning with an instant sense of panic and fear. My fight-or-flight instinct has kicked in because in a few hours I know I have to deliver our pitch to Chip Martin at Gliders, and I can think about nothing else. I have been sitting at my desk for half an hour, staring at the detritus Allie and I pulled together until late into the night, before I even realise I haven't had my regular hit of caffeine. It takes another fifteen minutes to be able to drag myself down to the kitchen and to put the kettle on.

The rest of the world flows around me like waves against a stubborn rock that won't be moved. Brett passes in a blur as he prepares breakfasts and lunches for Luke and Caley, telling me about his plans for the day, but I don't register a single word.

'Honey, shouldn't you be getting dressed?' I catch as he pecks me on the cheek on his way out the door with the children. 'You've got your thing in a few minutes, haven't you?'

I stare down at my watch in disbelief. How is it half past eight already? I have been up for nearly three hours and am still in my pyjamas, my hair unbrushed, and only a half-drunk mug of tea to show for it. I know how important making a good first impression is, but I cannot seem to shift my brain out of neutral.

When Allie appears in the doorway, I can't tell if her frown is confusion or disgust, but she doesn't wait to explain, maybe sensing my need for maternal care in this moment. She takes me by the hands and leads me out of the kitchen and upstairs, sitting me on the bed, while she ransacks my wardrobe, laying an outfit on the mattress beside me, while giving me detailed instructions about dressing. It's like the most surreal out-of-body experience, and but for her forcing me to strip out of the pyjamas and into the trouser suit, I would probably have remained frozen to the bed until I finally caved to sleep.

I feel the teeth of the brush as she runs it through my unkempt hair.

'It's going to be fine,' she tells me over and over. 'And what's the worst thing that can happen?'

And therein lies the problem: I can't get past my mind catastrophising exactly what the worst-case scenario will be. The file will be missing from my laptop's hard drive; the broadband service will drop out and we'll lose connection, leaving Marcus to try and blag; I'll lose my voice; I'll forget my words; I'll make a complete mess of the presentation, and Marcus will realise what a fraud I am, and fire me and the whole team.

'I believe in you,' I hear Allie say next. 'Chip Martin isn't going to know what's hit him. Take these and wash them down with this glass of water.'

She presses two small capsules into my palm and although I have no idea what they are I don't resist when she pushes my hand up to my mouth, and I swallow the capsules with the glass of water she has provided. I am then led into the office and she sits me in my desk chair.

'What's your favourite song?' she asks, and it's one of those questions I always detest.

My favourite 'thing' is very much dependent on my mood and the context, and most people don't understand just how hard it can be to come up with an answer. I don't want to lie so I need to consider all my options, and that means I need the context. My favourite song to dance to isn't my favourite song when I need something calm and mellow to relax me into sleep. Similarly, my favourite piece of classical music would be rubbish if I was trying to work out at the gym. Why does she need to know my favourite song right now? I have too many other things to be thinking about.

'I know, what song did you and Brett do your first dance to at your wedding?'

I instantly picture the weeks leading up to our big day. Brett was terrified about our first dance, and we must have listened to more than fifty songs trying to find something he could ably move to, and it was only after practising various holds that we chose something with a good melody that meant something to us, but hadn't registered just how inappropriate the lyrics were for a first dance as husband and wife. By the time we realised, it was too late to find an alternative.

'We danced to "If You Leave Me Now", by Chicago.'

She stares back at me blankly, maybe trying to read whether I'm joking or being sarcastic.

'It was used in a television advert years before that always used to make us laugh,' I try to explain.

'Okay, well, let's go with that,' she says, flicking through her phone, and a moment later the song blares out of the small device. 'Close your eyes, and remember that first dance. Picture the scene around you. Think about the dress you were wearing and how proud and supportive your guests were seeing the two of you tie that bond. Think about the food you ate, the gifts you received, and the excitement of the honeymoon that was to follow.'

I feel myself swaying to the music, replaying that scene over in my mind, as I have done countless times before. And then when the song finishes, and I open my eyes, my mind is more settled, and I feel so relaxed.

What did she give me?

She switches on my laptop, and I log in, with five minutes to spare until the meeting is due to start.

'I can sit in with you if it would help,' Allie volunteers. 'I can perch down beside the desk so I won't be on screen. Not that you need me; just remember everything we discussed last night and you will knock them bandy.'

The call starts and I ball my fists beneath the desk when Chip and his team dial in, followed by Marcus a few seconds later. Although Chip and his team look relaxed in polo shirts and chinos – they are standing, rather than sitting – Marcus has opted for a full shirt, tie, and blazer, and looks like he has a court appearance to follow this meeting.

'Good morning, Chip,' I say, not waiting for Marcus to introduce me, 'I'm Jenna Morgan, and I am the Creative Director of Elite Artisans. Thank you for your time this morning, and without further ado, we'll begin.'

* * *

My pulse is racing as I conclude the presentation and invite questions from Chip and his team.

'Forgive me for saying, but Elite Artisans has a rather small turnover of staff right now, and I'm interested to know how you would plan to upscale to meet our needs,' Chip asks.

I can see Marcus desperate to answer, but I already have this one rehearsed.

'We are ready to grow the business immediately,' I say with a confidence I'm not feeling. 'We have a list of freelance designers awaiting our call. We plan to take them on a trial basis, so we can assess their work is up to standard and that they share Gliders' core values of integrity, sustainability, and out-of-the-box thinking. And the benefit of today's post-pandemic world means we can recruit from anywhere across the globe, because we are a dynamic business that doesn't force its employees into an office just for appearances' sake.'

I deliberately avoid eye contact with Marcus as I say this, and I can imagine how desperate he must be to interrupt me right now. It was something Allie and I discussed last night, and whilst there can be benefit to personal contact, it shouldn't be restricted by the old norms. I probably should have mentioned this to Marcus sooner, but I know he would have disagreed.

'And,' I continue, taking a deep breath, knowing that Marcus could explode at what's to follow, 'because we will be making you our premier client, and will be at your beck and call 24/7, it would make sense for us to give up our office space in London, and make use of the Gliders Headquarters building. You could essentially think of us as a subsidiary of Gliders, and whilst we will generally work remotely, we could feasibly have a presence in the building at all times to accommodate your needs.'

Marcus's eyes are so wide they're practically on stalks, but I focus on Chip and see him whispering something to the woman beside him who nods and scribbles a note on her tablet.

'Well, Marcus,' Chip says, turning back to face the camera, 'I have to say I'm very impressed, with Jenna in particular. She's a real find, and if you're not careful I might try to poach her for Gliders.' He adds a disarming chuckle, but I can't tell if he's being serious or just bantering Marcus for old times' sake. 'We still have a couple of other companies to hear from, but will have a decision for you on Monday. I'm very impressed, Jenna.'

I feel my cheeks blaze, and because I've never been good at receiving compliments, I grab Allie's hand and pull her into the view of the camera.

'I have to admit, I had help putting all of this together. May I introduce one of those freelance graphic designers I mentioned earlier. This is Allie Davis, and if you give us the green light on Monday, she'll be the first recruit into my new team.'

Marcus is frowning, but it's nice having someone else share the spotlight.

'Thank you all,' Chip concludes. 'Until Monday.'

The call ends and Marcus immediately calls me back.

'What the hell was that?' he shouts into his camera.

'Personally, I thought it went really well,' Allie says, 'and you should be praising Jenna for a job well done.'

'And who are you exactly?'

'Someone who sees Jenna's full potential.'

He gives her a withering look.

'Jenna, what happened to the presentation deck you shared with me yesterday afternoon?'

'I remembered – actually, Allie reminded me – that Chip hates presentation decks, and much prefers to see the nuts and bolts of how things work. Allie and I rejigged a few things last night to better meet the client's needs, and he said himself he was impressed.'

'And what was all that about giving up the lease on this place?'

'It came to me last night,' I say. 'You've been so worried about our balance sheet this year, and yet our biggest expense is office space. During the pandemic, we managed by working from home, and we won't only achieve profit this year by switching back to a remote model, but it will dramatically reduce costs in future years. None of our existing clients ever come to our office, we always go to them. So, really, the only reason we maintain that space is for staff meetings and occasional socialising. And if Chip signs on, we can maintain a small space at Gliders at no additional cost. It's a win-win.'

He opens his mouth to retort but changes his mind, maybe just angry that he didn't think of the idea first. I don't mention that the real reason for suggesting the business model change is so that I can have better access to my children and strive towards something like a decent work-life balance. And in truth, I don't know how much longer I can continue to put up with commuting to London. The bright lights, the big noises, it is an overstimulating environment and not beneficial to my needs.

Marcus signs off, telling me to keep my fingers crossed, and I throw my arms around Allie. Although I'm not a fan of hugging, I want her to know how grateful I am for all her support in the last twenty-four hours. I know there is no way that things would have gone as well as they have without her influence on me.

'I think this calls for a celebration,' she says, with a cheeky grin. 'Let's crack open a bottle of prosecco and celebrate.'

23

I know better than to drink alcohol so early in the day, but as I stir awake in unfamiliar surroundings, my head pounding, I am filled with regret.

The moment Allie suggested opening the prosecco to celebrate, I should have told her that it doesn't take much for me to feel inebriated these days. But she kept saying we deserved something a little naughty, and then she popped the cork and passed me a flute. I told myself I would only have the one glass, and that I would sip, rather than guzzle, but it didn't seem to matter how slowly I drank, my glass never seemed to get any emptier; every time I wasn't looking, Allie would top it up.

At first, the light-headedness was fun. Allie produced bagels and smoked salmon, and I made scrambled eggs, and it reminded me of cooking with friends at university. I vaguely remember us calling each of the team to tell them how well the pitch had gone, and introducing them to Allie; telling them Marcus had agreed for her to join the team, even though I don't think he's said anything of the sort. The combination of the alcohol and the buzz of the morning's pitch went to my head, and

I think I emailed Allie's CV to Marcus, telling him I'd offered her a job.

I sit up, realising now I'm lying on the sofa in the living room, a light blanket draped over my legs. An empty flute stands on the coffee table to my right, along with the now empty bottle of prosecco. My eyelids feel so heavy, but I can't stay like this. I'm supposed to be collecting Luke and Caley from school this afternoon, and I must look a state. I need coffee, a shower, and something to take away the pounding in my head. Throwing off the blanket, I swing my legs off the sofa, but as I attempt to stand, my head lolls to one side and I fall back down.

This is not good. If Brett comes home and sees me in this state, he'll be so disappointed. I can't believe I allowed myself to get drunk in the middle of the day; especially when I should be logged on. I can't even remember whether I was supposed to have any work meetings today. What would Marcus think if he could see me now?

I start again, sensing that I was falling back to sleep, and this time force myself to all fours and crawl away from the sofa in the vague direction of the kitchen. Brett keeps a supply of energy drinks on the top shelf of the fridge for days when he can't motivate himself to work. A boost of sugar and caffeine would be welcome right now, and so I pad into the kitchen like some errant pet, and it takes me three attempts to stand, using the countertop and drawer handles as ballast.

What is wrong with me?

This is more than just a hangover. It feels as though my head is buried deep below the ground. Everything I look at feels so far away, and all sound is muffled somehow. Straightening, I pull open the fridge door, but it takes more effort than I'm expecting, and when I'm bathed in the painfully bright yellow glow of the bulb it takes me a moment to remember why I came to the fridge in the first place. I'm about to close the door when the light glints off the metallic rim of the cans, and I grab one, flicking it open and pouring half the contents in my mouth. I wince at the bitter taste, but force myself to finish the can, knowing the sooner the caffeine hits, the sharper my mind will feel.

It only serves to heighten the pain behind my eyes, and as I take in the pile of washing up behind the sink, I spot another open bottle of prosecco standing beside the dustbin. No wonder I feel so awful. My eyes rise from the bottle, and up the wall until they fall on the clock.

No, that can't be right.

I raise my wrist to check my watch, but I'm not wearing it, so I then have to go in search of my phone, locating it on the coffee table back in the living room. I stare at the digits as they blur in and out of focus, and my heart skips a beat.

No, no, no.

How can it be four o'clock? I should have collected Luke and Caley half an hour ago. I stagger in blind panic towards the front door, slipping on a pair of trainers, no longer caring about my appearance, as I burst out into the warm and too bright outside. My car sits on the driveway, and despite my urgency, I'm in no state to drive. Diving back into the house, I grab my sunglasses and house keys, and then half-jog-half-stumble along the road, in the direction of the school.

My phone shows missed calls from the school, but when I try to return the call, it goes unanswered. I can't believe I allowed myself to get into this state. I knew Brett would be out all day, and it was my turn to collect the children. And I was planning to take them to the village café for an ice cream after school. Caley was so looking forward to it, as was I.

My heart is in my throat as I swing around the final corner, and see the school gates up ahead. There are a few parents still flittering about, collecting children or dropping off for the various after-school clubs. I scan the playground as I push my way through the gate, but I can't make out either Luke or Caley amongst the children in PE kits playing hockey. I am breathless as I make it to the door of the school office, but when I pull on the handle it is locked. There are two women chatting beyond the window, and I have to thump my hands against the glass to get their attention. As they buzz the door open for me, I catch sight of my reflection in the window, and am filled with shame. I pat down my hair as I enter, but I'm fighting a losing battle.

'How can I help, Mrs Morgan?' the woman with white hair scraped back in a tight bun asks, and I'm a little taken aback that she knows my name when I have no clue of hers.

'I'm so sorry I'm late,' I pant, realising now I have no excuse to make, so decide not to offer one. 'I'm here to collect Luke and Caley.'

She frowns in confusion, though it could also be at my less than savoury appearance.

'I'm sorry, Mrs Morgan, there must be some kind of mistake: Luke and Caley aren't here.'

I almost laugh out loud at the ridiculousness of her suggestion.

'Of course they're here. It's my day to collect them, but I fell asleep, which is why I'm late. You called me,' I say showing her the list of missed calls on my phone.

Something seems to click behind her eyes.

'That's right, we phoned when nobody had arrived to collect them, but then someone did.'

School protocol would be to phone both parents if the children aren't collected, so they must have called Brett.

'Someone? You mean my husband?'

Her frown lines deepen.

'No, it wasn't your husband. It was... oh, excuse me a second.' She heads back inside the office, emerging a few seconds later carrying a clipboard. 'They were collected by Miss Allie Davis at 15.45.'

Allie collected them? Why didn't she wake or tell me?

'She said you weren't very well, and had sent her in your place. She is on the list of approved caregivers.'

A wave of nausea rises the length of my spine, and I have to press my hand against the wall to stay upright. I don't say anything else as I plough back out of the door and into the cooler air, desperately hoping I don't vomit on school grounds. My face feels as pale as snow, and I stumble away from the building, trying to focus my gaze on my phone's display to call Allie and find out what's going on.

I hear the phone ringing and place it to my ear, but my call goes unanswered before the answering service kicks in. I don't leave a message, ending the call and trying again as I spill out through the school gates.

This time Allie answers, much to my relief.

'Where are you?' I say, appalled by the slur of my speech.

'Oh, hey, Jenna, how are you feeling now?'

'Where are Luke and Caley?'

'Oh, they're fine. The school phoned while you were passed out and so I said I would collect them. I left you a note to say I would get them, didn't you see it?'

I have no memory of any note, though that would have been helpful.

'Where are you?' I ask again.

'Caley said you were supposed to be taking them for ice cream so I said I'd take them to the café in the village so you could continue sleeping. We've just sat down, but you're welcome to join us.'

I feel envy bubbling near the surface, but swallow it down.

'Are you feeling any better?' Allie asks.

'W-what happened?'

'Um,' she begins, with more than a hint of awkwardness in her tone. 'Do you remember when you couldn't get going this morning ahead of the meeting with Gliders? I gave you some of my anxiety medication to calm you down. But then when we opened the prosecco, I forgot what I'd given you, and alcohol doesn't mix well with that particular narcotic. I realised too late that you were slurring your words and unsteady on your feet, which is why I made you lie down on the sofa to try and sleep it off. I felt so awful when the school phoned, so I thought I should make it up to you. But you're awake now, which is a good thing, I guess.'

I don't even remember Allie slipping me any pills this morning, but then I remember very little of today. It's no wonder I've felt so off since waking on the sofa. Even now, as I cross the park in the direction of the café, I feel as though I could curl up on the damp grass and go to sleep. I don't think I've ever felt this rough in my entire life.

I end the call, passing on my gratitude that she collected the children, but as I near the café, and see the three of them sitting at a table in the window, the breath catches in my throat when I see that Brett is with them. Although I can't hear it from out here, I can see his big laugh, as he leans closer to Allie and they share a glance. I can't get over just how picture-perfect the four of them look together. But what terrifies me the most is the prospect that Allie chose to drug me to keep me out of the way.

24

On the way home, we buy fish and chips from the takeaway next to the café, serving it on plates as the idea of eating it out of the grease-covered paper makes my skin crawl. I don't think Caley has stopped telling Allie about all the different things she got up to at school, in the same way she used to chew my ear off. Luke seems more chill, less impressed by Allie, the would-be surrogate auntie.

There's part of me thinks I should tell Caley that her newfound friend won't be around forever and that she shouldn't allow herself to become too attached. After all, once Allie has found a new place to live, I don't imagine the children will see much more of her. And that's the moment I remember sending the email to Marcus and demanding he hire her. I shouldn't have allowed myself to get so carried away. Allie's ideas definitely helped with the presentation to Chip and his Gliders team today, but the truth is I still know so little about her that I shouldn't be making such impulsive decisions. I'm usually so careful about who I trust with my time and energy and yet for some reason I've allowed Allie to bulldoze her way into our lives without doing my due diligence.

I did try to look her up and didn't get very far. But maybe the offer of employment is my opportunity to get some real information about her. It is expected that a would-be employer would ask her for things like her date of birth, National Insurance number, and references. If she is hiding something, this will be my opportunity to find out everything I need to know. Deep down, I know it's possible that my drug-addled subconscious was already three steps ahead of me when it sent the email to Marcus, but it could just be a turn of good fortune.

Caley beams as Allie listens and asks clarifying questions, and I hate the feeling of envy that is once again rearing its head in the back of my mind. I should be pleased that Caley is finding it so easy to talk to Allie when she's usually so introverted around strangers. I still remember my own lack of sociability around strangers when I was growing up; something that remains with me in adulthood.

Luke declares he's going for a shower before bed, and Brett says he will wash the plates while I take Caley upstairs for a story. Caley whines that she wants Allie to read to her instead, and I'm about to put my foot down and insist when Allie tells her she needs to make an important phone call, but promises she'll read to her tomorrow night instead. Satisfied, Caley takes me by the hand and leads me upstairs and to her room, where I help her change out of her uniform and into pyjamas.

Luke's shower is noisy next door to Caley's room, but I know he won't be more than a few minutes in there. I can hear the vague sound of his music and he never stays in the shower for longer than one song.

Settling Caley in bed, I pick up *The Velveteen Rabbit* and continue the story from where the bookmark pokes out. She snuggles with her favourite teddy, a giant, furry bumblebee that Brett's mum knitted for her years ago. There was a time when Caley wouldn't leave home without Mr Bumble pressed into her hands.

Although I continue to read the words to Caley, my mind is elsewhere, and I can't stop glancing at the bee, thinking about all the years my own mother has missed. Although I've told her she has grandchildren, I stopped sending photographs a while ago, when she wasn't responding to the cards and update letters I was sending. Is she actually aware that she has grandchildren? I don't know what kind of state her mind is in now, nor whether the hospital will have given her what I sent.

And so now I'm feeling overwhelming guilt as well. If Tom is right, and her mental health is improving with the regime of medication, then I have been a terrible daughter. I haven't visited in forever, or even phoned to check up on her. It would break my heart if I ever lost contact with Luke or Caley, and maybe that's exactly what she's experiencing now too. That's not to mention how much grandparental time the two of them have also missed out on.

No, I can't do this to myself! I broke off contact to keep my family safe. Mum was a danger to both herself, and to Tom and me. That is why she was sectioned, and I shouldn't be allowing these feelings of guilt anywhere near my conscious mind.

I look at Caley as I reach the final word on the page, and see her eyes are clamped shut and her breathing has reached a steady rhythm. I gently close the book and stand it beside the foot of the bed, before tucking the duvet around her frame and kissing her forehead.

'Good night, my little doodlebug,' I whisper, stealing myself away, knowing I could spend the rest of the night just watching her sleep.

The bathroom door is open when I emerge back onto the landing, a plume of steam still hanging in the air, even though Luke's shower is long since finished. I flick on the extractor fan, as he's clearly forgotten again, before heading to his room to say good night. He's already in pyjamas, his hair a spiky mess and his eyes glued to the game of football he's playing on his television.

'Just one match and then it's lights out. Yes?'

'Yep. Night, Mum,' he replies, his eyes not leaving the glare of the screen.

I kiss the top of his head, and he squirms, complaining that my leg is blocking his view, and then I leave his door ajar. I'll come back up to check he isn't still playing in ten minutes or so, but I trust him to stick to the rules.

I find Brett just finishing the dishes when I enter the kitchen, and am relieved there's no sign of Allie, though I am curious about the important call she claimed she needed to make. I don't know if that was just to get out of reading to Caley or whether she's maybe found a new place of her own to rent. I feel bad thinking it, but the sooner she gets back on her feet, the better for everyone. I think I've coped well so far with the changes to our careful routines, but her staying here isn't a long-term solution.

'Do you want a coffee?' Brett asks.

'I'll make drinks,' I offer, conscious I haven't helped clear away dinner, and reach for our mugs. 'How was your day?'

'Not as impressive as yours, by all accounts. Allie said you smashed your presentation out of the park this morning.'

I can't help the smile breaking across my cheeks.

'There are no guarantees they'll go with us though,' I temper, not wanting to get my hopes up, only to have them dashed on Monday. 'I'm pleased with how it went, and I gave it my best shot.'

We both turn to look at one another when the doorbell sounds, not used to visitors so late on a Friday evening.

'I'll go,' he says, leaning across and pecking my cheek, as he knows I don't like unexpected calls.

I hover by the door, listening in, trying to work out whether it's some kind of late delivery, or a neighbour returning one of Luke's lost footballs. But it's almost impossible to hear anything with the kettle boiling, so I end up flicking off the switch and returning to the edge of the door to listen.

'And is it just you home?' a voice I don't recognise asks.

'No, my wife is here too. She's just putting our children to bed. I'm sorry, what is this all about?'

I press my ear to the gap between the door and its frame.

'Have you noticed anyone unfamiliar hanging about; either outside or near wherever you work?'

The knot in my stomach twists. The late call; the official-sounding voice; why are the police here?

'No, I can't say I have.'

'And I can't see any sign of a burglar alarm at the property; do you have any other kind of home security installed at all? Maybe a security camera or one of those video doorbells?'

'No, nothing like that. Rownhams has always been a fairly safe area. Has there been a spate of burglaries then? Is that why you're here?'

'No, not exactly that, Mr Morgan. We're actually searching for a woman, who we believe may be in the area. We have a picture we can show you.'

My mind clicks into gear. Allie's ex Clark is in the police, and now there are officers here asking questions about her. She warned me he would use his personal influence to paint her as the villain to find out where she's hiding.

But Brett isn't aware of the backstory or exactly what happened between Allie and Clark, and I don't want him to let something slip. I burst out of the kitchen and squeeze in beside

Brett. There are two uniformed officers at the door, one male, one female. Both look as though it's not long since they left school.

'Hi, I'm Jenna Morgan,' I say before the officer can show Brett the picture and he gives the game away. 'Is there something I can help you with?'

Inside my slippers, my toes are balling as I try to mask my outward behaviour and appear as normal and relaxed as possible, when I'm feeling anything but.

'Good evening, Mrs Morgan,' the female officer says, a small red LED glowing on the camera attached to her uniform. 'We're sorry to disturb you, but we were just asking your husband whether he's seen—'

I don't want Brett to catch me in a lie, so I quickly turn to face him. 'Luke asked if you'd go up and say good night.'

He gives me a curious look but doesn't challenge me in front of the officers. I wait until he's at the top of the stairs until I turn back to face them.

'Sorry about that. Do you have a picture of this woman you're looking for?'

The male officer removes something from his pocket, before unfolding it and handing me a printout of Allie captured on a security camera.

'Do you recognise the woman in this picture, Mrs Morgan?' he asks.

I force myself to frown, desperately hoping they don't see the obvious signs of recognition. I don't know if the police are trained to read body language or not.

'No, I'm sorry, I've never seen that woman before in my life.'

I grind my teeth; there is nothing that ties Allie and me together apart from that moment on Tuesday morning. Is it possible they could have found footage of us both disembarking at Basingstoke that morning and then they've traced our steps back to his flat in Winchester? It seems too incredible, and yet isn't that exactly how Allie has described what Clark is capable of?

'Are you sure?' the female officer asks. 'Look again.'

I make a show of scrutinising the image, the cogs in my head whirring, wondering where the image was captured, and whether they also have a picture of Allie and me together.

'I'm sorry, definitely not. What is it she's supposed to have done?'

The officers exchange looks, but neither answers my question. The female officer then reaches into her pocket and pulls out a small card, passing it to me.

'If you do see her hanging around here at any point, please contact me on either of the numbers on this card, or if it's an emergency phone 999.'

I accept the card, turning it over in my hands, enjoying the sharpness of the corners pressed into the tip of my thumb.

'I will do. Thank you.'

I close the door and wait until I've heard them walk away before letting out a huge sigh of relief, though deep down I sense this won't be our last dealings with Clark's colleagues.

'We need to talk,' Brett says, coming down the stairs and pointing at the kitchen.

I shouldn't be surprised that he has questions about why I'm lying to the police, and I don't want to keep him in deceit any longer. But he speaks again before I have the chance to come clean.

'I'm worried you're doing too much,' he says, once we're both inside and the door is closed. 'You're prioritising work over the welfare of your family, and I think you're spreading yourself too thin.'

It's sweet of him to worry, and I move my hand to his cheek to show I appreciate the support, but he whips his face away, his expression one of anger, rather than empathy.

'You can't keep putting work ahead of us.'

'I'm not,' I say back, but I'm not sure he hears me.

'First, you missed most of my library talk when you said you'd finish early to be there, then you weren't home yesterday when I needed you to watch the kids while I was being interviewed, and then today I had the school phoning me while I was out because you didn't show up to collect them.'

'Wait, hang on, that's not fair.'

'And worst of all you missed collection time because you were drunk. At three in the afternoon, you were passed out.'

When I met with them at the café earlier, he never mentioned any of this, so I assumed he didn't know. But Allie must have told him, and now he's making me out to be the villain. Well, I'm not standing for it.

'Can I speak now?' I say aggressively. 'Firstly, I didn't mean to miss your library talk, but you were supposed to be the one collecting the kids yesterday. Had you messaged me about the interview I would have come home sooner. I'm not a mind reader, Brett. And before you start accusing me of prioritising work over our family, just remember, *you're* the reason I have to work so damned hard! My income has allowed you to pursue your writing dream.'

'Oh my God, are you ever satisfied? You've spent all year criticising me for not writing my second book and promoting the first, and now that things are starting to move you're blaming me again.'

His cheeks are blazing, and I know we need to stop before one of us says something we might regret, and so I don't respond, taking some slow breaths to try and calm myself.

'All I can say is you're lucky Allie has been here to help us out,' he continues. 'So, if you're planning to push for this new account and your working hours are going to increase, then we may have to consider hiring a nanny to help us out.'

'A nanny?' I scoff. 'We're barely getting by as it is.'

'Yeah, well, things can't go on like this for much longer. And if we can't afford help, then the only alternative is to ask my mum to come across and help us out for a bit.'

It's like he's trying to push my buttons.

'The last thing we need is your mum here, judging me for not being a stay-at-home mum like she was.'

'Well, if you can't be here to pull your weight with the kids then we may have no other choice.'

He heads out of the room, leaving me alone with my thoughts.

25

I shouldn't be awake before seven on a Saturday, but my sleep was disturbed again, only this time it was Clark haunting my nightmares. In one, I was in the supermarket with Caley and we'd just turned down the confectionary aisle when Clark suddenly appeared, calling to my daughter with a huge tub of sweets, and despite my best efforts to hold onto her, she moved towards him in a trance-like state. I woke screaming out her name, with Brett panicking beside me because I'd woken him. And then in another, I was in the London office, working at my desk when Marcus's door opened and Chip Martin and Allie emerged, laughing at the tops of their voices, then they were joined by Marcus, draping his hands around their shoulders like they made the perfect team.

But what's more troubling than my subconscious trying to terrorise me is that I know Mum suffered with similar bouts of insomnia and bad dreams, and it was the lack of sleep that only served to heighten her paranoia. I wake thinking I should book an appointment to see my GP to discuss what's going on. Therapy isn't the dirty word it once was, and I am not prepared to follow the path my mother created for herself. I can't continue to have disrupted sleep, but I don't want to treat the symptoms with sleeping pills; I need to get to the root cause. And right now, that means getting Allie out of my house.

I want to help her, and I feel like I already owe her so much for how she's helped me at work this week, but I can't have Clark turning up on our doorstep and causing troubles for me and my family. I have to keep them safe.

And it is with this mindset that I decide I'm going to take Luke and Caley out for the day. I've been neglecting them both recently and I don't want them to ever question how important they are to me, so I'm going to take them into Southampton city centre for the day and spoil them rotten. Not that I want to buy their affection, but just want to spend some quality time with them both. They are growing up so quickly, and before I know it they'll be facing GCSEs and A-Levels and I'll have missed their best years. They need me now more than they'll ever need me in the future, and I want them both to know they are my priority.

'I'm thinking of taking the kids into town today,' I tell Brett over breakfast. 'Fancy coming with us and making a day of it? I thought we could hit the shops this morning, a spot of lunch somewhere, and then maybe bowling or the cinema to finish. What do you think?'

We haven't discussed last night's argument since we woke, and although it's still playing on my mind, Brett appears to be his usual chipper self this morning.

'That sounds great,' Brett says, but he's frowning.

'What?' I ask, unable to read why his lips would be saying one thing, and his forehead something different.

'Well, the thing is... I'd set my heart on writing today. I've reached a key part of the book and need to make sure I'm able to tie several of the plot points together in the next ten thousand words.'

I don't know why I'm so disappointed, as when I'd come up with the idea first thing, I hadn't pictured Brett being with us. I shouldn't feel jealous that he wants to work on his book – God knows, we need the money – but it does feel like he's rejecting us. And it's giving me flashbacks to when Mum would organise a day out for her, me and Tom, and then Dad would say he'd already agreed to play golf or watch the football.

'These last couple of days have been a real breakthrough,' Brett continues, 'and I know if I can get through these next couple of chapters, I'll be on the home straight and in a place where I can share the first draft with my agent.' He pauses, trying to read my face. 'But if it means that much to you, then I'll come along and postpone the writing until tomorrow.'

And now the guilt overwhelms me. After what he said last night, I don't want to be the reason he loses motivation for his writing again. Plus, the royalties from the second book may come in handy to make sure Mum stays at the Graveside Hospital.

'No, you should stay and focus on your writing,' I say, adding a smile to quell any feelings of guilt he may now have.

Allie appears in the doorway, stifling a yawn as she stretches her arms over her head. I chose not to tell her about the visit from the police, although I did eventually tell Brett about Clark and his controlling behaviour. And he told me Allie had already filled him in, though I don't understand why he didn't say anything sooner. We shouldn't be keeping secrets from one another.

In truth, I've been replaying last night's encounter over and over in my mind, and I can't be certain they believed me when I said I didn't recognise Allie. If they saw through my lie and reported as much back to Clark, then there's a possibility he will visit here at some point today, and that's another reason for me to want to be as far from home with Luke and Caley as possible.

Of course, I'm not sure I want to leave Brett here alone with her. The pyjamas she's wearing hang from her tiny and younger frame, and although I don't want to doubt Brett's loyalty, I can see how he might be tempted if she were to throw herself at him. But I don't want to be Mum and be having these kinds of thoughts all the time.

I shower and change and find Luke and Caley alert and waiting by the front door when I come down. I notice Allie has also dressed, a mini dress and cardigan, and she's plaited her hair in two pigtails.

'Are you two ready?' I say, reaching for my coat, wanting to cover the dowdy-looking jeans and sweater I'm wearing.

'Can Allie come with us?' Caley asks, and I wince at the unintended barb.

I don't immediately answer, uncertain how to phrase my answer without offending Allie. Today is supposed to be about me and the kids.

'I can't,' Allie says, when she sees me floundering. 'I've got house hunting to do.'

Caley pulls a sour face.

'Oh, please,' she whines, stretching the vowel sound. 'I can show you that dress I was telling you about in Primark. And Mum said we're going to get food as well.'

I can feel Allie trying to read me.

'Allie said she has plans,' I say, trying to break it to Caley gently.

'You don't need to look for a new home,' Caley persists. 'You can just keep living with us here. Problem solved.'

'Well, I suppose I could look at houses this afternoon, but it's up to your mum.'

I feel three pairs of eyes all staring at me now.

'You should come,' I finally say, as brightly as I can manage, determined not to be the reason that sour expression remains on my daughter's face.

* * *

We arrive just after ten and the place is heaving with other shoppers. I don't do well in crowded places, but Caley insists we go to Primark first, emerging with handfuls of bags full of reduced items, eventually calling in at HMV for Luke to peruse the games. He also chooses two games that are on a sale offer, so I allow him to get both as they're not that much more expensive than the cost of a new one.

Allie insists on buying lunch, and we allow the children to choose where we go, and so we end up at Nando's, and I desperately want to commit their smiling faces to my long-term memory. If I could bottle this moment, I would. They're even happy spending time together, which has felt quite rare recently. They have very different personalities, and they seem to be branching further apart as they explore their own interests. Luke is all about football and gaming, which Caley has no interest in. Where once I could leave them both playing a boardgame together, they seem to agree on so little these days.

The thought of working flexibly from home, able to take them to school or collect them most days, is just so much to hope for. I hate hoping for the best because too many times in my life it has resulted in greater disappointment when the positive things haven't happened. And so my response now is always to assume the worst will happen. With that mindset, I should be prepared for the likelihood that Gliders will disappoint us on Monday, and rather than Marcus seeing the potential of expanding the team, he'll still demand I make one of my team redundant.

These are the thoughts troubling me while we're inside Nando's.

'Penny for them?' Allie asks, when the kids go off to choose their drinks.

'Sorry, I can't stop thinking about Monday morning and what Chip is going to say.'

'You really don't need to worry about that. You've done all you can, and there's nothing more you can do to change the outcome. What will be, will be, isn't that what the French say? Stop worrying and just enjoy the moment. You don't realise how lucky you are to have Luke and Caley. They really are great children. You and Brett should be very proud of the way you've brought them up. I wish the kids I knew growing up were so polite and respectful.'

'What was your childhood like?' I ask. I've been looking for a way to ask more about her background all morning, and I'm not going to pass this up.

'I grew up in Cheetham Hill. Do you know it?'

I shake my head.

'It's to the north of Manchester city centre, and had huge problems with drugs and burglaries when I was growing up. The sort of place you never quite feel safe enough to leave home, but didn't want to stay in just in case. The girls in my school were skanks who picked on anyone who just wanted to keep their head down and earn qualifications. There were some really dark days.'

My heart goes out to her. My school life was no picnic either, but name-calling was the extent of it. This is the first glimpse of vulnerability I've seen from her since the day we met, and now it's making me feel guilty about questioning her motives. Brett, Luke and Caley have all warmed to her, so she can't be as bad as my paranoia is making out.

'Sorry, I didn't mean to dampen the mood,' she says next. 'I graduated school and got the hell out of there and haven't looked back. When I met Clark, I thought I'd found the one. You know? I could see us marrying and starting a family of our own. I never had any brothers or sisters growing up, so I want more than one child. But now that I've seen what you and Brett have, I can see that what I had with Clark wasn't love. Not really. I think I was kidding myself, but now I know what I want, and once I'm back on my feet, I'm not going to waste another second going after it.'

I'm about to thank her for sharing but Luke and Caley bundle back to the table, almost knocking over the bottle of ketchup.

By the time we've eaten, I feel exhausted, and Luke is so desperate to get home and play his games that I don't even mention bowling or the cinema. It wouldn't be the same without Brett here, and Allie did say she wanted to go looking at flats and houses this afternoon anyway. We head home and when I see our house with Brett's car on the drive, I'm filled with love for the little life I've carved out. Allie is right: I am lucky. And filled with this warmth, we enter to the smell of something sweet baking in the oven. It makes the place feel even more homely, but it surprises me that Brett has found the time to bake when he was so keen to focus on his writing. I head into the kitchen, my mouth dropping when I see the head of white hair in my apron washing up by the sink.

'Oh, there you are, dearie,' Judith says, drying her hands on the apron.

'Grandma,' Caley squeals from behind me, racing into the kitchen and throwing her arms around Brett's mum.

'There's my favourite granddaughter. Look how big you're getting. But still just as pretty as when I first saw you.'

When Brett mentioned her coming across from Ireland to help us, I thought it was a hypothetical question. He never said he'd actually invited her. And with Allie here, we don't have a room for her to sleep in. I can't believe he's gone behind my back and invited her to come and stay.

'Are you going to stand there catching flies all day, or are you going to come and give me a kiss?' she asks, and I can already feel her judging me.

26

'I didn't know she was going to come and stay,' Brett says in a loud whisper when I've dragged him to our bedroom five minutes later.

'Don't give me that,' I fire back. 'This is precisely what you wanted. You said as much last night.'

'That's not fair. Mum phoned yesterday and she asked if it would help for her to come and visit, and I told her we were fine. But it turns out, she heard what she wanted to and booked herself a flight first thing. I swear to you I didn't know she was coming until she rang the doorbell. At first I thought it was the four of you back early.'

I want to believe him, but it feels too coincidental that he hypothesised this scenario last night and now it's come to fruition.

'And where the hell is she going to sleep with Allie in the guestroom?'

'The kids can bunk in together for a few days and she can have Caley's room. And then when Allie moves out, she can have the guestroom.'

'It could take weeks for Allie to find and secure a new place. How long is your mum planning to stay?'

He puts his finger to his lips, and I realise now my voice is loud enough to be overheard downstairs.

'We haven't talked about it yet. Once she sees everything is okay, I'm sure she'll return home to Dublin.'

'Well, you could have warned me she was here so it wasn't such a surprise when I walked into my kitchen and found her re-washing the dishes I did last night.'

He holds his hands up in surrender.

'You're right. I'm sorry.'

He holds his arms out and I move into his embrace. After what has been an incredibly stressful week, my judgemental mother-in-law turning up on the doorstep was the last thing I needed.

'You know she's going to be her usual delightful self, don't you?' I say.

'That's why we need to stick together,' he says, kissing the top of my head. 'But do you know what? It might be good for the kids to spend some time with her. You know she likes making a huge fuss of them, and with your mum... well, you know... it won't be a bad thing for them to have a grandparent spoiling them a bit.'

My jaw clenches at the mention of my mother. It was my choice not to tell them she's alive, and I thought I'd done well to keep that part of my life locked up. But with my fortieth birthday approaching rapidly, and the fragility of my own mental health now in question, the ghosts of the past feel like they're catching up.

'We should head back down,' Brett says, breaking off the embrace, 'before she fills the children's stomachs with sweets and biscuits.'

'We had Nando's so I don't think Luke and Caley will have space for anything else.'

But it turns out that was wishful thinking, as when I enter the living room, I find Caley curled up on the sofa with half a chocolate chip cookie dangling from her mouth.

'Caley, you need to use a plate,' I remind her.

'Ah, no, it's fine,' Judith interrupts from Brett's armchair. 'Leave her be. I was going to whip the vacuum around the room in a bit anyway.'

'You don't need to, I was planning to do it in the morning.'

'My wee mammy always used to say don't put off until tomorrow what can be done today. And it looks like it could do with a tidy. It's no trouble.'

And so it begins.

'I'm perfectly capable of keeping my house clean, Judith, thank you,' I say between gritted teeth.

'Oh, I know you are, dearie. I wasn't suggesting otherwise. Oh, gosh, and now I've offended you. I really didn't mean to. I always forget how sensitive you are.'

It takes all my willpower not to react, as it will only make matters worse. What I need is for Brett to grow a pair and stand up to his mother once and for all, but he's never been one for confrontation, especially where she's concerned. Whenever I've asked him to pick her up on some of the snide comments she's made down the years, he always bows out with excuses. *She's not in great health; she's only trying to help; we're the only family she has left; she's still grieving Dad's passing.* It feels ironic that she considers me the one who's oversensitive.

Luke walks into the room and sees the cookie in Caley's hand.

'What? Why's she got a cookie? Mum, why's she got a cookie?'

'Ah, finally, there's my handsome grandson. Don't you have a kiss for your grandma?'

Luke hadn't even noticed her sitting there, but his face brightens from behind the cloud and he gives her a hug.

'There's a cookie for you in the kitchen too. But mind, they've not been out of the oven long.'

He hurries off, returning a minute later with a cookie, but at least he has a plate.

'How are you, Luke? You're getting so big now. You'll be taller than your dad soon. You know, you're the spitting image of him at that age. Good genes.'

As opposed to my bad genes, I think, but don't say.

'How is football, Lukey? Are you scoring lots of goals?'

'Yeah, a few,' he says, between mouthfuls of cookie. 'Coach reckons I'll be ready to progress to the next age group soon.'

This is news to me, but I don't say anything, assuming both he and Brett just forgot to mention it. But maybe it's just another sign of how engrossed I've been with work recently that I'm missing the key details in my family's lives.

'While I'm here, we must go out so I can buy you something you really want for your birthday. Maybe a football shirt for that club you support.'

Luke's eyes widen with glee.

'And of course, I'll have to get something nice for my favourite granddaughter too,' she adds, winking at Caley. 'What else are grandmothers for?'

Brett finally enters, a cookie between his lips and no plate, followed by Allie, though I've no idea where she's been since we got home. Probably just trying to keep out of Judith's way.

'And who do we have here?' Judith says, spotting her.

'Mum, this is Allie,' Brett announces. 'She's a friend who's staying with us at the moment.'

'It's nice to meet you,' Allie says, marching over and shaking Judith's hand.

'Well, aren't you just the prettiest wee thing,' Judith says, adjusting her glasses.

'Thank you. Brett and Jenna have told me so much about you. And Caley was saying just this morning how much she wishes she could see her grandmother more.'

'Was she? Oh, that's so sweet. I wish I could see more of my grandchildren too. Brett and Jenna as well, of course.'

I excuse myself and head out to the kitchen, opening the fridge door and spy the open bottle of wine in the door, but it's too early, so I reach for the carton of milk and put on the kettle.

'Are you okay?' Allie asks from behind me.

I force a smile.

'I will be. Sorry, I should have introduced you when we got home, but seeing her here threw me.'

'No need to apologise. I can see how tense she's making you.'

I frown at this statement, wondering whether Judith can also pick up on the tension.

'When has Brett mentioned Judith to you?' I ask.

'Oh, he hasn't,' she says quickly. 'I was trying to help; just telling her what she wanted to hear. I didn't even realise her name was Judith until you just mentioned it.'

She smiles, and it slightly disturbs me just how easily she can shift her persona to fit any environment, much like a chameleon. Maybe I should take a leaf out of her book when it comes to dealing with my mother-in-law.

'It'll be nice for Luke and Caley to have their grandmother around for a few days,' Allie continues. 'And it will free up your time to be focused on work too. Her timing couldn't have been better really.'

I wish I could agree, so I say nothing instead.

'Do Luke and Caley get to see much of *your* mum?' she asks next.

'No, she passed,' I say quickly, sticking to the story.

'Oh, I hadn't realised. I'm so sorry. I was sure you mentioned her previously and I got the impression she was still alive. When did she die?'

'Just before Luke was born, so neither got to meet her.'

'You must miss her a great deal.'

My jaw clenches as I force my head to nod. I hate that I'm lying to Allie, but I can't let the delicate house of lies I've built come crashing down around me. I don't want anyone else to know the problems that I may have inherited from her.

'Oh, that's such a shame. But even more reason for them to make the most out of Judith's visits then.'

The kettle boils and I make tea for the grownups, whilst Allie fixes squash for the children. We carry it through to the lounge on a tray, but Luke has disappeared back up to his room, and Caley is sitting on Judith's lap, allowing Allie and me to sit down beside Brett on the sofa.

'I'd best find myself a hotel,' Judith says after a moment.

'Nonsense,' Allie interjects. 'You're family, and I'm the imposter, I'll find myself a hotel, as I've already outstayed my welcome.'

'Don't be silly,' Brett says. 'We have plenty of room, which means nobody needs to go searching for a hotel. Luke and Caley will bunk in together, and Mum can go in Caley's room.'

'I don't want to put anyone out,' Allie says. 'Judith should have the guestroom as she'd benefit from the en suite. And it isn't fair for Caley to be booted out of her room.'

'But you can't afford to pay for a room in a hotel,' Brett says.

'Well then, I'll sleep on the sofa. I really don't mind. I can sleep anywhere.'

'That's very kind of you, Allie,' Judith says, giving her a warm smile she's never shown to me before.

'You can have my room, Allie,' Caley says, now sucking on a lollipop, which she must have been given by Judith. 'I don't mind sleeping on the airbed in Luke's room.'

'Well, what a generous wee lady you are,' Judith coos, giving her a squeeze. 'I guess that's settled then.'

I hate that I've become a ghost in my own home, but I know Brett is right about Allie not being able to afford a hotel in the area. And Judith certainly can't afford to stay in one, and we can't afford to pay on her behalf. I'm not sure Luke will be so keen to have his sister cramping his style, but I'll speak to him privately and find a way to convince him, even if it involves more retail bribery.

'Well, hopefully it will only be for a few days,' Allie says, sipping from her tea. 'I might find the perfect place this afternoon when I go out. I don't suppose you want to come with me, Jenna? I'd appreciate a second opinion.'

Despite my exhaustion, the thought of staying home, trapped with Judith, feels a worse choice.

'I'd love to,' I say, quickly standing. 'Shall we get going now?'

27

We both stare at the light brown stain on the wall across from us, and I don't know about Allie, but I'm hoping it's tea.

'The landlord has assured us he will have the flat freshly painted before anyone moves in,' the short man in the too-large grey suit and spectacles says. He doesn't look old enough to be allowed out on his own, let alone to be showing flats to prospective tenants.

Even if the stain is tea and not something worse, it still doesn't explain how or why it is so high on the wall.

'It isn't the biggest living space we have on the market,' Elliott the estate agent continues, 'but it's actually just below the budget you gave me, so you'd be able to save a little extra every month.'

'The website described this as a one-bed studio flat,' Allie says, 'but I can't see a door to the bedroom, so have I missed something or is it some kind of hidden door in the wall?'

It's a fair point. The room we're in is about four metres squared, which includes a table, a chair, and a small countertop with sink, microwave and two cupboards hanging from the wall above.

'That's the beauty,' Elliott says proudly. 'Would you mind stepping over to the window?'

We oblige, and Elliott carefully places his tablet on the countertop, before crossing to the wall opposite the stain. He raises his hand above his head, and pulls on a small black handle screwed to the wall, and that section begins to come away with him, until the bed and mattress are down and taking up the lion's share of the floor space.

'Ta da,' Elliott says, wiping the sweat from his forehead with a handkerchief.

One corner of the mattress is now squashed against the table in the corner, so the only way to get back across the room is to lift the bed back into the wall.

'Clever, right?' Elliott says, misreading our confused expressions. 'It really does maximise the space, doesn't it? So, during the day you have all the space you need for working, entertaining, and relaxing, and at night, you don't waste that space, but transform it into a haven for rest and sleep.'

He speaks so confidently that I feel as though he genuinely believes the bullshit he's feeding us.

'This is not a one-bedroom flat,' Allie declares.

'The keyword in the description was studio,' Elliott says. 'Think about it: how many people make use of their living rooms and kitchens during the night? They are wasted real estate, whereas this seamlessly transforms one into the other.'

Having briefly seen the flat Allie was sharing with Clark, this place isn't even a third of that size.

'Can we have a few minutes to talk?' I ask Elliott, and he raises the bed back into the wall, before taking his leave, though he leaves the door to the hallway ajar, so we'll have to keep our voices down.

'I know you want me out of your place as soon as possible,'

Allie says, as if reading my mind, 'so, if you think this is the best I'm going to get, then say and I'll sign the agreement today.'

'Don't be silly,' I say unconvincingly.

'With Judith now visiting, the place is overcrowded, and with the pressure at work, you don't need me adding to your woes at home.'

She has a point, but I'm surprised she's even considering this flat. It's arguably the smallest of the three we've looked at this afternoon, though not the worst. It's walking distance from Southampton Central train station and the city centre, which is probably why the rent is as high as it is, despite the diminutive nature of the flat. Even as a student I would never have thought twice about somewhere so small.

'You don't need to go with this place though,' I counter meekly. 'What about that flat above the takeaway we looked at last? It's a bit further from the station, but it was bigger than this and at least had a separate bedroom and kitchen.'

'Did you not smell the fumes from the fish and chip shop reeking through the carpet? It wasn't unpleasant for a few minutes, but that smell is going to end up permeating all my clothes, and everyone will smell it all day. Plus it's over the budget I'm able to afford. Of all the places we've looked at this afternoon, this is the only one within budget.'

'Then we keep looking. I can't see you living somewhere like this. And assuming Marcus does take you on when you meet on Monday, then your budget might increase.'

What is wrong with me? She was giving me a way out, and I'm now the one convincing her to stay.

'Are you sure? I don't want you coming to regret helping me because I'm getting under your feet.'

'Don't worry about me.'

'But it isn't just you, it's Brett, Luke and Caley too.'

'Luke and Caley love having you with us, and if Brett was here right now he wouldn't want you leasing this place. We'll manage until you find your right home.'

She steps forwards and throws her arms around my neck and awkwardly pulls me into her.

'Thank you so much,' she whispers.

This is the moment Elliott pokes his head back around the door.

'Do we have a decision then? Should I draw up the paperwork?'

Allie releases her grip and turns back to face him.

'No bloody way, pal. If this is the only thing you have within budget, then we'll look elsewhere. And you really need to update the description on your website, because it's misleading.'

Allie grabs my hand and marches me out of the room, and we brush past a floundering Elliott, until we're outside in the warm afternoon glow of the sun. But she doesn't stop at my car, instead pulling me further along the road until we reach a small pub on the corner of the small high street. Inside, she orders two large glasses of wine before I've had chance to argue, and then she tells me to head towards the beer garden, finding a table at the back of the patio space, away from the smokers.

'I really shouldn't,' I tell her when we're seated.

'Nonsense. Your choice is to sit here with me and enjoy a glass of wine, or return home to Judith's Spanish Inquisition. And instinct tells me this is by far the lesser of two evils.'

Heat rises to my cheeks as I realise my views on my mother-in-law must be far more overt than I realised.

'What's the deal with the two of you anyway?' Allie continues, clinking the rim of her glass against the one before me.

I reach for the glass and take a sip.

'I don't imagine our relationship is much different to the usual mother and daughter-in-law relationship.'

'Does she not think you're good enough for Brett?'

I almost spit out my wine.

'Oh, no, I don't think it's personal, like that. To be honest, I don't think anyone would ever have been good enough for her little boy.'

The truth is I've never really thought about why Judith is always so judgemental of me, but maybe there is more to her disapproving of me. I take another sip of the wine, enjoying the acidic aftertaste on the back of my tongue.

'She's part of that generation that doesn't believe in neural differences. When I first told her I was autistic, she totally dismissed it out of hand. "We never had issues like that in my day," she said. "We all just knuckled down and got on with things." It felt so invalidating, but she's one of those people who it doesn't matter how much you argue with them, there's no changing their mind. Do you know what I mean?'

She nods.

'I used to have a friend who was very much like that. She would argue the world was flat, even when seeing views of the earth from space. What does Brett say about her?'

'Behind closed doors, he agrees that she's a challenge, but he loves her dearly and knows she won't be around forever, and is so resistant to challenge her back. He doesn't see the point.'

'Which presumably means when she's rude to you, you just have to accept it?'

I nod, conscious that I shouldn't be unburdening my soul on Allie, but it's been so long since anyone really listened to me that it's hard to keep my thoughts to myself.

'I was so nervous the day Brett first took me to her house to meet her. I'd made a cheesecake for dessert, as I thought it would show her I would be able to take care of Brett long term. She thanked me for it, but the look of disgust on her face was hard to miss. I wondered whether I'd inadvertently offended her in some way – like, was she lactose-intolerant and Brett had forgotten to mention it? – but there was no explanation offered. Anyway, we finished the shepherd's pie she'd made, and then she carried through a massive bowl of trifle. Brett asked her where the cheesecake was, as he wanted a spoonful of each, and she told us she'd left it unattended on the side and her cat had eaten it. Now, that could have been true, and I was too anxious to say anything, but it just felt a little too convenient. I mean, she could have said she doesn't like cheesecake, and I wouldn't have been offended that she didn't want to eat it, but I'd gone to real effort to prepare it, so that really upset me. Brett and I argued about it on the way home, and he just didn't understand.'

'Did your mum ever meet Judith?'

'No. The thing about my mum is...' My words trail off because I don't know how to answer why I've been lying to Judith for all this time, without making myself sound like some kind of sociopath. I've always been so desperate for Judith's approval that telling her about Mum's poor mental health felt like it would be a bit of an own goal.

'Mum wasn't very well in the final years of her life, so there was never a moment that seemed right for the two of them to formally meet.'

I study Allie's face for any sign that she doesn't believe my lies, but I can't read what she's thinking.

'It must be tough for you not having your mum around to talk about these things with. My relationship with my mum wasn't great, but there isn't a single day passes that I don't miss her. She was always just there at the end of a phone if I needed to rant or chat through an obstacle. It can't be easy for you not having someone you can talk to about problems.'

How can someone so much younger be so insightful?

'I've never been good at sharing my feelings, and I don't know that Mum ever knew how hard things were for me growing up,' I say in a moment of honesty. 'I find it hard to trust people.'

'I think you're doing yourself a disservice there. I actually think you're very good at sharing what's on your mind, and if you ever need someone to just vent at, I'm a good listener. And you can trust me.'

She reaches across the table and gives my hand a gentle squeeze.

'Does Brett know how hard you find it when Judith imposes?'

I shrug.

'He knows, but it doesn't make a difference.'

'Her heart seems as though it's in the right place, though, right?'

I return the near-empty glass to the table.

'I don't have an issue with who Judith is really. She spoils Luke and Caley rotten, and she gave Brett a good and loving upbringing, so the shadow that she casts over my life is a price I'm prepared to pay. I just wish she would be more open-minded and reflect a bit on the things she says and does, that's all. I don't mean to sound sour. And Brett's right: she won't be around forever.'

'I can say something to her if you want?'

My eyes widen at this suggestion.

'Oh, God, no, please, I don't want that. I've probably spoken out of turn, so please don't say anything to Judith or Brett. I probably am just being oversensitive, and neither of them would understand.'

I watch her, waiting for an acknowledgement, but she drains her glass instead.

'Promise me you won't say anything, Allie,' I try again.

'I won't,' she says, but now I'm filled with regret for being so open. What if she drinks too much later and something spills out? I'm going to spend the rest of the day worrying.

'Do you fancy another?' Allie asks, but I'm already feeling a little lightheaded and still need to drive home.

'No, listen, I have a better idea. You can't keep living out of the few clothes you snagged from your flat on Tuesday. Why don't we drive there now and collect your remaining stuff?'

'What? No. I don't want to go anywhere near that place. Clark might be there.'

'But he's not going to do anything with me there.'

'You don't know him. Trust me, I'd sooner never see those things again and replace the lot.'

'Okay, okay, fine, then we'll head home instead,' I say to appease her.

Her reaction isn't untypical of someone who doesn't want to see their abuser again, but I can't help thinking there's some other reason Allie doesn't want to go back there, I just can't figure out what.

28

I catch sight of my face in the rear-view mirror as I'm parking outside the house, and I can't get over how much I look like Mum right now. My cheeks look drawn, with clear bags puffed beneath my eyes from disturbed sleep this week, and my skin so pale despite exposure to the afternoon sunshine. It's no wonder Brett is so worried.

'If Judith's fussing gets too much, just give me the nod and I'll make some excuse to get us out of there,' Allie says. 'I've got your back.'

'Please promise me you won't say anything about what we discussed. It would cause more problems than it would fix, and ultimately won't improve the situation because Brett and Judith are just so blinkered.'

She fixes me with a firm stare.

'I told you, Jenna: you can trust me. Okay? I won't go sharing what we've discussed. You've been so good to me this past week, and I owe you. Just let me know what you need and I'm there. Okay?'

I'm still not totally convinced that she'll keep quiet and I wish

I hadn't opened my mouth in the beer garden. I know I'm probably just catastrophising things again, but predicting the worst outcomes is my only shield in this confusing life.

We head inside, and I immediately spot the open patio doors into the back garden and can hear Caley shrieking in glee as she bounces on the trampoline. The air is filled with the smell of charcoal and burning fat, so Brett must have the barbecue on. Allie says she's going up to her room to change and so I continue out to the garden, where I spot Brett and Luke by the barbecue, and the scene looks perfect. These are the images that make me happy: my family together and enjoying the sunshine. And I'm over the moon to see Luke detached from his Xbox.

'Hey, you're back at last,' Brett calls over. 'Now we can get the burgers cooking. Mum's in the kitchen preparing salad and the buns, so sit down and just take it easy. I don't want you lifting a finger.'

I feel my cheeks instantly tighten into a smile, remembering that Brett does love me and it's unfair for me to be criticising him for not being firmer with Judith. He isn't my father and shouldn't be tarred with the same brush.

I cross to the wooden picnic bench and sit, facing the sun to try and give my skin a little colour, and Allie slides in across from me a moment later, a fresh bottle of wine and two glasses in her hands.

'See, not as bad as you thought it was going to be, is it?' she whispers, and I hope that's the last we'll talk about our earlier conversation.

I take the bottle and pour measures into both glasses, passing one to Allie and raising my own to toast her.

'Oh, Jenna, you're back, thank God,' I hear Judith call over from the patio doors. 'Would you mind giving me a wee hand in the kitchen?'

I glance over to Brett to see if he's going to stand up for me, and tell her that he wants me to sit and relax. But he's disappeared off into the garage and I can see him leaning over the freezer, searching for the burgers.

'I'll go and help her,' Allie offers, in the process of standing.

'Allie, you relax with Brett and the children, Jenna and I should be fine on our own.'

My shoulders tighten, but I take a deep breath and down what's in my glass, before topping up and standing.

'I'll be fine,' I tell Allie quietly through gritted teeth.

The kitchen is in a real state with a stack of pans on the counter, another on the stove, the fridge door wide open, and a selection of plates, cutlery and condiments scattered across the table.

'I don't know how you find things in this kitchen,' she mutters under her breath. 'No rhyme or reason for where things are.'

She's wearing my apron again, so I lift down Brett's from behind the kitchen door and tie it around my waist, leaving my glass of wine on the table.

'What is it you're looking for?' I ask, half sighing.

'Dijon mustard,' she says, still shuffling items around in the fridge.

I move to the cupboard where we store tins and jars and lift the mustard out.

'Here it is.'

Judith looks from me to the open cupboard door.

'Why the hell is it up there? If the jar is open, it should be kept in the fridge, no? Ketchup too.'

'Well, we keep them in the cupboard because they contain all the necessary stabilisers and additives to be stored at room temperature. Besides, Caley doesn't like cold ketchup. What do you need the mustard for anyway?'

'I'm making a dressing for the salad.'

'Oh, we have salad dressing in a bottle in the fridge.'

'No, I mean real dressing. Homemade. You can't trust these companies that mass produce such things. It'll be lovely, and it's really no bother.'

Just breathe.

'Can you stab the potatoes for me, Jenna, and see if they're done?'

I pick up the sharp knife from the counter and do as I'm instructed, and it comes away easily, so I withdraw the pan from the heat and drain the water.

'Just so you're aware, Luke and Caley don't like boiled potatoes, so we might have to make them some chips.'

'Don't be ridiculous, Jenna. A chip *is* a potato. What's not to like?'

'They don't like the texture, that's all. It's fine, we have some frozen fries I can quickly cook in the air fryer.'

'But I've cooked enough potatoes to feed an army. I'm sure they'd like them if they give them a try. I think you could be a bit tougher with what they eat instead of pandering to their every want. Brett used to be funny about textures too, but once he got used to them he was fine. Trust me, we'll get them eating these.'

I return the pan to the hob with a clunk as my frustration simmers near the surface.

'I should carry some of these plates out,' I say, looking for an excuse to escape.

'Before you do, I wanted to have a word with you...'

Tension pulls at my shoulders.

'Sit down for a moment, won't you?'

I pull out a chair, and instantly reach for the wine, taking a swig for courage. I see Judith's disapproving stare as she sits in the chair perpendicular to me.

'Brett told me you're struggling at the moment.'

I didn't expect her just to bowl out with what's on her mind, and mine blanks as I search for a response.

'It's okay to admit that you're finding things tough, dearie, we all do from time to time. It's nothing to be ashamed of. But not asking for help is a road to trouble.'

I wish the ground would just swallow me whole. I don't have to sit and listen to this interfering busybody judging me, and yet the sudden manoeuvre has my mind frozen, and my body won't respond to its commands. I just need to tell her to mind her own business, stand up and go to any other room or back outside. I don't think she'd dare have this conversation in front of Brett, and especially not the children. But I cannot move.

'That's why I've come to help you,' she continues, oblivious to my internal monologue. 'I can stay as long as you need. Get things running like clockwork here so you can do your wee job and Brett can fully focus on his new book.'

I want to tell her that it's my *wee job* that pays all the bills in the house, but my lips remain tightly shut.

'Brett tells me you're working all the hours God sends and if he won't tell you then I only feel it's right that I tell you: you can't do everything. I knew a man once – well, he was more like a cousin than a friend – and he used to work morning, noon and night and dropped dead at the age of fifty. Is that what you want too?'

She has no idea what I'm going through, but instinctively I've assumed the role of errant child being scolded by a parent. I'm a grown woman, and I should be able to tell her to leave well alone.

'I had another friend whose motto in life was work to live, don't live to work. Have you ever heard that expression before?'

Of course I have, I want to scream.

'That's the approach you should be adopting. Wee Luke and

Caley will be grown and gone before you know it, and you'll spend every day after wishing you'd made more of their youthful exuberance. God knows I wish I could turn back the clock with Brett. Not that I'm not extremely proud of the father and provider he's become, I just miss having him curl up and fall asleep on my lap.'

Stop patronising me, Judith.

'Even now, look at how tightly wound you are. Like a coiled spring waiting to explode. I noticed it when you came home earlier too. It's not healthy, Jenna, and you mark my words: if you don't do something about it – learn to relax – you're going to burn yourself out.'

You've no fucking idea!

'And given the family history of mental illness, I do worry that you're going to go the way of your mother.'

My mouth drops at this.

'Brett told me, dearie,' she says casually. 'You and your brother ended up having her committed for her own safety, and I can see signs of you losing your grip on reality.'

I can't believe Brett has gone behind my back and spoken to her about Mum. I want to drag him in here right now and demand to know what else he's told her. My mum's poor mental health is nobody else's business, and I hate that she's speaking like some omniscient expert. Not even Brett knows just how bad things were when I was growing up, because I've shielded him from those things, so whatever information he's provided her isn't even halfway close to the truth.

'Breathe, dearie. Nice and deep. I'm here to help.'

I wish Allie was here right now, but I can't see into the garden from here and have no way of signalling for her to come to my rescue.

Judith moves her hands across the table and tries to take hold of mine, but I whip them back in an instant, almost toppling the chair backwards, but it gives me the momentum to stand and cross back to the countertop, my back to Judith, trying to block out the voices of insecurity screaming in my head.

'You're not well, Jenna, dear,' I hear Judith from behind me, and I snap round and glare at her.

'I'm absolutely fucking fine, Judith, and if you spent even an ounce of the energy you waste judging me, you'd see you're the reason I'm on edge right now.'

The blood drains from her face, but it's too late to shut the floodgates.

'My mum's mental health is none of your fucking business. Who are you to judge me? I work my arse off to provide a home and stable environment for my children, far better than the childhood me and Tom had. I've learned to be better than her, and you have no idea how difficult it can be. And your beloved Brett is a good father, but we'd be homeless if it wasn't for me. So stop judging me for being an absent mother, and celebrate me for working so damned hard.'

I stop when I see Brett and Luke in the doorway, shocked expressions on both their faces. I instantly regret my tirade, and wish I could go back just five minutes and stay in the garden.

'I'm sorry,' I finally say, sighing heavily, aiming the apology at Brett, and feeling a lump form in my throat.

He steps slowly into the kitchen his arms wide, and his hands waving in a passive gesture.

'Put the knife down, honey,' he says, and at first I don't know what he's talking about but then I follow his gaze down to my hands and catch the glint of silver in my right hand, pointing in Judith's direction.

I hadn't realised I'd picked it up, let alone that I was holding it in a threatening gesture.

'No, wait,' I say, throwing it towards the kitchen sink, wanting to get it as far from me as possible. 'It isn't what you—'

'I think you should come outside with me,' Brett says, still slowly closing the gap between us.

I look over to Luke, hopeful that he'll be the one to concur that they're blowing this out of proportion, but he takes an unsteady step out of the room and then sprints away back to the garden.

My heart shatters into a hundred pieces, and I know I just need to get away from all of this. I race forward, darting around Brett and rush upstairs, slamming the door behind me, collapsing onto the bed, sobbing.

29

I start awake, my chest burning, and my throat dry. I don't remember getting beneath the duvet, and judging by the dark night sky beyond the window, I've been asleep for several hours. Pushing the blankets away, I try to take several deep breaths to clear the fog in my head, but end up coughing instead. There's a rancid taste in my mouth; usually a telltale sign that I've been snoring. Brett has told me before that I only tend to snore when I'm unwell – migraines and colds the prime culprits. I reach over to check if he's also awake, but am disappointed to feel the cold space beside me.

When my snoring is at its height, he's been known to seek solace in the guestroom, as his mood is less affable when he's deprived of sleep, but with Judith in there, he can't be.

I push myself out of bed and head to the bathroom, using my electric toothbrush to try and clear the horrid taste from my tongue, and then rinsing with mouthwash. My phone tells me it's after two, so I'm surprised Brett hasn't come to bed yet.

He's probably hooked up with Allie.

My mother's voice in my head is like a slap to the face.

No, Brett wouldn't do that; and I don't want to believe that Allie has any desire to break up my marriage. I've gone out of my way to help her this week, and she'd have to be some kind of heinous bitch to stab me in the back like that. Besides, Brett is at least a decade older than her, and whilst I will always fancy him, middle age has brought on a paunch and balding crown. And given her last boyfriend was tall, dark, and athletic, I'd argue Brett isn't her type.

But remember how cute they looked together; how much he's been laughing with her around. He wouldn't be the first man to have his head turned.

I haven't physically spoken to my mother in years, and yet it is definitely her voice in my head. Is this what schizophrenia feels like? When people hear voices, is it their own, or do they hear it in different accents and intonations? Am I actually losing my mind?

I run the tap until the water is cold, and then splash handfuls against my cheeks, savouring the icy sting against my warm skin, before finally stepping back and staring at my reflection in the mirrored doors of the medicine cabinet above the basin.

I don't know when I started to look so tired. In my head I'm still in my early twenties: young, free, and with sixty-plus years of life ahead of me. But the woman staring back at me looks slightly gaunt, wrinkles bunching at the corners of her eyes. And I now see just how much I look like Mum. This is the woman everyone else sees, and it's no wonder that Brett is worried I'm following in Mum's footsteps.

Your father started straying when I started looking my age.

Her voice is so loud, breaking through my own thoughts, that it's like she's standing in the corner of the room behind me. I physically turn to check that she isn't there and this isn't some intense nightmare, but I am alone in the room.

I can't remember the exact moment when Mum stopped trusting my father, but I remember the snide comments she'd make when he broke the news he was having to stay away for work. It was never that regular, maybe a day every other month at first. She'd demand to know who else would be staying away for the conference. He was always quite vague, avoiding naming names, but as much to protect her as just to avoid arguments. And I don't know if she ever believed him, but I remember the Monday night she belted Tom and me in the car and drove to the conference hotel in Worthing. She dragged us to reception and demanded to see a list of hotel guest names. When the staff refused to comply, she started shouting until someone must have called Dad, because he came down, his face burning with anger and marched us up to his room in an effort to prove he wasn't having an affair.

He told me years later, after he'd moved out, that it was Mum's constant accusations that finally drove him into the arms of another woman. He joked that if he was going to be charged with doing the wrong thing, he might as well get some fun out of it. I hated him for saying that. No matter how mentally unwell Mum was, she didn't deserve to be cuckolded. I didn't see much of him after that. He tried to stay in touch, but I stopped agreeing to visit him, blaming university and then, when I found Brett, I broke off all contact. I blamed them both for the breakup of their relationship, and vowed I would never allow my marriage to suffer in the same way.

I hate that I'm now asking similar questions of Brett when he doesn't deserve my mistrust. He's never given me any reason to question his loyalty, and I shouldn't start making irrational leaps in judgement.

Where is he then? You were unwell, so he should be looking after you.

My head snaps around again, but there is no ghostly figure hovering beside the door. These voices aren't natural, and whilst I've always had competing thoughts in my mind, they've never manifested in this way before. And it terrifies me that the woman I've been avoiding for all this time may have experienced these exact same voices before we realised just how mentally unstable she was.

I exit the bathroom and return to bed, sitting on the edge, listening for any sound of where Brett could be. He's been known to fall asleep on the sofa while watching a film before, but I can't hear the vibration of the soundbar through the floor, which would suggest the television isn't on.

You can't blame him for straying. She's younger and prettier than you.

'Shut up!' I shout through gritted teeth.

This isn't healthy. That much is becoming obvious. I need to speak to my GP and let him know what is happening. My mum refused to seek treatment until she was sectioned, but maybe if she had – if she'd realised how ill she was – she could have got help sooner and things would have been different. I owe it to myself – and to my family – not to ignore my own doubts.

I grab my phone from the side and open the app for the GP surgery, searching for the next available appointment, but there are none to be booked. I will just have to phone the surgery on Monday morning, explain what is happening and ask for an emergency appointment then. Locking my phone, I try to lie back on my pillow, but it isn't just my mum's voice I can hear in my head now.

What if Chip Martin decides to reject the pitch and Marcus demands the name of someone to be made redundant? How are you going to choose one of the team? What if Mum's mental illness is hereditary and you've now inadvertently passed it on to Luke and Caley?

Will they suffer in the same way? What if Clark is outside the house right now, waiting to pounce? What if he already has and that's why Brett is missing?

I sit up at this last thought. If he knows where we live, what's to stop him coming here to exact revenge? Maybe while I was passed out in bed, he came to the door and attacked Brett and Allie.

I bury my face in my hands. I know my imagination is playing tricks on me, but now that I've had the thought, I can't ignore it. I need to find my husband and check he is safe.

Standing, I'm still half asleep as I drag myself from the bed and narrow my eyes when I open the bedroom door and am confronted by the bright landing light. Switching it off brings scant relief, and I check on Luke and Caley, finding them both peacefully asleep in Luke's room. The Xbox remote is still on the edge of Luke's bedspread, and I move it so it won't fall off in the night and land on Caley in the airbed.

The door to the guestroom is closed, and I hover outside of it for several minutes, my ear pressed against the wood, trying to hear any sound beyond, but there's nothing. From the top of the stairs, I can hear the low rumble of voices in the lounge but can't make out whose. I creep down the stairs, stopping at the door when I hear Brett.

'Of course things aren't like they used to be. I never expected they would stay the same. Marriages evolve, you know. It goes from lust to love to companionship.'

'Jenna's very lucky to have found such a talented and understanding husband. And the way you are with Luke and Caley... you're a great father.'

'You're going to make me blush,' he says, adding a chuckle at the end.

'I'm not saying anything that isn't true. My own father is

nothing but a footnote in my life story, and I was never my mum's priority, so I speak from experience when I say you and Jenna are doing a great job. Luke and Caley are very lucky.'

It goes silent for a moment, and I physically press my ear against the wooden pane of the door.

'I think you're right to be worried about Jenna,' Allie then says. 'I think Judith being here isn't helping and I don't know how much more she can take before she tips over the edge.'

'That's the whole reason I asked Mum to come and help out. I mean, you've been incredible this week, and I don't know how we would have coped without you picking up the slack, but it isn't fair for us to be taking advantage of you like that.'

'I really don't mind. I was happy to help, and it's the least I could do with you both coming to my rescue like this. In fact, I'm happy to stay on a bit longer and provide any support you need, if it means Judith can finish her visit earlier. Would that help? I'm here for you, Brett.'

Silence descends again, and in the darkness of the hallway I see images of a naked Allie seducing Brett flashing before my eyes. My visual imagination always felt like such a gift when I was younger, but right now it is killing me.

She touches her hand to his face, and although he is reluctant at first, she whispers that he doesn't know what he's missing out on, and she moves his hand to her breasts, forcing him to cup them, as she slips his free hand between her legs.

I burst through the door, ready to charge at them, and find the two of them standing by the table, their bodies only inches apart. Have they just kissed? Was what I was seeing right?

Allie takes a step back, her face shocked as Brett turns to face me, a tumbler of whisky in his hand.

'Jesus, Jenna, you nearly gave me a fecking heart attack,' Brett admonishes in a playful manner.

'Are you feeling better?' Allie asks.

'W-what's going on?' I manage to stutter, locking away the images in my head, but aware that they could return at any moment.

'Sorry, I hadn't realised how late it was. Did we wake you?'

I'm searching his lips for any hint of lip gloss and betrayal.

There is an almost empty bottle of whisky on the table beside them, but there's no sign of a glass in Allie's hand, so I can only assume Brett has consumed the lot himself.

'It's my fault,' Allie says, standing and coming to my side. 'I've kept Brett talking about his writing process. Would you like me to make you a drink?'

I take a step back. Who does this woman think she is to be offering to make me a drink like I'm a guest in *her* home rather than the other way around?

Maybe this was her plan all along? Push all your buttons until you're convinced she's trying to replace you like a cuckoo. Maybe showing an interest in writing is just her first step in seducing Brett.

I clamp my eyes shut, trying to silence Mum's voice.

'I'm going to go up to bed,' Allie says when I don't respond, 'and give you two some space. Good night.'

I watch as she slinks away, but I can't stop picturing her hand on Brett's face. And I can't stop imagining what would have happened had I not burst through the door when I did. One thing's for sure, until I know more about her, she can't be trusted.

30

My hopes for a relaxing lie-in are crushed by the sound of the neighbour's lawnmower shortly after eight, and although Brett snores on oblivious, my brain has taken the hint and starts in again.

Brett and I stayed up a little longer after Allie had withdrawn, but no matter how many times I tried to explain that I wasn't threatening Judith with the knife, I don't think he believed me. I tried to get him to open up about his concerns in the same way he had with Allie, but he offered very little. I can't remember when we stopped talking about the important stuff. Most of our conversations these days focus on Luke and Caley's schedules and working out which of us will be taxi service for which.

I should be telling him of my own concerns about my mental health, but I'm terrified that will only firm up his fears that I'm turning into Mum. I need his support, not his judgement.

As much as I was hoping to drift back to sleep, I seemingly woke on the hour every hour, my hand shooting out to check for a presence in the bed beside me.

One thing I'm certain of is I can't allow these thoughts to take over my life. I either need to trust the pair of them, or get Allie out of the house to remove temptation. I can't speak to the GP until tomorrow as they're closed on Sunday, and I'm not sure my mental health concern can be classed as an emergency. I get up and close the bedroom window, but the hum of the lawnmower continues to vibrate against my bones, and I know I won't be able to get back to sleep now. So I head downstairs, finding Luke and Caley stretched out on the sofa in the lounge, Luke playing on his dad's console, and Caley reading a book.

'What's for breakfast?' my daughter asks the moment I enter the room.

'I don't know. What do you fancy?'

'Fruit salad.'

It's such a left-field request from a girl whose comfort food is Coco Pops and toast that I actually laugh out loud.

'What are you laughing at?' she says, a wounded frown swiftly stretching across her face.

'You're serious?'

'Allie says fruit for breakfast is a healthier energy boost first thing in the morning than cereal.'

I try not to show my frustration. The number of times I've tried to get Luke and Caley to eat more fruit and failed. I swear that woman could tell Caley black is white and she'd believe her.

'I'm not sure we have any fruit in the house, sweetie,' I say sympathetically. 'But I can go and buy some when the shops open. Is there anything I can fix you in the meantime?'

She considers the question with deep concentration before replying, 'Toast, please.'

'And Luke, what do you fancy?'

'I already had a croissant,' he replies sullenly, his eyes never leaving the screen.

I should speak to him privately and try to explain why I was arguing with Judith, but I know he won't be receptive if I interrupt his game, so I leave him to it and head out to the kitchen to fix Caley two rounds of toast, enjoying the feel of the sun's warmth through the window on my face. It gives me an energy boost I'm not expecting and instinctively I know what I need to do.

I head upstairs and dress quickly, managing to avoid disturbing Brett's bearlike grizzling, and then I grab my keys and head out to my car. Although Allie has told me about their relationship and why she's so terrified of Clark, she's only one source, and there are two sides to every story. I vaguely remember where the taxi dropped us in Winnall Close in Winchester, and if I can trace my way back to their flat, then maybe I will finally find the answers I'm looking for.

It takes forty minutes through stop-start traffic to reach my destination. I thought taking the back roads to avoid the M3 would save time, but two accidents along the way confirm I made the wrong decision. I'm conscious that Brett might be stirring by now, and I really should have left him a note to say where I was going and when I might be back. Despite my mistrust of Allie's attraction to Brett, it's not like I've left them alone. I'm sure Judith's beady eye and Caley's obsession with Allie will dampen any flames.

I wish it was that easy to extract the images of the two of them from my mind. In the harsh light of day, I desperately want to believe that nothing happened in the room during the night, and that their close proximity was nothing other than them trying to keep their voices from waking the rest of the house. Surely Brett would have been full of apologies and guilt if he'd just crossed that line, but in the haze of sleep I can't be certain what was real and what was imagined.

I park in an open-air pay and display car park, and complete the rest of the journey on foot. I felt so confident when I left home, but the nearer I get, the more doubt has crept in. The plan was to knock on the door and fire questions at Clark, but he may not be alone, might refuse to answer me, or worse still, lunge at me for even knowing Allie. Had I told Brett what I was planning he would have told me not to bother and that Allie is better off without that monster in her life, and he definitely wouldn't have agreed to come with me. I tried to convince Allie yesterday but I felt like she fobbed me off. There has to be more behind her motives for not wanting to return.

I remember now how affluent an area this place looks with large detached properties scattered left and right, and a luxury cars in every driveway. I instantly feel out of place in jeans and a hoodie.

I locate the building the taxi dropped us by on Tuesday, and I study the directory outside the main door. Clark's flat is 415 on the fourth floor, and I press the buzzer beside the number. I take a deep breath, running through the script I prepared in the car, but nobody answers the intercom. I try a second time, now realising that he could be at work for all I know, and that I shouldn't have been so impulsive this morning. There's still no answer and I feel like a prize fool for driving so far with no result, but just as I'm turning away, a woman in cycle shorts and a helmet appears at the door. She's struggling to hold her bike and get the door open and so I take the handle and pull it wide while she engages the release button.

'Thanks so much,' she calls over her shoulder, without a second thought, hopping onto the saddle and pedalling away. The fact that he hasn't answered the intercom probably means he isn't home, but this feels too good a chance to turn down, and I dart through the door and call the lift. Butterflies flutter in my gut as the lift ascends to the fourth floor, and as I step out I feel like an intruder, but continue along the pale blue corridor until I'm standing outside 415. I bang on the military-grey door, and press my ear to it, straining to hear the sound of movement inside. But if Clark is inside he must be in a virtual coma.

I could hang around and wait to see if he returns, but I don't know how long I should wait before yielding and heading home. The lift opens as soon as I press the button, and it quickly descends and I'm back out in the cool morning air in no time. There are no shops or cafés where I can wait, so I start walking back in the direction of the car park, promising myself I'll buy a takeaway tea from Winchester Services for my journey home.

I turn the corner and almost bump into the man coming the other way who quickly apologises without looking up from his screen, but I recognise him regardless, my pulse on high alert. My fight-or-flight is telling me coming here was an awful idea and I should just hurry back to the car without looking back, but then I'm reminded of the image of Allie with her hand on Brett's face and I stop.

You'll never get a better chance to find out the truth about her, I hear Mum tell me.

'Clark?' I hear my voice say uncertainly as if someone has choked the word out of me.

The man stops and slowly turns, a deep frown on his face as his eyes meet mine.

'Sorry, what did you say?'

It's too late to run away, but I'm not in control as my feet move me closer to him.

'You're Clark, right? I'm a friend of Allie's.'

'No, sorry, you must have me confused with someone else. My name's Charles. Wait, I know you, don't I?'

I study the man's face and I swear it's the man from the

picture Allie shared with me, and yet this is the same man I followed across London on Thursday.

'Sorry, I'm usually really good with names and faces. We met recently, didn't we?'

I should just apologise and get going, but he snaps his fingers together.

'Wait, weren't you the person who took the photograph of my wife and me in Covent Garden? Oh my, what a small world.'

He doesn't look worried by our second chance encounter, and I can't get a sense of him as the violent and controlling monster Allie has described.

'I know about you and Allie,' I hear Mum's voice say. 'And unless you want me to tell your wife about your sordid little affair, you'd better start talking.'

His brow furrows, and he gently shakes his head.

'I'm really sorry, but I don't know anyone called Allie. I really think you may have me confused with someone else.'

I hear Allie's voice in my head: *He's manipulative. He has a way with words that wins people over. He's like the devil in that way.*

'You live in this building, right? Flat 415?'

I'm giving him an out, but he nods.

'Yes, yes, I do, but how did you know that?'

'I was in 415 on Tuesday morning with Allie. She told me about your fight.'

'I really don't know what you're talking... wait, did you say Tuesday?'

I nod.

'We came and collected some of her things. You must have noticed she'd moved out.'

'Wait, you were here on Tuesday with this Allie person? Can you describe what she looks like?'

'Quit playing games, Clark.'

'Listen, I'm sorry, but I don't know who this Clark is, and I genuinely don't know anyone called Allie, but when I returned to my flat on Tuesday morning there was an intruder inside. A woman. Maybe five foot five, blonde, curly hair, slim build, petite. She attacked me with a frying pan, almost cracking my skull. When I came to, she'd gone, and I had to call an ambulance to take me to hospital. You know this woman, don't you?'

Allie warned me he'd try to twist the story and he'd make out like she'd attacked him, and yet, the way he's speaking, I don't sense that he's lying. But it doesn't make any sense.

'I'd been back in London for a long weekend, and it looked like the woman had been squatting or something. When I told her to get out, she tried to seduce me, and then when I told her I was married, she flew into a rage. I was lucky not to be killed.'

She's been lying to you, Jenna, and now Brett's her next target.

'You're lying,' I say to both Clark and the voice in my head. 'You're a police officer and a coercive controller.'

'I'm not in the police. I'm CEO of an IT company. I did report the attack to the police, I gave them a picture of her taken outside this building, but they said there was little they could do unless I knew her name, but you know who she is. You can come with me and confirm her identity...'

But I don't hang around to listen to any more, spinning on my heel and racing back towards the car park, praying he doesn't give chase.

31

Traffic on the journey back to Rownhams is even slower than on the way, with the M3 jammed in both directions due to an accident involving a tractor, a caravan and an articulated lorry. By the time we're all diverted off and through Chandlers Ford, it's already after lunch. I'm desperate to get back home and have it out with Allie. I want Brett to be there when I reveal what I've learned from Clark, no wait, I mean Charles. After I saw him on the train on Thursday, I can't believe I almost managed to convince myself that I'd followed the wrong man. I even asked Allie whether her Clark had a brother, such was the striking similarity between the man in the photo and the one in real life.

On Thursday night, when I told her about who I'd followed, she could have come clean and said that she'd lied about who he really is, but what I still don't understand is why she lied. When I first found her on the train, she was indeed bruised and bloodied, but what was she hoping to gain by lying to me? She must have thought I'd be more likely to help if I saw her as a victim. And maybe now the lie feels too big to admit the truth; much as Brett avoids telling Judith how rude she is.

I don't want Luke and Caley to overhear the conversation, so I'll ask Judith if she can take them out to the park for a bit. Hopefully, Allie will be more honest with only Brett and me around.

I could have phoned home from the car and told Brett what I'd learned, but I don't trust him not to let something slip to Allie, and I don't want to give her time to fabricate more lies to cover the originals.

I inwardly cringe when I remember introducing her to Marcus and Chip at the end of Friday's presentation. I was so desperate for her to share the recognition I was receiving, but now I've given them reason to believe she's trustworthy. And worse still I vouched for her when I emailed Marcus in my drugged state and demanded he hire her. Maybe that was also part of her plan: slip narcotics into my system so I'd be little more than a hand puppet for her. How's it going to look if I now have to tell Marcus I was wrong about her? He'll assume I'm a poor judge of character and give him more reason to question my future at the company. But if I don't blow the whistle, anything she then does while employed will reflect as badly on me as it will her. I'll always be remembered as the one who pushed her through the front door.

I feel like such a fool!

I'm exhausted when I pull up behind Brett's silver classic Mercedes. It's so old now that only a collector would likely pay anything if he ever tried to sell it, but it was the first car he ever bought, and he's too sentimental about it. I kill the engine, and take a deep breath in, holding it for several seconds before exhaling. I need to be sure about what I'm going to accuse her of. I left here this morning because there are two sides to every story, I just didn't realise how vastly different the two sides would be.

Allie claimed she'd been in a relationship with him for several months, and that he'd slowly been gaslighting her and taking control of her life. And according to her, on Tuesday morning he snapped and tried choking her to death until she retaliated by hitting him with the frying pan in self-defence. I remember how easy it felt to believe her story; after all, she had the injuries to support the claim. But, according to Charles, he found her squatting in his flat after time away and when he demanded she leave, she attacked him and left him for dead.

I can't correlate the gentle and sincere man I met with the monster Allie has been describing for the last five days. I would never describe the man I just met as violent and coercive, but Allie did warn me that he's manipulative and able to mislead people.

One of them is certainly lying to me.

I'm generally good at spotting small changes in behaviour – even if I don't always understand the cause of the change. I feel like I'd know if Allie is lying when I tell her what Charles said. She didn't want to report his crime to the police because she claimed he was in the force himself, but he doesn't look like a policeman. His hands and fingernails didn't resemble those of someone who regularly has to handle himself on the street. He looked to all intents and purposes like a businessman, which makes his claim about being CEO of an IT company more believable.

My mind is all over the place, and I feel lost. I don't want to believe that Allie has been betraying the trust I put in her, and I can't be certain that what my mind is seeing is completely real. I remember how certain Mum was that Dad was cheating on her, and yet by his own admission he didn't ever break his vows until after she'd driven him out.

What if I'm the one jumping to all the wrong conclusions about both of them?

I gasp when I see a dark shadow fall across my window, and then see Brett making a goofy face at me.

'Are you planning to sit out here all day, or what?' he asks, opening the door.

'Where's Allie?' I ask.

'Um, she's out still, I think. Do you want a cuppa?'

I follow him into the house, part of me relieved I can share the news with him first, to help get my thoughts clear in my head.

'Where've you been for so long?' he asks, filling the kettle at the sink.

'I went to Winchester, but got stuck in traffic on the way home.'

'There was a pile-up on the M3,' he tells me, as if I didn't know. 'Pretty nasty one according to the news.'

'I know,' I say, sighing and dropping into one of the chairs at the table. 'I went to see Clark, the man Allie *claimed* was her boyfriend.'

He blinks at me several times, before placing the kettle on its stand and switching it to boil.

'He didn't hurt or threaten me,' I continue when he doesn't say anything, 'but he told me some things about Allie that I think you need to hear too. For starters, his name isn't Clark, it's Charles. And he wasn't in a relationship with Allie. In fact, he says he doesn't know anyone called Allie. He said he found her squatting at his place and she attacked him with the frying pan when he tried to evict her.'

'Of course he said that. The guy is full of shit! Allie told us he would try to manipulate the truth to paint himself as the victim.'

'I know that's what she said, but you didn't see him today. He sounded genuine, and I'm inclined to believe him.'

'Oh, you meet a guy for a few minutes and you think you can tell if he's a straight shooter or not?'

'It's not just today. I saw him indirectly on Thursday as well.'

'What? You met him on Thursday? Why is this the first I'm hearing about it?'

'No, I didn't meet him. Well, not exactly. I saw him on my train and I followed him and his wife across London.'

'I thought you were working in the office on Thursday.'

'I was. This was before that.'

'So, when I needed you to finish early so I could do that radio interview, you were off galivanting like some vigilante?'

'No, I just wanted to get a sense of who he was.'

'And then you decided to meet with him again today?'

'No, I went to his flat so I could demand some of Allie's things back, and that's when he told me what really happened.'

'No, stop right there. What *really* happened is what Allie told you happened. You've no reason not to believe her just because her abuser says so.'

Charles could have come up with any number of stories about what happened that morning. He could have outright denied that anything bad happened, and that Allie has lost the plot after a mental breakdown; he could have claimed that it was just a misunderstanding; or he could have admitted it was true but that he was now seeking help for his behaviour. Those all sound more believable and possible than what he's said. Either he's really bad at constructing lies, or there's more to his claim than Brett's giving him credit for.

'So, according to the man Allie has told us was psychologically abusing her, she's what? Some kind of crazed stalker?'

'No, not a stalker, but someone who's potentially dangerous and we should probably ask to leave for everyone's safety.'

The kettle reaches a crescendo, but Brett makes no effort to make the tea.

'Just take a moment, Jenna, to really think about what you're saying here. Okay?'

The truth is I don't know what to believe any more. There have been times when I've just wanted to wrap Allie in cotton wool and treat her as one of my own children; there have been times when I've felt like I've found a new best friend; and then there have been times where I've not trusted her, and worried about the future of my marriage.

'I've thought about nothing else these last few days. There's something not right about her, but I wasn't able to put my finger on what until now.'

'Well, this is the first I'm hearing of it.'

He's right that I've played my cards close to my chest, but I wanted to be sure of my own thoughts before sharing.

'I'm telling you now, and it would be nice to hear you supporting me.'

'Darlin', you know that I love you and I support you in everything you do. But have you heard yourself? Allie has gone out of her way to help us. You with your work pitch; me with school pickup and my writing; and the children with their homework. That doesn't scream of someone dangerous.'

He's not listening, and it hurts to hear him taking her side over mine, even with her not in the room pulling his strings.

'Don't you think I know that?' I shout, slamming my hand against the table in frustration. 'But something doesn't add up. And when I tell her she has to go, I want you to back me.'

He turns his back and proceeds to pour steaming water into two mugs.

'Where are Luke and Caley?' I ask, suddenly aware that the house is far too quiet for a usual Sunday afternoon.

'Allie took them swimming,' he replies without looking back.

My mouth drops open.

'You what? You let her take them?'

He turns and offers a pitying stare.

'Yes. They both said they wanted to go swimming, and I know how much you hate the leisure centre because it's so loud and full of people. When Allie offered to take them, it seemed like a no-brainer.'

'Which pool have they gone to?'

'They went by taxi, so I assume they've gone to Romsey Rapids.'

'You assume? You mean you don't know?'

He comes across, and crouches down by my legs, taking my hands in his.

'I didn't want to say anything before, but I'm really worried about you. It's been ages since we properly spoke and you unburdened yourself. I know how hard you've been working and I can see the toll it's taking on you; all the trips to the office, and the late returns. You're burned out, and none of that can be good for your mental health. You used to vent to me about Marcus being a dick, but I can't remember the last time you did. It's not healthy to be keeping all of this bottled up.'

'I don't have time for this, Brett. You've allowed our children to be taken by a virtual stranger who could be a psychopath for all we know.'

'Can you hear yourself right now? Do you know who you sound like?'

I pull my hands free of his.

'How dare you? This is nothing like my mother. My concern is real.'

'Is it though? Allie has given me no reason to doubt her credibility. She didn't ask to take the children out today; she did it as a favour to me. I was hoping the empty house would give you and me the chance to catch up and be intimate with each other. The children aren't here because I asked her to take them out. You're overreacting and I don't know how to pull you back from the edge.'

I inwardly cringe at the thought that he's been discussing our dwindling sex life with Allie, but I'm also smarting from his comparison to my mum's irrational behaviour.

'I think...' he begins, before taking a second to choose his words. 'I think it might be time for you to speak to the doctor. I want to support you, Jenna. I want to help, but I don't know how. I'm so worried about you right now. I don't want things to get worse.'

I don't want to listen to this. It's one thing for me to acknowledge concerns about hearing Mum's voice in my head, but for my nearest and dearest to echo those concerns is more than my mind can handle right now.

There's only one thing I need to focus on: getting my children back.

32

I can't believe Brett can be so blasé about the fact that Allie is out there with our children, and he doesn't even know where. What if we've totally misjudged her trustworthiness and she's abducted them? If Charles was telling the truth about Allie this morning, then she isn't the person we thought and that means she could be capable of absolutely anything.

You never should have trusted her. I tried to warn you.

My mother's 'I told you so' speech isn't helpful right now. I'm probably just overacting – at least I hope Brett's right about that. But I'd far rather be proven wrong for the first time in my life. I can't even bring myself to consider the possibility that I'll never see Luke and Caley again.

'You should phone the police,' I tell Brett as I unlock my car and pull open the door, the cool breeze a slap to the face.

'The police? Seriously, Jenna, this has gone too far. The children are fine, and I bet they'll be home any minute and then you'll see just how ridiculously you're behaving.'

I glare at him.

'And what if you're wrong, Brett? Every passing second could be putting more distance between us and our children.'

'I'll phone her,' he says, fumbling in his pocket, and then pressing the phone to his ear.

I hover with one leg in the car and one out, waiting for any shimmer of light at the end of the tunnel. He lowers the phone and tries again.

'It's going straight through to voicemail,' he says, and it's all the confirmation I need.

Starting the engine, I connect my own phone to the Bluetooth and dial her number for myself.

'Her phone's probably in a locker and it just doesn't have any signal,' I hear Brett hollering as I accelerate away.

He might be right, but I won't be satisfied until I'm holding Luke's and Caley's hands. There are a couple of leisure centres with swimming pools in the area, and although Brett said he assumed they would go to Romsey Rapids, he doesn't know for sure and that isn't the closest pool to us. But it is the one I usually take the children to. It's where they had swimming lessons, and so I set that as my destination, using the back roads to avoid traffic on the main road.

I try Allie's number again, but her answerphone cuts straight in.

'Hi, Allie, it's Jenna,' I say, trying to sound calmer than I'm feeling. 'Brett mentioned you've taken the kids swimming. I was hoping I might be able to tag along. I'm on my way to Romsey Rapids, so can you call me when you get this so we can arrange to meet up? Thanks.'

I end the call, instantly regretting how shrill my voice sounded. Will she notice? There's no way she can know that I've spoken to Charles, but if she senses that I suspect she's lying, there's a chance it could tip her over the edge.

I desperately try to push the thoughts out of my head, turning up the radio, hoping music will distract my overactive imagination. The car in front brakes suddenly, and it's all I can do to slam my foot on the pedal, stopping just shy of the bumper in front. Looking up, I see the roadworks sign, and the imposing figure of the temporary traffic lights. If I'd known the road had been dug up, I would have taken the next turning, which runs perpendicular to this one. I look at the rear-view mirror to see whether I can back up and turn around, but I see two eyes staring back at me, and scream.

Swivelling around in my chair, I find the back seat empty, as it should be, and when I look back in the mirror, Mum's ghostly face is no longer there. My heartrate doesn't slow any though. It was like she was there, leaning forwards, within touching distance of me.

The sound of a horn from the car behind draws my attention back to the green traffic lights, and I hold my hand up in apology and pull forward, continuing my journey towards Rossmore. I keep glancing back up at the rear-view mirror, double-checking she really isn't there. Hearing her voice in my head is one thing, but hallucinating is on another level. The sooner I speak to the GP the better. I'm not ashamed to admit my mental health is struggling, but what if it's already too late? I saw what happened to Mum when she went untreated, and I know I've been ignoring the signs for too long.

It could be a brain tumour.

My brow furrows at the intrusive thought. No, I'm sure there would have been other signs – nausea, seizures, sensitivity to light – but then I think about last night's meltdown and feel my thoughts spiralling. I almost miss the turn for the leisure centre, braking quickly, and clipping the kerb as I pull the car around the bend and beneath the barrier. I circle the car park and find a space a stone's throw from the building's entrance.

Caley was having lessons here last year, but I found the acoustics of the place too intense, and Brett had to start bringing her instead. Locking the car, I hurry across the car park, and in through the automatic doors. There are two people talking to the teenager in the orange polo shirt behind the reception desk. I stand behind them, chewing at my nails, willing them to just get on with it and stop asking questions.

'Can we get some change for the locker,' the man says, just as his friend is starting to move away. He drops a five-pound note on the counter, and the teenager proceeds to open her till and exchanges the note for five coins.

They finally move on, and I crash into the counter.

'I need to know whether my children are here,' I say, cutting to the chase.

The teenager frowns at me, probably not trained to deal with a manic woman who fears her children have been abducted.

'Um, I'm not sure what to say,' she finally stammers.

I pull my phone out of my pocket and flick to a recent picture of Caley, and show it to her.

'This is my daughter, Caley. She would have been with her brother Luke who's a couple of years older, and a woman in her early thirties with blonde curly hair. Have you seen them?'

She's still frowning as she looks at the phone's screen. I rotate it back, searching for a picture of Luke, but the only one I can find is from Christmas, and has him sitting at a table, so it's impossible to get a sense of just how tall he is for his age. I show her the picture and hold my hand out at shoulder level.

'He's about this tall. Do you recognise them? Have they been through here today?'

'I'm sorry, my shift only started ten minutes ago, and I haven't seen them come through.'

'Who was on the desk before you? Can I speak to them?'

She shakes her head again.

'No, I'm sorry, Shannon went home ill, that's why I was called in. I don't usually work the front desk.'

'What about CCTV? You have security cameras, right? Can I see them?'

She glances back over her shoulder as if she's hoping someone is going to come to her rescue, but the door to the administration office remains ajar.

'No, I'm sorry, I can't let you back here.'

I can feel my frustration building, and the air inside here is so warm that I can feel my clothes adhering themselves to my body.

'Listen, I need to know if my children are here. I just need to view your security feeds for this morning, and if they're here then I can go and collect them. And if they're not, I will move on to the next pool. Okay? I won't be five minutes.'

'Why don't I go and get my manager and he can probably help you.'

She hops down from her stool before I can argue and disappears through the door. There are now three people queued behind me, but they can wait as long as it takes. I keep my eyes glued on the stairs that lead to the changing rooms, in case the three of them emerge while I'm waiting. I could just run up the stairs and head through to the changing rooms, but the complex is so large, with three different pool areas, plus a jacuzzi, flumes and wave machine that I could totally miss them in passing.

'How can I help you, madam?' a young voice asks, and when I look up, the owner of the voice doesn't look much older than the girl who fetched him. He is donning a badge that describes him as the deputy manager, but I swear he can barely be in his twenties.

'I need to view your security camera footage,' I say plainly, like it's not the most unreasonable request he's likely to hear today.

'I'm sorry, that's not something I can allow.'

The girl has returned to her stool and is doing a lousy job of hiding her eavesdropping while she serves the next customer.

'I need to know if my children are here,' I say firmly. 'If I can just view your security recordings for the front desk, I'll be able to see if they came through here today. Please, it's an emergency.'

'I'm sorry, madam, but I can't allow you to view our recordings. If you want to buy a ticket, we can let you through and you can go and search for them. Or we can announce their names through our speaker system and ask them to identify themselves to one of the lifeguards.'

'I didn't bring my purse with me, so I can't buy a ticket,' I say through gritted teeth, struggling to keep my voice even. 'Please, I'm desperate. I just need to know if they're here.'

'I can't let you through if you don't buy a—'

'I want to see my children,' I scream, cutting him off midsentence.

A deathly silence falls over the girl and the woman she's serving beside us.

'I understand your frustration,' the deputy manager says. 'And as I said, we can ask them to head to the nearest lifeguard if they're here.'

I don't wait to listen to any more and sprint off towards the stairs. I've barely made it to the top when I see Allie and Caley skipping towards me. I can't be certain it isn't another hallucination, and so I hurry over, dropping to my knees, and scoop Caley into my arms.

'Mum, what are you doing here?' I hear her angelic voice say as hot tears splash against my already warm cheeks.

'Are you okay?'

'Yes. Why wouldn't I be?'

I look her over, checking for any sign of trauma or fear, but she looks perfectly well.

'You're okay,' I say, burying my face in her shoulder.

'Of course, I am. What's going on, Mum?'

I suddenly realise there's a Luke-sized gap.

'Where's your brother? Caley, where's Luke?'

'Getting changed,' she says, and a moment later, Luke is beside us, swinging his kit bag in a circle like he's wielding a hammer.

'Oh, hey, Mum,' he says, and I pull him over to Caley and me.

'Is everything okay, Jenna?' I hear Allie asking innocently.

'You had Mummy worried,' I whisper to them.

I feel Caley trying to peel herself away, and when I look at her, I see her confused brow, and her reaching for Allie's hand.

'Don't be scared,' I tell her. 'I'm here now, and I'm not going to let you out of my sight ever again.'

She glances nervously at Allie.

I kiss my children's cheeks, and straighten, taking their hands in mine.

'Come on, let's go home,' I say, pulling them back down the stairs with me as I march towards the automatic doors.

'What about Allie?' I hear Caley say, but I'm not going to address that problem until I know Luke and Caley are belted into the car, safe.

'Go get in,' I tell them once I've unlocked the doors. I wait until their doors are closed before I turn and look at Allie.

'Is everything okay?' she asks. 'Brett knew I was taking the kids swimming. Didn't he tell you?'

'Oh, he did, but that was before I went and spoke to Clark, or Charles if we're using his *real* name.'

She stares back at me, unmoved by the statement.

'I went to your flat this morning and had a really interesting conversation with the man you attacked there on Tuesday morning. His name is Charles and he's married. He isn't in the police, and he's never heard of you before.'

I study her face, looking for any twitches that will tell me if she's worried, but it remains expressionless.

'You spoke to Clark this morning?'

I nod.

'And he told you his name is Charles and he's never met me before?'

I nod again.

'I knew his name was Charles, but Clark is a nickname his friends use, because he looks a bit like Clark Kent. You know, from Superman? And I knew he was married, but that didn't stop him sleeping with me.'

I was expecting her to crumple when I called out her lies, but she looks totally unfazed.

'You said he was in the police.'

'Okay, I lied about that bit because you kept banging on about me having to report him. I knew that if I filed a complaint, the police would speak to him but take no further action. It would have been a waste of time. I'm sorry I lied, but you don't know what he's like.'

'He doesn't know who you are, Allie. Apart from someone he found squatting in his apartment.'

'Is that what he claimed?' she scoffs. 'Don't you see? This is what he's like. I told you he would try and manipulate the facts to paint me as the villain. He always has to control the narrative. I can't believe you're falling for his lies.'

In that instant I picture Mum's reflection in the rear-view mirror. With the way things are, how can I be certain what to believe?

33

The journey back from the leisure centre is made in virtual silence. I try asking whether they've had a good time, but Luke is monosyllabic and Caley looks like she's swallowed a wasp, such is her scowl. Allie is just staring out of the window. I will try to explain to them why I was so worried, but only once Allie is out of the way. God knows I don't want to make things any more awkward.

The children hurry inside as soon as we're back, but Allie hangs back and waits for me by the door.

'Listen, I'm sorry for any misunderstanding this morning,' she says, her tone less bright than usual; wounded maybe. 'And I understand that you now feel differently about me after speaking with Clark. I know it won't make a difference, but this is exactly what he's like: sowing enough doubt to make you want to question yourself.'

This isn't just about what he told me though; it was the doubts I already have that drove me to the flat this morning, but then I can't be certain those doubts are legitimate with the ghost of Mum hanging over me.

'It's probably best if I accelerate my plans to move out. I've already overstayed my welcome. And if we are to work together, then it's probably not healthy for us to be sharing a home.'

My need to people please has me wanting to disagree and tell her to stay, but I bite my tongue.

'I'm going to go out now and find somewhere to live. I might catch the train to Basingstoke and see what's available and in budget there.'

She heads away, and I force myself not to offer her a lift to the station. Knowing Luke and Caley are safe and back home fills me with huge relief, and I feel tears brewing at the corner of my eyes when I close the door.

What I'm not expecting is to see Brett pulling on his anorak, and Judith with a made-up face, clutching her handbag.

'Are you going somewhere?' I ask, unaware of any prior engagements.

'Mum wants to take the kids to town to treat them, so I said I'd drive.'

'Oh, but we've just come home, I'd have thought...'

My words trail off when I see Luke and Caley appear from behind Judith. I shouldn't be surprised that the promise of her spending money on them has persuaded them to go straight back out again.

'Where's Allie?' Caley asks, her expression quickly spoiling when she looks at me.

'She's gone to look at some more flats,' I say, as much for Brett's awareness as hers.

'You're making her move out.'

'No, sweetie, I'm not. It's for the best. Allie was only ever going to be here for a few days. She has her own life and needs her space.'

I had hoped to speak to both Luke and Caley about the incident at the leisure centre, but I'm not prepared to raise the subject with Brett and Judith watching on. A bit of time to myself should help me carefully compose what I want to say.

'We might eat out,' Brett says, clearly also in a mood with me. 'I take it you're okay fixing something for yourself?'

So, I guess in his eyes, my erratic behaviour now means I'm excluded from dining with my family.

'That's fine,' I say, forcing a smile, not wishing to rock the boat further. 'Have a good time.'

Brett makes no attempt to kiss me goodbye, and both Luke and Caley shrug off my attempts to hug them as they pass. And then I'm alone in the house, and I can't say I don't deserve for them to shun me. I can remember how embarrassed I used to feel when Mum had had one of her episodes outside the school. It was like her shadow was a stain I didn't want to be anywhere near. And now I know how she must have felt when Tom and I wouldn't want to speak to her. What is it they say about the sins of the parent being revisited on the child? If I don't sort myself out then one day Caley might grow up to be like me and then we'll be trapped in a perpetual loop of tragedy.

I move into the kitchen and switch on the kettle, before crossing to the fridge to collect the milk. But when I see the chilled bottle of Pinot Grigio in the door, I take that instead and leave the kettle boiling while I take a glass and head to the living room.

I'm through one glass when a knock at the door startles me out of the half-sleep. Assuming Allie must have changed her mind, I head to the door and pull it open, trying to ready myself for an honest conversation, but double take when I see Tom on the doorstep.

And for the briefest second, I wonder if I've totally lost it and am imagining him here now. But then a memory of our call fires to the front of my mind.

My flight arrives at Gatwick on Sunday morning.

He takes a step forwards, and I throw my arms around his neck, and pull myself into him.

'Well, this is a lovely welcome,' I hear Tom say, choking for breath, 'but do you think you could release me so I can come in?'

I let him in, wiping away my tears with the sleeve of my sweatshirt so he won't see, and then lock the door behind him again. I follow Tom into the living room, only now realising he doesn't have any luggage with him.

'Where's your cases and bags?'

'I left them at the hotel,' he says.

'You could stay here,' I say, before remembering the house is already full with Allie and Judith.

'I know, but I figured you probably didn't need me getting under your feet, what with Brett busy with his new book. Where is he, by the way?'

I can't contain my emotion, and hug him again. As much as I don't enjoy physical contact with other people, Tom is different. He always used to hold me tight when Mum and Dad would argue, or when I'd wake from a nightmare, screaming. He always had a way of making me feel safe.

'There, there, it's okay,' he whispers, gently rubbing his hand across the small of my back. 'I didn't realise you'd missed me this much.'

I chuckle at his self-deprecating humour, and finally some of the tension eases in my shoulders. He hands me a clean handkerchief, and I dry my eyes again.

'Is everything okay, sis? You don't seem yourself.'

I want to tell him all about the stress I've been feeling these last few months, culminating in my encounter with Allie, but I really don't know where to start. He knows better than anyone how much my paranoid thoughts sound like Mum's and I don't want him to start believing I'm following in her footsteps, and that I'm the next one who is going to need committing for psychiatric help.

He takes me by the hand and leads me to the sofa, sitting me down, and squeezing in beside me.

'Tell me all about it. I'm more than happy to listen.'

I try to shuffle my thoughts into a coherent order, but my mind is racing ahead and already pre-empting his responses to what I might say, and there's no way the conversation ends with him not worrying more about me.

'Is everything okay between you and Brett?'

I don't even know where to begin answering that question. Up until a week ago I would have said I have the perfect marriage. But now every time I think of him I can't help but picture Allie seducing him. And with him now questioning my mental health, things are far from perfect.

'Jenna?'

'Everything's fine,' I say, my voice breaking under the strain. 'Tell me about you. How is life in Geneva? I really should make more of an effort to come and visit you.'

He studies me for several seconds before relenting.

'Living in the mountains has the odd drawback, but I wouldn't swap the clean air and water for anything.'

Looking at him now, he's never been in better health. There are no rings beneath his eyes, unlike mine, his hair is light and fluffy, and he's the thinnest I've seen him in decades. I can't believe how envious I feel. He looks happy, and what I wouldn't give for a spoonful of whatever he's taking.

He narrows his eyes. 'So, did you think any more about what we discussed the other day? About Mum, I mean.'

My heart sinks. I'd hoped it would take him a little longer before he addressed the elephant in the room. The truth is, in the small hours between bursts of sleep when my brain wakes itself, it's all I've thought about. How will Mum react to me just showing up? I don't know if she'll be pleased I've made the effort, angry that I haven't come sooner, or just hopeful that I'm willing to give her a second chance.

I've wanted to discuss it with Brett, but with everything that's been going on with work, with Allie and of course Brett's newfound inspiration, I just haven't found the time.

No, wait, that's a lie. I haven't wanted to find the time to discuss it, because it's easier blaming distractions than admitting why I don't want to think about visiting Mum.

Tom's eyes are fixed on mine, and it feels like his stare is boring into my soul. I don't want to disappoint him, but I just don't think I can bring myself to go and see her.

'I don't think now is the right time,' I eventually say, meaning I'd rather prepare myself before answering the question, but he misunderstands.

'She'll only turn sixty-five once, you know. I get your reluctance after everything that she put us through, but she was unwell, and I don't think we should judge her for that.'

'It was different for you though, Tom. She didn't keep tabs on all of your movements in the same way she did mine. It was like having my very own stalker, keeping track of everything I did and everyone I spoke to.'

'I know it wasn't easy—'

'That's an understatement. I don't want to expose myself or my family to that again.'

'Please just come and visit her with me. We need to speak to Dr Yates about her long-term care plan anyway, and regardless of how her illness made her behave, she is our flesh and blood. We're all she has left.'

34

I'm already awake before the alarm sounds, the whirlwind of thoughts racing through my mind since before dawn. Tom stayed until Brett and the children returned, but took his leave soon after when Judith started questioning why he isn't married yet.

I now find myself, once again, on the train from Southampton Central to London Waterloo, only this time Allie is in the seat beside me. Marcus emailed me late last night to say Chip Martin has flown back to the UK because he wants to meet us today to go over our pitch again. Marcus said we shouldn't read too much into it yet, but a face-to-face would suggest there's definitely some interest from their side. Marcus said he wants the whole team in early so we can make sure we can deliver everything I claimed we could during Friday's call.

'I don't think you have anything to worry about,' Allie says again, my own little cheerleader. 'Don't you remember what the Gliders CEO said at the end of the call? He warned Marcus that he might try to poach you to go and work for Gliders directly. Even if he doesn't offer the contract to your agency, he may offer you a position in the company. Either way, it's a win-win for you.'

I wish I could bottle some of her positivity and swallow it down every morning. Having spent a lifetime with voices of negativity in my head, it's a real struggle to accept encouraging feedback from anyone. I always assume I'll be rejected so it's easier to bear when it happens.

I should probably be giving Allie tips on how she should behave when Marcus finally meets her. If I want her out of my house, I need Marcus to offer her a job. And yet I don't think I need to give her any advice, and she'll have Marcus eating out of the palm of her hand.

He has a way with words that wins people over. He's like the devil in that way.

For all she said about Clark being able to manipulate people, those words seem more befitting of Allie herself. I hate myself for thinking it, but I really don't know who to believe any more.

I see Allie brace in the chair beside me, her knuckles white from how tightly she is gripping the arms of the seat. It's only when I hear the train guard's voice through the loudspeaker that I understand why.

'Ladies and gentlemen, we will shortly be arriving at Winchester, where we will wait temporarily while a fault is repaired. The doors will remain locked until the fault is repaired. Thank you for your patience.'

Six days ago, this was the moment where Allie came bursting into this carriage, clearly distressed by what had just happened to her. But it's also the place where I saw Clark waiting on the platform on Thursday. Until now, I hadn't even considered the prospect that he could be here today. I don't know how he'll react if he sees Allie and me sitting together. He might board the train and lash out at the two of us, or he might attempt to drag one or both of us from the carriage. If he's as unbalanced as Allie has made out then he could be capable of almost anything.

I'm about to lean over and try to say that everything will be okay, but Allie stands, telling me she needs to use the facilities, and I don't blame her for wanting to hide in the toilets where the door can be locked from the inside. I wish I'd thought about it earlier as I could have joined her. But once the doors open this carriage will fill quickly given it's the busiest train into London each morning. I don't want to be forced to stand for the eighty minutes it will take to get to London. So, I remain seated, keeping my head turned away from the window. Whilst there's a part of me that wants to know whether Clark is here again today, I dare not risk letting him see me.

The train judders as it couples with the other, and then I hear the whoosh as the doors are unlocked and several passengers form a conga line and exit the train. I take a brief glance towards the window, but the queues of passengers waiting to board are six deep, and it's impossible to see beyond them. If Clark knows this is the train we usually catch, there's nothing to stop him boarding at one end and then searching each carriage while the train jolts along, so even if I don't see him on the platform, it doesn't necessarily mean we are in the clear.

I dare a second glance out of the window as the carriage fills around me, but there's still no sign of him. A large man tries to squeeze into Allie's seat, but I quickly tell him it's already taken. He gives me a disparaging look before huffing and stalking back along the carriage in search of another. I divert my eyes back to the window, now eagerly scanning the platform for any sign of Clark. I don't know what I'll do if I do spot him. Duck down maybe? Pray that he doesn't notice me is more likely.

Still the train remains stationary, almost as if fate is trying to buy him time to get here and discover us both. When the train does finally judder into motion, my nails are chewed to the quick, and I'm on edge as someone tries to slide into the seat beside me, until I realise it is Allie returning. When we first met, I silently judged her for falling into the trap of a relationship where she'd yielded control, and yet now find myself in a similar position where the prospect of Clark has me jumping at every shadow.

'You look pale, are you okay?' Allie asks.

I puff out my cheeks.

'I will be once the meeting with Gliders is over. My stomach feels like it's in knots.'

'I'd offer you one of my magic pills, but I don't want you passing out again like Friday. Maybe half a pill?'

I shake my head; I want my wits about me all day, even if they are slowly driving me to the brink of insanity.

There's a real buzz in the office when we arrive, lots of chatter amongst the team. I sign in Allie with reception and then lead her up to Marcus's office. Although him interviewing her is little more than a formality, he still doesn't invite me to sit in on the interview, and so I return to my desk, but can't keep my mind from picturing what they could be discussing inside. If he offers Allie a job, then she'll have no reason not to find a place of her own, and will be out of our hair, and yet I'll be forced to see her every day at work.

My phone buzzes, and I see a message from Tom, telling me he's planning to visit Mum today, and checking I don't want to go with him. The message includes an image of the three of us that I haven't seen in years and I almost don't recognise Mum. Her hair is much darker than I remember, but tied back in a ponytail, and with a little makeup, she looks... normal. She's smiling in the picture, a far cry from the last mental image I have of her screaming and crying as she was admitted to Graveside against her will. She called me every name under the sun that day, and I've never forgotten that venomous look she gave me.

The guilt of not being there on her sixty-fifth birthday overwhelms me. I told Tom I can't see her, but would it really be so unbearable to swallow my pride for an hour? Maybe I could tell her about all the crazy thoughts peppering my own mind to understand whether this is what she experienced before things crashed around her. And if medication has now helped level out her mind, there's hope that my own muddled thoughts might respond to treatment.

I'm about to phone the GP surgery to ask for an appointment when Marcus's door opens, and a beaming Allie emerges.

Marcus looks like the cat who got the cream as he calls me over. I can't keep my eyes off Allie's face as I cross the room, and she steps out of my way to allow me to enter Marcus's office.

'You wanted to see me?' I say breezily, still not sure how I feel about the prospect of Allie joining the team, especially after what Clark told me yesterday.

'I've decided we should hire Allie,' he tells me, like he's Newton and the apple has just bounced off his head. 'You've been telling me I should put my money where my mouth is, and on this occasion, I think you're right. She's got lots of ideas of things we can offer Gliders – should things go well today – and I think hiring someone straight away shows how serious we are about working with them. One of Chip's questions on Friday was how swiftly we can scale up our operation, and a new face within a day shows what's possible.'

I glance at Allie wondering exactly what she's said to win him over in such a convincing way. I was sure I'd need to step in and fight for her, but he's taken the decision out of my hands.

'With all due respect, Marcus,' I say, turning back to face him, 'we haven't checked for Allie's references yet.' I force a smile in Allie's direction to show I'm not trying to pop her balloon. 'I'm sure there won't be any problem getting a reference from her previous employer, but there are protocols we need to follow.'

'I can give you a copy of my references,' Allie pipes up. 'I asked them to forward me a copy when I handed in my notice. I had a feeling I would be needing them sooner rather than later and I know how slow HR can be in that place.'

'There you go, you see,' Marcus grins back at her. 'We've got her references already.' He pauses. 'Allie, do me a favour and find Rose. She'll be able to get your laptop connected to the network and access to the folders and files you'll need.'

Allie leaves the room, closing the door behind her.

'I thought you'd be pleased, Jenna,' Marcus says when we're alone.

'I am,' I say quickly, though not even I'm convinced by the tone of my words. 'It's just...'

'It's just what? You were the one saying we need to speculate to accumulate and that by growing the team we'll have a better shot at nailing larger clients. Pitching to Gliders was your idea, and unless you're now telling me that everything you told them on Friday was bullshit—'

'No, I didn't lie on Friday, but...'

How do I tell him what Clark told me yesterday? How do I explain that I don't trust her without seeming like I'm losing the plot?

'I have a really good feeling about today's meeting with Chip and the others,' Marcus continues. 'The fact that he wants to meet us so soon can only be a good thing.'

I do hope he's right. For all we know right now, the meeting might just be Chip's way of showing us respect: letting us down face to face. I instantly hear the voice of catastrophe in my head; like an old friend back to keep my feet firmly on the ground, even while everyone else is floating away. Maybe that's why I find it so much easier to buy Clark's claims: because they lead to a darker ending than the prospect that he's the one lying to me.

'I've told Allie she should come with us to the meeting,' he says. 'That okay with you?'

I want to say no, but in fairness, if it wasn't for her intervention and reminder that Chip hates slideshows, we wouldn't be in the position we are now.

'Can you get her up to speed on our other clients, introduce her to the team, and then make sure everything about our pitch is locked down?'

His question is rhetorical, but I offer a nod as I leave the office, closing the door behind me.

* * *

Two hours later and Marcus has gathered Allie and me in the conference room to make sure the laptops are hooked up to the projector and speakers. My stomach is performing cartwheels, but Allie is the picture of calm as she chats to Marcus about her other ideas for the account; ideas she hadn't yet shared with me. I can't help thinking that she's going to prove herself more resourceful than me, and soon Marcus will be making the decision to replace me with her.

Shut up, Mum! I say internally to the voice in the back of my head.

Marcus leaves the room to wait for Chip and the Gliders party in reception.

'Can you believe how well today is going?' Allie says, hurrying over, her hands flapping with excitement. 'I don't know how to thank you for everything you've done for me, Jenna. Helping me when I was at my lowest ebb; taking me in; and now helping me secure new employment. You're like my guardian angel.'

Or the biggest mug to ever walk the earth, I think, but don't say.

'Are you all right? You look a bit peaky?'

'Nerves are wreaking havoc on my gut,' I tell her.

'Why don't you nip to the toilet and freshen up. You've probably got a couple of minutes before they get here.'

I nod, extricating myself and hurrying to the bathroom, where I use the toilet and then splash cold water on my face. I should have brought my bag and applied some lippy, but I don't like wearing makeup. Ironically, I've spent so much of my life wearing a mask that I don't feel the need to paint on an additional one. I'm not used to things going so well, and the voice of catastrophe that lives within my head has been nurtured as I've lurched from one disaster to another. It was born out of trauma and tries to prepare me to better deal with potential future disasters. And the worst part is, it's not often wrong.

I practise smiling at my reflection, silently reciting the script I've been working on all morning. I'm determined not to appear quiet when Chip and his team arrive and have been working on questions I can ask to generate small talk. I've studied the BBC News app on my phone so I have a better idea of world events that I can interject to ask Chip's opinion. I'm as ready as I'll ever be. Drying my hands on a paper towel, I head back towards the conference room, panicking when I see everyone else has arrived, is seated, and waiting for me.

'Speak of the devil,' Allie says, and I instantly feel the heat rise to my cheeks.

I try to recall my planned script for Chip, but my mind is blank, so I approach and offer to shake his hand, before remembering that he isn't a handshaker. I quickly withdraw my hand, hoping he didn't notice.

'Shall we begin?' Marcus interjects. 'Chip and his team have other meetings to get to.'

'Of course,' I croak, my throat suddenly a desert. I open one of the bottles of mineral water, taking a sip, almost gagging when I realise it's sparkling.

I unlock my laptop, but the file I'd left set up on the screen has vanished. I'm sure it was open when I left, but now the file is missing from my desktop.

This can't be happening! Where has it gone?

I search frantically for the file, knowing there should be a copy backed up on the main server.

'Is there a problem?' Marcus mutters under his breath in the seat beside mine.

'No problem,' I say, more breezily than I'm feeling.

I don't understand where the file has gone. It was on my desktop and was open before I went to the bathroom, I'm sure of it. I lower my laptop lid, suddenly wondering if I'm sitting in the wrong space, but this is definitely my laptop. What must Chip be thinking? He has brought three people with him this morning, but I missed the introductions because I was in the bathroom. This is so unprofessional, and I can feel the weight of their stares on my shoulders.

'I'm sorry,' I say, realising the only right thing to do is fall on my own sword. 'There seems to be a problem. I can't seem to find the program we were going to show you.'

'No worries, Jenna, I have a copy,' Allie says eagerly. 'Pass me the cable and I'll flash it up on the screen.'

'Pass her the HDMI lead,' Marcus grizzles under his breath, and I oblige, my mind already racing with a dozen different questions, unable to focus on a single one.

Allie plugs in her lead and a moment later the program is loaded and on the projector screen. I should be talking everyone through it but overwhelm has taken over and I no longer have the processing power to speak. I look at Allie, pleading with her for help, and to my relief she starts speaking, and it's like hearing my own words in her tongue.

There is no logical way the program could have disappeared from my desktop, unless my laptop performed some kind of software update, but I can't see how that is likely. Could someone have deleted the program to make me look bad in front of the Gliders team? I hate how paranoid that sounds, but it's the only way I can explain what has happened. But Allie has nothing to gain from embarrassing me in that way, especially given everything I have done for her.

I can't stay in the room any more, and I stand, unable to verbalise what is going on in my head, and hurry from the conference room, bursting through the toilet doors, staring at my paling reflection in the mirror. And a moment later I'm expelling the contents of my stomach into the basin. When I look back up, I see my mum's face staring back at me.

I need to know if this is what happened to her as well. I unlock my phone and dial Tom's number.

'I need to see Mum. Today.'

35

I'm grateful that Tom isn't a little miffed that I didn't reach the decision to visit Mum earlier, and he agrees to collect me from Winchester as it will be quicker to reach Graveside from there than me returning to Southampton first. I send an apologetic email to Marcus and Allie, blaming it on menstruation, knowing that Marcus won't dare to challenge it. I reassure him that Chip and his team are in great hands. I know I should be in the room with them, answering any of the trickier questions, but I just don't have the processing power to focus on work right now.

I can't keep ignoring my worsening mental health, and if hearing voices isn't a big enough reason to seek help, I have to be honest and admit I no longer trust my own judgement. For all I know, both Clark and Allie are lying to me, and I can't keep leaping from one outrageous conclusion to another. And giving Mum a chance to share her experiences might just help me explain to my GP what I'm going through.

The lunchtime train bound for Weymouth is virtually empty and I practically have a carriage to myself. That doesn't stop me sitting in my regular seat, close to the toilet end of the carriage, should I need to dart towards it. Alighting at Winchester is a huge risk, given Clark could be lurking, but given he's supposed to have a day job, he can't spend all day, every day searching for Allie. And if he still suspects I'm harbouring her at my house, I think it makes more sense that he's more likely to be waiting in Southampton than Winchester.

My fears are quashed as the train pulls into the station, and I hurry from it, up and over the stairs towards the car park where Tom said he would be waiting. He gives me a concerned look as I climb in, throwing my laptop bag onto the back seat.

'Are you okay? You look like you're going to be sick.'

'I'm fine,' I lie, lowering my window for some much-needed air.

I look away, allowing my vision to blur as I fight back grateful tears. I've spent so long running from the past that I never thought I'd find the strength to see Mum again, and I wouldn't be going if my big brother wasn't there to protect me.

'How's work?' he asks, trying to break the silence, but I don't respond, not wanting to upset myself further.

He eventually takes the hint and turns on the radio, searching until he finds an oldies station and Johnny Cash blares out. It reminds me of trips we took growing up; Dad was such a huge country and western fan, and Mum would complain that she'd married a cowboy.

Tom sings along to the stereo absentmindedly, and it temporarily takes my mind off what's about to happen.

We arrive at the gates to Graveside fifteen minutes later, and I shudder at the weathered stone gargoyles that still look down at all who enter. When she was first admitted, the gothic feel to the grounds and former country estate building seemed quite apt, but now they only serve to remind me how horrifying poor mental health can be. Tom says he phoned ahead to say we would be visiting so the nursing staff could make sure Mum was up and dressed. It is raining when we arrive, and so Tom hurries inside, while I take another cursory look at the grey mass that somehow seems to swallow the sky beyond it.

Is this where I'm going to end up one day? Will Luke and Caley realise it isn't my fault?

I step inside as the rain worsens and am greeted by something akin to the smell of an old persons' nursing home, mixed with cleaning products. It certainly isn't a scent I ever want to be accustomed to. Tom introduces me to Dr Yates, who asks to speak to the two of us before we leave. I'm assuming that relates to what Tom warned me about in terms of Mum being released from the facility. I don't know if I'm ready for her to be let back into my life. With my own issues, I don't have the capacity to shoulder anyone else's burden as well.

One of the nurses shows us along the corridor, and to a door that says Dawn's Room, and Tom knocks twice before opening it and peering in. He pushes the door wider and steps in, but I don't immediately follow, trying to summon the courage to enter. This is it: the moment I've been dreading for so long. I wish I'd asked Brett to attend too now. I could really do with one of his arms to clutch hold of and cower behind. Tom is frowning at me, and so I take a deep breath and force my feet to move forwards.

My hand shoots to my mouth the moment I see Mum standing by the large floor-to-ceiling window. The light streaming through casts her like a ghost; her skin so pale it looks as though she hasn't seen even a hint of sun in a decade. Was she always so pale? I really can't remember. In fact, I can't even picture her younger face in my head. Her once dark hair is now light grey and much thinner, hanging down over her shoulders like a veil.

She reaches out a trembling hand and grasps the back of a

chair facing the window, and she looks far less steady than I recall. I can't get over just how old and frail she looks.

'Hello, Jennifer,' she croaks.

'It's Jenna, now, Mum,' I correct, instantly regretting the decision and expecting a backlash.

Her mouth forms an 'O' shape, as her other hand reaches out for Tom, who takes it in his and steps forward to hug her. Tom helps her into the chair, offering the other to me, but I shake my head, perching on the edge of the pink quilted bed instead, keeping him between the two of us for her protection as much as my own.

'How have you been since I last visited?' Tom starts, sitting in the vacant chair, but adjusting it so he can see us both.

'Fine, thank you, dear,' she says meekly. 'And you? How is work?'

I'm not sure she has any real idea what he does for a living, but he tells her it is fine. I wish even more that I'd brought Brett and my children to show off what I've managed to make of my life despite her influence. If I'd known I was coming here today I'd have brought a copy of Brett's book for her to see too.

There is a knock at the door and the nurse who showed us here carries in a tray containing cups, saucers, a jug of milk, and a tea pot. She sets it down on the table between the two of them.

'Shall I be mother?' Tom asks, reaching for the pot, but Mum quickly shakes her head.

'I'd like to do it,' she says, standing and filling the cups. 'Do you take sugar?'

I start when I realise she's speaking to me.

'Um, no. Just as it comes is fine,' I reply, standing and collecting the cup and saucer she's holding out to me, noting that her hands are no longer shaking. I wish my own were steadier, almost dropping the cup.

I reclaim my place on the edge of the bed, sipping from the cup, and willing my mind to think of something to say. It's been so long since I saw her here – and whilst she certainly appears in better health, mentally, than I remember – I don't know how to begin to unpack everything that's happened since then. I don't feel as though I should apologise for not visiting, and yet the guilt is eating me up inside. As far as I'm aware we have no shared interests, despite our history, and I'm not prepared to rake up the past at this juncture. It wouldn't be fair on either of us.

It's at this moment I feel her eyes burning a hole in my head, and I look up.

'I can't believe how much you've grown,' she is gushing. 'You're so beautiful.'

I look away, never certain how to react to a compliment; always trying to guess whether the provider means it or is secretly trying to butter me up for some other ulterior motive. I remember not believing Brett for weeks when he told me he'd fallen head over heels in love with me.

'Thank you,' I eventually say, 'you look well too.'

'And my boy is the spitting image of his rugged father,' she says, smiling at Tom and patting his leg in the process. 'I'm so thrilled that the two of you have remained close... despite everything that happened between me and your dad.'

'Well, that's all in the past,' Tom says, far more positively than I'm feeling. 'There is no use in crying over spilled milk. What's important now is that you're doing much better, Mum. And Dr Yates really feels you're ready to finally find a new home. And I know how excited you are by that prospect.'

'Oh, yes,' she says, nodding. 'I feel so much more in control now that I'm on this new medication. It's so odd not having all that noise in my head. To think this is how everyone else lives. They don't know how lucky they are!'

What I wouldn't give for a few moments of inner quiet each day. I'm curious to know what medication they have put her on, but I don't know how to ask without revealing to Tom what I'm going through at the moment.

'It's really good news, Mum,' Tom continues. 'It really feels like this could be a fresh start for all of us.'

I know the comment is aimed at me, even though he doesn't look over. In fairness, we've been sitting in here for over five minutes and she has yet to shout or scream, or blame the world for her predicament, which is longer than she's ever managed before in my experience.

'Would you both excuse me?' Tom says, standing. 'I need to go to the little boys' room.'

'It's along the corridor,' Mum says, 'last door on the right.'

He leaves, and I glare at the back of his head as he does. I've been wanting a moment alone with Mum, but I didn't realise it would come so quickly, and I've yet to figure out what I want to say to her. My mind instantly fills with voices, each shouting questions at me.

'Tom tells me you're a mum too,' she says, and I immediately remove my phone, open up to a photograph of Luke and Caley and hold it out for her to see.

She puts on her glasses and stares at the screen but makes no effort to extract it from my hand.

'Oh, Jennifer, they are so beautiful. And they look so happy. How old are they?'

'Luke's nine and Caley is seven.'

She smiles at the thought, but I can read the disappointment behind her eyes as well; disappointment that she's never met them.

'They are both so smart and kind,' I say, pocketing my phone and wishing I'd brought a framed picture of them that I could have left for her.

'And their dad?'

'Brett is a bestselling author, and he dotes on them so much. I know how lucky I am.'

She leans in conspiratorially, glancing back at the bedroom door.

'And you trust him?'

The question sends a chill along my spine.

36

I stare at her for what feels like an age, questioning whether I actually heard her speak, or whether it was just her voice in the back of my mind.

'Brett is a loyal and loving husband,' I say, though there's an unexpected edge to my voice when the words emerge.

She narrows her eyes, before leaning back and taking a sip from her cup, silence once again returning to the room. It can't be coincidence that she saved that question until we were alone.

'Brett isn't Dad,' I say, more firmly this time.

'That's good, darling. As you said: you're clearly a lucky girl.'

She isn't looking at me as she says this, so I can't read her face to know whether she means it or is just saying what she thinks I want to hear. Tom was adamant that Dr Yates said the medication is working and that she's in a much better place, and yet...

I can't put my finger on why but something doesn't feel right. That, or I'm seeing things that aren't there.

I stand, wanting to try and clear the voices in my head, and cross to the small dressing table in the opposite corner of the room. The house was sold when she was admitted to Graveside, and what we couldn't sell to fund her treatment was donated to charity. So, everything in this room is the sum total of her worldly possessions. Tom and I were both over eighteen when she finally signed the divorce papers, so she received no child support, and the solicitor she hired did a lousy job of securing any additional funding from Dad. In fact, he walked away from the mess of his marriage relatively unscathed; another reason why I didn't try to keep contact with him after he left us.

There is some perfume, which appears to have been decanted into plastic containers, presumably so she can't break and use them to harm herself. There is a box of tissues, and a small bag of makeup, although she doesn't seem to have made any effort with her face this morning, unless that's why her skin looks so deathly pale. I'm secretly searching for any clue as to what medication they have her on, but it was naïve to think they would leave patients with access to their own meds. And I don't imagine she knows what they're prescribing, though I'm sure I can ask Dr Yates for the specifics when we meet her later.

'What are you doing over there?' I hear her call out and realise she's scowling at me.

'Oh, sorry, I was just looking,' I say, lowering my hands and backing away from the dresser, instantly feeling like my twelve-year-old self, caught red-handed stealing a biscuit from the tin before dinner.

'Stay away from my things,' she barks, crossing the room in an instant, and scanning the contents. 'I bet that's the only reason you've come here: to see what you can steal from me.'

'No, Mum, that isn't why—'

She fixes me with a hard stare, and I'm forced to look away.

'You think I was born yesterday? This is my stuff and you're not having any of it. You think you can show up here after years of ignoring me and act like everything is okay?'

Where is Tom? This is exactly how I thought she was going to be, and I'm amazed at how quickly she's allowed the mask to slip from her face without him here.

'I don't want any of your stuff, Mum,' I say, stepping further away, willing Tom to return to the room and see her in her old state.

I knew she wasn't ready to come out yet.

'You're just like your father,' she continues, holding one of the plastic perfume containers to her chest, 'saying one thing and acting another. He thought I wouldn't learn the truth about him and those whores, but I could smell them on his clothes.'

'Should I fetch one of the nurses, Mum?' I ask, concerned at how quickly she's escalating.

The mention of the nurses stills her instantly, and she returns the container to the table, shuffling back to her chair and retaking her seat as if this episode didn't even happen. Tom isn't going to believe me when I tell him what I witnessed, and although I don't want to make matters worse for her, Tom needs to see that she's pulling the wool over everybody's eyes.

I join her at the table, sitting in Tom's chair.

'When did you start suspecting Dad of cheating on you?'

'Oh, I knew what he was like when I married him. I was naïve to think he'd settle down and stay loyal. And after you and Tom arrived, he had me trapped at home. He saw me as someone who cared for his children and prepared his dinner. That's all I was to him. And although he paid for the house, I never had any money of my own, apart from the scraps of change I could steal from his wallet so I could buy you and Tom sweets every now and again.'

I remember Mum not having a job when we were growing up, but that wasn't that unusual. I had several friends whose mums were housewives, so our situation felt normal. I didn't understand why we never had any money until Dad eventually moved out.

But this serves as a reminder that mine and Brett's situation is very different to what I witnessed growing up; I've battled hard to make sure that's the case.

And yet I've had horrible suspicions about Brett straying with Allie, even though I know they're totally unfounded.

'He was a wrong-un, your dad. I know I shouldn't speak ill of the dead, but I imagine he's roasting in hell for the way he treated us.'

I'll never understand why he chose not to mention his cancer diagnosis to us. I don't remember him being distant until she started accusing him of sleeping around, and he always swore she was mistaken, and he wasn't cheating. I remember in the run-up to the divorce he took Tom and me to one side and swore on his own mother's grave that he never cheated on Mum until after he left home. I had no reason to doubt the statement as it didn't serve his purpose to lie to us at that point.

'You want to watch that husband of yours too. All men are the same when you boil it down. They're like chimpanzees; always looking for the next branch to swing to.'

I leap to my feet, unable to listen to any more.

'My Brett isn't like that, Mum,' I yell. 'I love him, and he loves me. We're not like you and Dad.'

'Sure, keep telling yourself that, sweetheart. Don't come crying to me when he proves you wrong.'

I race out of the room, my vision blurred from the tears waiting to break through. I rush down the stairs, past the reception desk, and out into the pouring rain. I hate getting wet when I'm wearing clothes as it sends me into a sensory meltdown, but I keep running. Away from the gothic building. Away from the car park, and out through the gates with no sense of purpose or direction.

* * *

I finally stop running when I reach the car park of a village pub, and head inside to shelter. I'm panting as I reach the bar and order a large glass of wine, carrying it to a small table by a fireplace that's unlit. I have several missed calls from Tom, who I can only imagine returned to the room to find me gone and is panicking. I can only hope that Mum admitted what she said, but something tells me she fixed her mask back in place the moment I bolted.

I don't message Tom back until I've consumed half the glass and my hands have stopped shaking. I send him the address of the pub, and he arrives a few minutes later, his face the picture of concern.

'She's lying,' I tell him. 'The moment you went to the toilet she started on about Dad and how he was always lying to her about sleeping around. It was like I was fourteen again. And she had the nerve to question my relationship with Brett.'

He listens without interruption, but I can see there is something he wants to say, so I quieten and wait for him to speak.

'Mum said you started yelling at her and knocked all of her things from her dressing table, before running out screaming.'

My mouth hangs open, but no words emerge.

Was that her ploy all along?

'I never... I...'

I try to replay the memory through my mind. I know I raised my voice but only because she was pushing my buttons. I didn't knock anything from her dresser, did I?

Stay away from my things.

No, I would have remembered that. Everything was on the dressing table when I left. She must have knocked the things off to frame me as the villain.

'I didn't knock anything to the ground, I swear,' I say, but even I can hear the desperation in my voice. 'You have to believe me, Tom. She's lying. She isn't better. She's just faking being well so she can get out of Graveside.'

Tom reaches across the table and rests his warm hands on mine, and they stop vibrating.

'It's okay, Jenna. Just calm down. Everything is going to be okay. Take a deep breath for me.'

I obey, inhaling deeply and making a show of exhaling loudly, aware that I need to keep him on my side and not hers.

'A couple of the nurses said they heard you yelling at Mum, and they were about to come and check on you when you ran out of the room, shrieking.'

I wasn't shrieking, was I? I don't remember. I just needed to get out of the room and out of the hospital.

'There's more going on here, isn't there?' Tom continues, his deep voice calming like a late-night radio host. 'You can tell me anything; you know I won't judge.'

If I tell him, he'll think I'm as crazy as she is.

'No, Tom, I'm fine. She upset me when she questioned Brett's loyalty, that's all. But I promise you: she is just pretending to be better. It's all a big lie.'

'Dr Yates still wants to speak to us. I said I would drive us back—'

'No, Tom. Please? I don't ever want to go back to that place. I know you said you can't afford to pay the fees on your own, but I can find a way to help you cover the costs. Would that be okay? We could come up with a finance agreement, or whatever, so I can pay you back some of what you've covered for the last few years.'

'Dr Yates assures me that—'

'She's lying to all of them. Why can't you see that? I'm telling you she's not better yet, Tom. If you saw her the way I did, I wouldn't need to convince you.'

Deep crevices form in his forehead, and he looks at me for a long time before he speaks again.

'Okay, I will tell Dr Yates that we need to get home, and I will arrange a call with her later in the week. Okay? I take it Brett is at home? Or Judith? I don't want to leave you on your own when we get there, Jenna. I'm worried that there's more you aren't telling me.'

'Brett will be at home,' I say, forcing a smile to try and placate him.

He lets out a long sigh.

'Very well. I'll take you home now. But please know that you can speak to me at any time. I want to help you if I'm able to.'

I nod, but after today's incident, I'm not sure who to believe: did Mum trash her room to make it look like I'm the one who's unwell? Or am I the one who's lying to everyone?

37

'Are you sure you don't want me to come back with you?' Tom asks as he pulls up outside Southampton Central station so I can collect my car from the car park.

Conversation on the way home has been stilted, with Tom desperately searching for answers to my behaviour at Graveside, and me unable to put into words how I'm feeling right now. I know I need professional help to better understand what is going on, but I'm not yet willing to share with those closest to me. I don't doubt that Tom loves me, but I don't want him thinking less of me. For years, I've managed to keep things ticking over, but right now it just feels like everything is getting on top of me. Earlier, I could feel the meltdown coming, and in those situations I've learned to remove myself until I am able to get things straight in my head, but I felt powerless to escape Mum's control, just as I was for all those years growing up. I know I don't want to ever feel that way again, but if I can't prove to Tom and Dr Yates that Mum is just telling them what she thinks they want to hear, she'll be released and I don't even want to think about the havoc she'll wreak on my life if that happens.

He suddenly leans across and hugs me, whispering into my ear.

'You don't have to do this alone. I am here for you and ready to listen whenever you're ready to talk.'

If only it was that easy.

We break apart and I hurry from the car before he can see my watering eyes. The ground is slick with rainwater, though I can smell damp in the air, which usually means a heavy downpour is due, so I hurry to my car, driving as fast as I can back to the safety of home. Once inside, I fall into the door, relieved the day is almost over.

I'd had such high hopes for today, and I can hardly believe that it's already gone five. Where did the time go? I've had no response to my email to Marcus and Allie, and my mind is already projecting what that might mean. My inability to locate the pitch on my laptop, Allie coming to the rescue, my running out of the conference suite and not returning – how can they see me as anything but unprofessional? And what if Marcus now shares that belief? Allie seemed to blow him away in her interview, so maybe he'll decide she's less trouble than me and replace me. In the space of a day I've gone from being a shining light to an embarrassment. It's no wonder Marcus hasn't messaged to check how I am.

But given the way I know my mind works, all this catastrophising could be disproportionate to the real situation. Maybe Marcus has been injured in an accident and that's why he hasn't messaged; maybe his phone ran out of battery; maybe someone stole his phone in a random mugging; or maybe he and Allie are too busy celebrating to even give me a second's thought.

I push myself away from the door, dropping my coat and bag to the floor, walking zombie-like into the kitchen and searching the fridge for wine, frustrated when I don't find any. I head into the living room, locate an open bottle of Brett's favourite Scotch, and pour myself a measure into a tumbler. I knock it back and immediately wince at the burn in the back of my throat, before pouring a second measure and slumping down onto the sofa. I just want to quieten the noise in my head. I call out to the speaker and ask it to play Johnny Cash's 'Ring of Fire' at full volume, and when his voice fills the room, I slowly close my eyes and focus on the lyrics. I see my dad in the front of the car crooning along as we drive along the motorway. Young Tom is beside me trying to sing along, while Mum moans at the pair of them for being so out of tune, but that only makes Dad sing louder. The memory slowly warms my heart, though that could also be the Scotch.

I start as I feel a hand press down on my shoulder, almost spilling what remains of my drink. I open my eyes and see Allie staring down at me, her face upside down, and her blonde hair in wet ringlets, framing her cheeks. Her lips are moving but I can't hear what she is saying until I shout for the speaker to pause the song.

'I didn't hear you come back,' she says now, still looking down at me. 'How are you feeling?'

'Fine,' I say, keen to resist my usual tendency to overshare, and tell her how hopeless I'm feeling at this moment. 'I'm sorry for bailing on you.'

She brushes away the apology with her hand, no obvious trace of anger or frustration in her face as far as I can tell from this inverted position.

'Forget about it. I just wish you'd said you were feeling off before we got started. We told Chip you'd been called away for a family emergency, and he was fine with it.'

I wish they hadn't lied; family emergency suggests that I put my family before work, and that's not a good impression to leave with a future client.

'Was Marcus angry?'

'No, not at all.'

'He didn't reply to my message.'

'That's because I told him not to. He was going to message to ask when he'd see you back again, but I told him that he shouldn't put that kind of pressure on his staff. I got the impression that he really doesn't understand employment law particularly well, and I learned today your company doesn't even have a Head of Human Resources.'

'We used to – Pamela something – but she resigned and was never replaced. That was a few years ago. Marcus said we could continue to use the policies she'd written, and would eventually hire someone else, but I guess he just hasn't got round to it.'

'Well, I've told him in no uncertain terms that he's going to have to hire someone now, or I won't accept his job offer.'

I grimace at the thought of Marcus being handed another ultimatum.

'I'm not sure you should be threatening him so soon after he offered you a job. He doesn't tend to—'

'He knows he can't withdraw his job offer, unless he wants to kiss goodbye to the Gliders account. There's no way Chip will sign the contract if you and I aren't heading up the relationship. That's why I've told Marcus he needs to give us both pay rises or we'll walk and take Chip's money with us.'

I'm not following what she's saying, and sit up, turning so I can see her properly.

'You did what?'

She nods excitedly, joining me on the sofa.

'Chip said he wants us leading their new campaign. He loves the concept you pitched on Friday, and the detail I provided today. He thinks we make a brilliant team. I've told Marcus he needs to give you at least a 20 per cent pay rise, and he said he will chat to you once you're back. I've told him not to contact you until you're feeling better, so you can take the next couple of days to ride it out.'

It's been years since Marcus paid anyone in the team more than a paltry 2 per cent annual pay rise, and I find it hard to believe that he'll agree to 20 per cent, but even 10 per cent could help keep Mum at Graveside.

'So the pitch went well?'

She nods excitedly, the ringlets bouncing.

'So well. I wish you'd been there to hear all the wonderful things Chip was saying. He's told Marcus to scale up at speed, and he wants the three of us to fly out to their New York office in a couple of weeks for an official media announcement. How cool is that?'

My mouth hangs open. Of all the scenarios my mind had conjured as to why I hadn't heard from either of them, I never got close to the truth. For all of Clark's warnings about Allie, she's really come through for me; I feel awful for daring to believe his lies...

I freeze as I take in Allie's appearance. She's wearing my bathrobe. The one that hangs on the door in mine and Brett's en suite bathroom. Brett's car was on the driveway, but I haven't seen or heard from him since I got home.

You want to watch that husband of yours too... They're like chimpanzees; always looking for the next branch to swing to.

Why is Allie wearing the robe from my room, and where is my husband?

I stand quickly and hurry out of the room and up the stairs, the Scotch swilling in the glass, but I don't care if it splashes on the carpet. I *need* to know the truth. The door to our bedroom is ajar, so I barge into it, searching the unmade bed, and then the en suite, but there's no sign of him. My imagination conjures images of the two of the rollicking in our bed, and then Brett with his hands all over her naked body in the shower. I hurl the glass against the wall and watch as it shatters into pieces, just like my heart.

I hear Allie on the stairs and she stands in the doorway a moment later.

'Where is he?' I yell at her.

But she stares back at me with confusion.

'Where's who?'

'Brett. You two slept together. Where is my husband?'

She's about to respond when I hear the front door opening, and Brett's voice urging Luke and Caley inside, telling them to change and leave their wet clothes in the washing machine.

'Brett wasn't here when I got home,' I hear Allie saying, but it's like she's speaking in a vacuum, because I can barely hear the words. 'I got soaked walking back from the station and so I had a shower. I don't understand...'

'Get out,' I yell at the voices in my head. 'Leave me alone!'

Allie backs out of the room, the blood draining from her face, saying something about going to get Brett to help. I slam the door shut as soon as she's gone and then I collapse to the floor in a heap and sob until I'm numb.

38

When I wake, I desperately hope that what happened last night was just an intense nightmare, and that I didn't really accuse Allie of sleeping with Brett, before I had a full-on meltdown. I replay the scene over in my mind, looking for clues that it wasn't real, and was simply my subconscious mind playing tricks on me.

But then I roll over and open my eyes, instantly seeing where the glass shattered against the wall; the outline of an amber-coloured stain evidence of what I did.

The voices in my head tell me how much of an embarrassment I am to my family; how I'm cracking up just like Mum did; how my actions are forcing a divide between me and Brett, rather than keeping hold of him. And the voices only grow louder, as I realise Brett isn't in the bed beside me.

I still remember the day Dad finally packed his bags and left, telling Tom and me how sorry he was, and blaming Mum's actions for driving him away. I don't think Brett would ever leave our children behind, but I could imagine him taking them and leaving me behind instead.

I shower and dress, still saddened to see the space where my antique perfume bottle once stood on the dressing table. I'm more certain than ever that Allie must have been the cause while snooping around my room. If she was willing to put on my bathrobe like it was her own, it's possible she's been treating more of my stuff as if it was hers as well.

Last night's imagined scene of Brett and her rollicking in our bed crashes to the front of my mind. Brett did eventually come up last night to check on me, and said he hadn't been home all afternoon. He collected the children from school and took them out for a burger and fries because he assumed Allie and I wouldn't be home until late. The children corroborated his story, so Allie and him together was all in my head. Never have I hated having such a visual imagination more than now.

He told me I should apologise to Allie, which I eventually did, but it was so tough to admit that I'd leapt to the wrong conclusion. She brushed it off as nothing, but I could see hurt behind those eyes. She's the first person who's tried to strike up a friendship with me in years, and my reaction is to assume she has bad intentions towards me and my family. I can't keep running away from the truth that I need help. I have the benefit of seeing what happened to Mum, and I don't want that to happen to me.

For the second time, Brett told me he's worried about my mental state. He says Judith has noticed it as well and wants him to arrange for me to be seen by a specialist. He says he thinks I'm in autistic burnout, probably as a result of all the pressure I've been putting myself under with work, and the ever-building guilt that I'm not spending enough quality time with Luke and Caley.

And I know he's right. It's like I'm trying to juggle bowling balls, and it won't be long before they come crashing down and destroy everything close to me. It would certainly explain the exhaustion I'm feeling at the start and end of every day; the fact that I'm struggling with basic tasks such as eating and brushing my teeth; my short-temperedness; and why everything I try to do feels like I'm wading through tar.

Brett wants me to take a break from work to recover. He said I should book a few days' holiday and just relax, and I know he's right, but with us now taking on the Gliders account, there couldn't be a worse time for me to take time off. Chip Martin is taking a huge chance on our agency, and I don't want to be the reason the relationship fails.

That is why I am going into the office today. I overheard Allie telling Brett that Chip has invited her and Marcus to their office near St Paul's today to meet some of the rest of their creative team, and I need to prove to Chip that I'm not a manic case he can't rely on.

I go downstairs, finding Brett snoring on the sofa, a blanket half kicked off to the floor. The bottle of Scotch is empty on the coffee table beside him, and I guess he either decided he would give me some space last night, or was too repulsed to join me in our bed. Either way, I know I have a lot of repairing to do. I want to tell him everything that's been going on in my head, but I don't want him to think I'm losing my mind and have me committed like Tom and I did to Mum.

'Oh, hey,' Allie says when I enter the kitchen and she catches sight of me while spooning cereal into her mouth. 'I thought Brett said you were taking a few days to yourself.'

'No, I'm fine,' I say, forcing a smile, like it's all water off a duck's back. 'Are you ready to go? I'll drive us to the station.'

She shovels the rest of the cereal into her mouth, leaves the bowl beside the sink and follows me out to the car. Conversation is stilted because I feel insanely guilty about accusing her of sleeping with Brett, and I guess she's also not sure how to get past that bullet.

'About last night,' she finally says as I'm parking in my usual spot in the car park, 'I want you to know that I would never do something like that. You and Brett and the kids have been so kind to me, I would never throw that kindness back in your faces.'

She is trying to make eye contact, but it's too painful for me to meet her stare.

'I know, and I'm sorry,' I say, focusing on the steering wheel, enjoying the texture of the leather between my fingertips. 'I had a bad day yesterday and... Please, just know I wasn't in a good place last night, but I'm better today.'

I don't think either of us is convinced by the lie, but Allie opens her door, and we head to the station in silence. It's only when we're seated and the train pulls away that I even think about the possibility that Clark could have been waiting for us to board.

* * *

The Gliders office building really is something else. A stone's throw from St Paul's Cathedral, the carbon net zero tower is the first of its kind in this part of London, and it's hard not to be impressed as we are welcomed by Chip at reception. He tells us how they are planning similar projects in key cities around the globe, leading by example with the latest sustainable technology in use.

'There are solar panels strategically placed around the building and acting as a canopy on the roof terrace,' he proudly tells us. 'Wait until you see the view from the terrace. It really is quite the spectacle on a sunny day. Hopefully some of this cloud will burn off later and we can all go up for an afternoon drink. There is a fully licensed gin bar up there, though it doesn't open until four.'

The building is sixteen storeys, and he deposits us on floor ten, explaining that only four of the floors are occupied right now, as they plan to lease out the remaining levels to companies with similar core values to their own. I can't deny how much of an upgrade the floor space feels compared to what we're used to. The ceiling is high, making the space feel more airy, and well-lit as the entire floor is surrounded by floor-to-ceiling windowpanes. Even from here I can see the Thames and the London Eye.

Once we're settled, and connected to their network, Marcus joins us, and confirms the contract is now under review by both sets of legal teams, but the deal is 99 per cent complete. He has tasked Allie and me with recruiting at pace, and has asked Allie to make contact with some of her former colleagues at Acorns to see if any are willing to join our exciting new project. Based on their preliminary conversations, we are going to need at least six more recruits before Christmas just to get up to speed with Gliders' initial plans. There is so much going on that I feel overwhelmed, and yet exhilarated at the same time. I'm amazed when Chip appears, telling us it's lunchtime and where we can log on to order our free lunch. I order a protein-packed salad, which arrives twenty minutes later. Allie smirks as her ribeye steak and fries arrive.

'I went for what looked like the most expensive thing on the menu,' she says, chuckling at something on her phone.

'What's so funny?' I ask, suddenly aware that I don't recall Allie ever mentioning other friends.

'Oh, nothing,' she says, putting her phone face down, and tucking in to her fries. 'Sorry, do you want one?'

I look away with a curt shake of my head, and stare down at my own food.

'How's your salad?'

'Delicious,' I say.

'If the food offering is this good, I can see myself coming into the office more regularly,' she says, marvelling around the room.

And I know what she means; I don't know if it's just because the building is so new to us, but I definitely feel lighter here than I have in our old premises, and I imagine my team will love the idea of a free lunch for coming in to work. But the thought of being there when Luke and Caley head off to school, and being home when they arrive back is far more appealing than a fancy lunch.

Allie is chuckling at her phone again, this time typing out a reply, but even when she catches me looking over, makes no attempt to share the joke.

In truth, I think I'm a little envious at how relaxed and happy she seems. It's been exactly a week since she changed from the poised, perfect women on Platform 8 with the glamorous life I'd visualised in my head, to the woman shaking in terror in that toilet cubicle. I'd be interested to know whether she's even thought about what happened that morning seven days ago. I don't want to ask in case it triggers trauma for her.

I continue to eat my salad in silence, and carry the container to the recycle bin, and when I return Allie tells me she's heading up to the roof terrace for a breath of fresh air, but I decline the opportunity to join her, keen to complete my list of tasks so I can get away at a reasonable time. I desperately want to read to Caley tonight, and if I'm back in time, I'll feel as though I've accomplished something today.

A phone vibrates on the desk and I immediately reach for my own, only there are no notifications. I glimpse Allie's phone on the desk, partially covered by the leftover napkins from her lunch. She must have forgotten to take it up with her. I start to reach for it, before snapping my hand back. She may have left it there on purpose so that she can enjoy the air without being disturbed.

But curiosity burns into my soul, and I push the napkins away and look at the notification, but it's not what I'm expecting to see. I read the message again and again, shaking my head and blinking rapidly, practically hearing my mother's voice over my shoulder.

You want to watch that husband of yours too.

The message is from Brett, and all it says is:

> Don't tell Jenna x

39

Mum's ghostly laughter echoes all around me, and even slamming my hands against my ears won't keep it out.

Brett wouldn't do this, I tell myself over and over. I love Brett and he loves me. I've always trusted him. I don't want to believe that he would cheat on me.

But Mum's words are getting louder: *All men are the same when you boil it down.*

I remember that first day when I came back from collecting Caley from school and caught the pair of them laughing in the kitchen, and Allie playfully slapping Brett's arm like they'd been friends for years rather than two people who'd only just met. I remember seeing the heat rush to my husband's face, like he'd been caught red-handed. Was that when it started? An innocent touch of his arm sparking something animalistic inside of him? How many other innocent brushes of hands or more have there been that I've missed or ignored?

I hear Mum's words again: *They're like chimpanzees; always looking for the next branch to swing to.*

Has it been there this whole time, staring me in the face? Of course Brett would be attracted to Allie; she's young and beautiful and confident; all the things that I'm not. With her long blonde curls, and hourglass figure, yet to be disrupted by the strain of childbirth. And with none of the fucked-up family history of mental illness to contend with. Why wouldn't he think about trading me in? Allie would certainly be an upgrade.

I'm suddenly remembering a wildlife programme Brett and I saw late one night. He said he was watching it for book research, and my mind was largely elsewhere, but the presenter was talking about how cuckoos often lay their eggs in the nests of other species of birds, tricking the host into raising the baby cuckoo who eventually pushes the eggs of her adopted siblings out of the nest in a murderous rampage. Allie is the cuckoo in my story, tricking Brett into choosing her and slowly pushing me out of my home. But once I'm gone, what if she then targets Luke and Caley?

I can't allow that to happen. I've worked too hard to keep my family together, and I'm not prepared to give them up without a fight.

Snatching up Allie's phone, I rehearse the conversation in my head as I stalk towards the bank of lifts, and jump in as the doors open, stabbing at floor sixteen. I don't recognise the two men already in the car, but their conversation instantly stops when they see me. I don't know if this is because their conversation is confidential or because they can see the angry heat escaping from my every cell.

They both exit at the next floor, leaving me alone, ruminating on exactly what I'm going to say to Allie. I have the proof in the text message from Brett, but I expect she'll deny an affair at first. Of course she will; she won't want to acknowledge that I'm onto her.

Charles warned me about her, but I chose to believe her over him. I have allowed her to manipulate me into letting her stay at our house, and now I've enabled her to get a job with Marcus and the team. How long until she's manipulating the rest of them into thinking she's an upgrade on me? And then I'll have nowhere I can turn.

The lift doors can't open quickly enough, and I march forwards, with no idea of where I am going. The corridor banks to the right and I suddenly find myself in a large sprawling space, with tall tables and stools to one side and a shuttered bar area to the right. The floor-to-ceiling windows to my left are bordered by a large patio space, with raised concrete flowerbeds, and that's where I see Allie, leaning over the edge of the tall metal wall puffing out smoke. Beyond the tall tables are lower tables and vacant sofas, and beyond that a pair of large glass doors that I now head towards. The strong wind blows me sideways as I step through, and follow the path to the left in the direction of Allie.

I call out to her, but either my voice doesn't travel on the wind, or she chooses to ignore me. I really don't want to move that close to the edge of the terrace in case this is the moment she's planning to push me over, like the baby cuckoo in that documentary. But as I'm watching her, she takes a final inhale on the cigarette before flicking it over the edge, starting when she turns and sees me standing here.

'Oh, Jesus, Jenna, you frightened the life out of me.'

I don't answer, holding my ground, the wind whipping my hair left and right as it pummels against me. In hindsight, I should have just waited inside, as she'd have to have passed me on her way back to the lift. But even though I now know this, my feet remain planted. In my head, this conversation happens outside, and I'm not prepared to change my plan last minute.

'Are you okay?' she calls out, moving slowly towards me. 'You look like you've seen a ghost.'

I hear Clark's words in my head again: *She flew into a rage. I was lucky not to be killed.*

I need to be mindful of exactly what this woman is capable of. All this sweeter-than-sweet attitude is a façade to lull me into trusting her. I can't allow her to make a fool of me any more.

'Is everything okay, Jenna?' she asks again when I don't respond. 'Do you want a cigarette or something?'

I shake my head, conscious she's still closing the distance between us, and she's now only a couple of metres away. I suddenly question what I think I'm doing, and why I didn't tell anyone – Marcus, Chip – that I was coming up here to see Allie. I can't see any security cameras up here, so if one of us was to go over the edge, only the surviving witness could account for exactly what happened.

'Oh, is that my phone?' she asks, spying the rainbow-coloured case between my fingers.

I picture Brett's message in my head, but it's like the words are hovering in the air above Allie's head.

> Don't tell Jenna x

Why did he put a kiss at the end if there isn't something romantic between them? Brett isn't one for public displays of affection (thank God!) but he isn't one to put kisses on messages unless they're addressed to me or the children.

I clear my throat, desperate to stop her getting any closer.

'I know about you and Brett,' I say, and she stops dead in her tracks.

'What do you mean?' she replies, but she's suddenly less self-confident.

'He messaged you,' I continue, holding the phone aloft. 'Don't tell Jenna, kiss.'

She frowns at this, before a smile breaks out.

'Oh, that,' she says, and I can't believe she's now so relaxed about this.

'Is that all you have to say?'

'I'm not sure what else I can say. I promised him I wouldn't tell you.'

There's a part of me wants to throw the phone at her, picturing it striking a blow against her forehead, at which point she stumbles backwards, concussed and confused, and suddenly she's falling over the edge of the building to certain death.

I take a step backwards, appalled at how visual the scene is in my head. Is this what it was like for Mum when she thought about my dad's affairs? Did she picture herself attacking the women who broke their marriage apart?

'I want you out of my house,' I say, firmer than I'm feeling.

'I'm sorry I didn't tell you, but he begged me not to.'

I've told her so many times that she should leave my house, but I've allowed her to manipulate me into changing my mind. This is her twisting the situation again, as she did with what happened to Clark when she claimed he'd attacked her, when by all accounts she was the one who attacked him. She's going to try and blame all of this on Brett, but I know what Clark told me.

'My husband wouldn't have instigated an affair.'

Her face balls in confusion.

'What are you talking about? Brett's having an affair? Is that what you think I'm hiding? I swear to you, Jenna, I know nothing about Brett cheating on you. He wouldn't. He loves you and the kids too much.'

'Don't deny it. I knew something was off when I came home

last night and you were wearing my bathrobe. I know you've been snooping about in my bedroom too.'

She steps forward, offering a hand, but I take two quick steps backwards, out of her reach, and she stops.

'You must have thrown yourself at him to try and push me out of the nest,' I say. 'Was that your plan all along? Make contact with me on the train, pretending to be a victim to appeal to my maternal side and then once you'd weaved your way into our lives, force me out.'

'You are unbelievable! It's no wonder Brett thinks you're losing your mind.'

I snap and lunge towards her before I feel a pair of hands dragging me back.

'What the hell is going on?' I hear Marcus yell, realising he is the one with his hands on my shoulders.

'Ask her,' I glower.

'I'm sorry you had to see this, Marcus. Jenna is... she's not feeling herself.'

'Stop lying!' I scream, straining against Marcus's grip. 'I've seen his message. I know you're hiding something from me, and I know how you've been outrageously flirting with Brett. I get it. He's still very handsome, and a bestselling writer, but I promise you I won't give him up without a fight.'

'Wait, what? What's this about Brett?' Marcus asks.

'Oh my God! I swear on my life I'm not having an affair with Brett.'

I feel Marcus release my arms, but he quickly steps between us.

'I don't know what the fuck is going on between the two of you, but sort it now! How do you think this looks to Chip and his team?'

'Show him your phone,' I say, knowing Marcus will take my side when he sees the undertone of Brett's message.

Allie shakes her head slowly, dismissively, but then unlocks her screen and shows it to Marcus.

'I don't get it,' he says, scrutinising the text. 'What aren't you telling Jenna?'

'He wanted to tell you himself,' she says testily. 'His book has been optioned for film, and his agent says the signs are good that filming will begin next summer.'

'What? No, she's lying,' I say, unable to process this news.

How can she know this? Why wouldn't Brett have phoned me?

'He was planning to tell you when we got home tonight. He's got champagne chilling.'

'No, you're lying. He wouldn't tell you and not me.'

Allie shrugs at Marcus.

'I guess he felt he had to tell somebody but wanted to make a bigger deal of the news with the woman he's closest to. I'm sorry, Jenna, but that's the truth.'

The urge to just run away is overwhelming, and I turn and stare back through the windows towards the bank of lifts. But my feet are frozen. The voice inside my head is telling me to run, but my body is ignoring it.

I feel Marcus looking at me, and I don't know what to say. I was so certain that Brett was following in my dad's footsteps, but it's me following in Mum's.

'Is this going to be a problem between you?' I hear Marcus ask, and as much as I've been battling internally with that question, my actions have already answered the question.

I hear Mum's voice telling me I'm right not to trust Allie and that it was inevitable Brett would cheat on me with all the baggage I bring.

My heart is starting to race with overwhelm. It feels as though the roof terrace is starting to spin on an axis.

I can't stay here. I need to get out; to get away from Allie and allow my mind to process this information. I glance at the bank of lifts again, but this time my feet do move, and suddenly I'm sprinting towards the doors and then across the tiled floor, and don't stop even when I hear Allie calling after me. As the lift doors close, I type out a message to Tom, begging him to meet me.

40

I agree to meet Tom at his hotel in Southampton, but the train journey does little to temper my mood. I've sent a message to Marcus apologising for my outburst and promising I'll explain everything when I next see him. I realise I'm making a terrible impression to Chip and his team and the last thing I want to do is appear unreliable. But given the pressure we're now under to recruit into the team, Marcus will be hard pushed to sack me for my sudden strange behaviour.

Tom is waiting in reception when I arrive, wearing a troubled expression.

'Is everything okay?' I hear him ask, and I want to scream out that nothing is okay right now: I have a stranger living in my house who tried to murder a man because he discovered she was squatting, and now I feel like she's trying to steal my family from me.

'Is this about Mum?' Tom asks next, leaning closer and lowering his voice.

I still can't speak, as my mind races through every conversation I've had with Allie. I feel certain she's been pulling strings –

manipulating me – since the moment we met on the train last Tuesday. But has it been longer than that? I think back to that first time I saw her on Platform 8 at Waterloo. The moment our eyes met, I saw her as someone with her life together and started to envy her because of the mess I'm making of my own life. Did she pick up on my vulnerability that day? Was my seeing her on the platform the catalyst that started all of this?

I don't say any of this to Tom but the questions are all that fill my mind. I look at my brother, willing him to read my thoughts.

'I'm sorry, I hadn't realised,' he says. 'We can go up to my room if you want to talk in private?'

He stands and heads in the direction of the lifts, and my eyes once again fall on the revolving door. I could just leave, and message him later to apologise. I'm feeling so overwhelmed, and I can't process the heat of the room, the odd glances from the other people passing through reception. There's also the fact that I'm going to have to see Allie tonight when I get home and I have no idea what I'm going to say to her. It feels as though the entire world has me in its fist and is slowly tightening its grip.

It isn't fair for me to unburden all of my crazy on to Tom. He came here to visit and sort out Mum's future; he has enough on his plate. I shouldn't have come.

I stand and grab my laptop bag, thrusting it over my shoulder and sprint towards the revolving door. The cool air on my forehead when I am back on the pavement brings instant relief from the overly warm reception area, but now I can't stop thinking about how Tom is going to react when he sees I've disappeared. I don't have to wait too long to find out, as he quickly catches up with me while I'm still within the shadow of the tall hotel building.

'Wait up,' he says, adjusting his anorak. 'You should have said you wanted to walk and talk, I'd have got us some teas to go.'

He doesn't even realise I'm in full fight-or-flight mode; either that or he's well aware and is just trying to soften the blow.

'There's a park with some benches about ninety seconds from here,' Tom says. 'Can we go there to talk?'

I stop and look at him, my eyes filling as I force my mind to focus on addressing him.

'Go back to the hotel, Tom. I shouldn't have come here.'

'No, don't be silly. I can see that you're upset about something, and whatever it is, I want you to tell me.'

'You won't understand,' I say.

'Then help me to understand. Whatever is going on, you don't have to deal with it on your own.'

Before I can speak again, he grabs my head and pulls it into his shoulder, and holds me tight, just like he used to do when we were children and I was scared because Mum and Dad were arguing.

'We'll be okay, just you and me,' he whispers and I'm instantly transported back to his room. 'I won't let anything bad happen to you. I promise.'

I allow him to lead me across the road and into the gated park, and we follow the path around the grass and sit on benches a stone's throw from the empty playground of swings and climbing frames. At least we're alone now.

'I remember when we were kids and you'd have shutdowns like that. It used to drive Mum nuts! She'd ask you over and over what was wrong, but didn't understand that you were so overwhelmed you couldn't properly express your feelings. She'd end up shouting at you in frustration, which would only make matters worse. And then you'd come and find me in some dark corner, and whisper into my ear, and explain what was bothering you.'

I remember he was the only one I ever felt wouldn't judge me for being me. He made me feel safe enough to drop the mask.

'Do you want to whisper it now to me?' he asks, and I feel a lump form in my throat. How did I get so lucky to have a brother who genuinely cares and wants to help?

'I think I've got whatever Mum has wrong with her. With her mind specifically. I've just accused Allie of trying to steal Brett and the kids away from me.'

'Sorry, who's Allie?'

'She's the woman who... she's someone who's been staying with us for a few days.'

Tom leans back in the bench and runs a hand across his mouth and chin.

'So she's a friend?'

I don't know how to describe our relationship. There have been times when I've felt a genuine connection with her, as if we've known each other for years. Somehow she just seems to get me, and that's what makes her closeness to Brett all the more hurtful.

'Not exactly. We were on the same train last Tuesday and she looked in distress, so I tried to help her and she told me she'd been attacked by her boyfriend. She fought back, but was terrified that she'd be arrested because he is a policeman and she said he'd twist her words. I felt sorry for her and told her she could stay with us for a few days.'

'That I was not expecting. Wow, that's a lot to unpack. So, prior to last Tuesday she was a complete stranger?'

'That's just it: the way she is, somehow it feels like she's been around for much longer than that.'

'Tell her she can't stay with you any longer, and then focus on getting better. I've never seen you looking as frazzled as you are right now. I noticed it when we went to see Mum yesterday. I'm worried about you, Jenna. The stress of holding down a job and raising a young family isn't easy to deal with. You need to give yourself a break from time to time.'

'It's not as easy as that. She lost her job and now she's working with me.'

'In the space of a week?'

'Everything happened so quickly, but she helped me out with a priority project and I thought it would help her get back on her feet.'

He considers this for a moment before speaking again.

'The Brett I know wouldn't cheat on you, Jenna. He's not the type.'

'And Dad was? He told me it was Mum's behaviour that drove him into the arms of another woman. What if my behaviour is pushing Brett towards Allie?'

I lean into him and he puts his broad arm around my shoulder. Like Brett, Luke and Caley, Tom is one person I don't mind hugging.

'Brett isn't Dad. And his claim that Mum drove him to it is horseshit. I saw him in the arms of another woman a couple of times when we went to watch the football. He'd tell me it had to be our little secret, and he'd buy me a chocolate bar to keep my silence.'

I try to pull away, angry that his actions helped Dad to keep up his pretence, but he holds me there. I remember how bad she became after he walked out, but I don't really remember what she was like before that.

'You were probably too young, but she didn't just accuse him of affairs and stalk him, she could be quite violent as well. If he came home late, she used to fly off the handle because he hadn't forewarned her, and she would have had dinner ready at a set time. She was a real stickler for routine, and couldn't handle things changing at the last minute.'

The hairs on the back of my neck stand, as I think about my own implosions when routines change suddenly. But what's most scary is the prospect that the apple hasn't fallen nearly as far from the tree as I'd hoped. What if all of what is happening right now is leading to where she wound up?

'I know now I should have spoken up, but the longer it went on the harder it became. I knew Mum would be cross with me for not saying something sooner, and I didn't want to become the target of her attacks.'

'What are you talking about?'

'She used to hit Dad. That was usually how the arguments would end. She'd slap and punch him, or throw something at him.'

'No, you're lying. Mum wasn't violent like that.'

'I saw the bruises, and one night after the arguing had stopped and you'd fallen asleep, I snuck downstairs and found her standing over his body, a patch of blood leaking out from the back of his head. I thought she'd killed him, but she was just standing there, unresponsive. I ended up phoning for an ambulance which came and took him to hospital. That was the day Dad decided to finally leave.'

I have no memory of Dad being in hospital, but I do remember the argument at Easter when he just wasn't around any more. And it was several weeks before Tom and I were allowed to go and see him at the hotel he was in.

'How did I not know about any of this?'

'Because I tried to shield you from as much as I could. She wasn't well, and although it took longer than it should have, we got her the help she needed.'

I think back to me throwing the glass of Scotch against the wall of my bedroom. Is that how it started for her? An act of violence that she started to funnel towards Dad?

'I'm more like her than you realise,' I say next.

'No, you're not. I think you're feeling the pressure right now, and maybe you need a break; a chance to recharge your batteries. Can you speak to your boss and take a few days?'

I scoff at the suggestion.

'Work's never been so busy. He won't agree to that.'

'Then maybe you need to go and see your GP and have them sign you off, before you burn out.'

I definitely need to get help from somewhere, but I hate the thought of leaving Marcus and the team in the lurch when they need me the most.

'Have you spoken to Brett about any of this yet?'

I shake my head.

'And I'm guessing you've probably not told him about what happened with Mum yesterday either.'

Sometimes his ability to read my thoughts can be a curse as much as it is a blessing.

'Tell me if it's none of my business, but my advice to you is to go home and talk to Brett now, and then when he understands the situation, make a plan of how to handle things together. I think that was one of the reasons Mum and Dad's marriage broke up. They stopped communicating and drifted apart. Brett's a good guy and I'm sure he'd benefit from knowing what's on your mind.'

I know deep down he's right, and I snuggle in closer to his chest.

'How did you get to be so smart?' I tease.

'Well, you got the good looks, so I suppose one of us had to get the brains.'

He roars with laughter, and he sounds so much like my memories of Dad laughing that it's a little unnerving. I wonder how much of Mum he sees in me, and whether it freaks him out more.

41

The wipers are on their top speed when I pull up on the drive, but I really don't remember any of the journey home from seeing Tom. It's almost like one second I was there and now I'm here, with no memory of the intervening passage. The house looks so dark, the windows reflecting the granite-coloured sky overhead. But at least I'm home where I'm safe to be myself, where my loving family waits just beyond the door. Tom is right: it's time I spoke to Brett about what's really going on in my head. It will be easier to face the challenge head on with him by my side.

There's no let-up in the rain, and I try to use my laptop bag as a makeshift umbrella as I hurry to the door. Once inside, I realise I can't remember the last time that Luke and more latterly Caley came running to the door to give me a hug and excitedly tell me about their day at school. I can't hear them, so assume they must be in their rooms. I want them to know that whatever I'm going through and will have to face over the coming weeks, I love them both dearly and that will never change. Mum became so obsessed with Dad's behaviour that I don't recall a single occasion when she told me she loved me or that she was proud of me. I don't want my own children to experience that coldness. Maybe I should take Caley for a pampering session at the local spa, and maybe I can try and get tickets to take Luke to watch some Premiership football; make a day of it like Dad used to do with Tom.

I'm about to pop upstairs and check on them when I hear Brett talking to someone in the living room. The door is ajar, and as I push it open, I'm surprised to see Allie sitting beside him on the sofa. But she's leaning forwards, elbows on knees, a mangled tissue between her fingers. I wouldn't have thought she'd be back from London by now. She starts as she sees me.

'You're home early,' I say.

She doesn't reply, pressing the tissue to the end of her nose.

'Perhaps you should sit down,' Brett says, his voice soft, yet firm.

I perch on the armchair so I'm sitting diagonally to the two of them. There's a bag of yarn and knitting the other side of the armchair, which tells me Judith hasn't returned to Dublin yet.

'What's going on?' I ask. 'Has something happened?'

Brett sits forward and I see him gently pat Allie's hands, and I resent their closeness. A shiver shoots down my spine as I picture Brett telling me that my worst fears were right and he and Allie have been having an affair.

'Allie told me what happened at work,' he says, his brow furrowing as he looks at me for an explanation.

I suppose I shouldn't be surprised that she's told him I confronted her on the rooftop, but the fact he still hasn't told me about his book news speaks volumes.

'I saw a message from you and jumped to the wrong conclusion,' I say, with more hope than certainty. 'I'm sorry I got the wrong end of the stick.'

I wait for Allie to acknowledge the apology, but she is staring at her hands as they pull at the tissue and Brett just glares at me in silence.

'Is that all you're going to say?' he eventually asks.

I don't like his tone, and in my defence had he messaged me about his book being optioned, rather than Allie, I wouldn't have jumped to the wrong conclusion.

'I don't know what else you expect me to say. I was hurt when I saw your message to Allie and the added kiss at the end. You know I have a tendency to catastrophise everything and my mind immediately jumped to the prospect that you were hiding something pretty major from me. Congratulations, by the way. You must be delighted.'

The crevices in his forehead thicken as he continues to stare at me.

'Don't try to deflect what you did, Jenna. You frightened poor Allie half to death.'

It's my turn to frown. What has she told him?

'No, don't be silly, you weren't really scared,' I say, half-expecting one of them to burst out laughing at this most impractical joke.

She still won't look at me, and my own maternal instinct wants to check why she's so upset. She certainly didn't look scared when we were up on that roof terrace. She was calm and relaxed.

'Jenna, you... I can't believe I'm even going to say this... you threatened to push Allie off the roof.'

My mouth drops.

'No, I didn't.'

Allie's tearful eyes snap up to mine.

'If Marcus hadn't shown up when he did, I don't want to think what might have happened.'

I blink several times, trying to replay the scene in my head.

We were near the edge of the terrace, but I didn't threaten her. I just wanted her to admit what she'd done. Didn't I?

Mum said you started yelling at her and knocked all of her things from her dressing table, before running out screaming.

'I didn't...'

But I can't formulate my words.

'And then there's what happened at the pool on Sunday,' Brett continues.

'Wait, what happened at the...?'

'Poor Caley was terrified,' Allie pipes up. 'You were screaming at the teenager behind the desk and you were physically shaking when you saw us. You kept checking Caley all over, and kissing her.'

'No, that's not...'

'Caley told me you really scared her on Sunday, Jenna,' Brett says. 'That's why she's hiding in her room right now.'

Wait, she's hiding from me? I know she was quiet on the way home from the pool, but I didn't do anything to frighten her. Why would she tell Brett that?

I stand.

'Where are you going?' Brett asks.

'I want to see Caley and make sure she's okay.'

'Don't. Mum's with her, and I think that's for the best right now.'

I think of Tom holding me tight when we were kids and Mum was losing her shit with Dad.

'I'm really worried about you, Jenna. Your behaviour these last few weeks...' He shakes his head and sighs. 'Maybe I'm to blame for putting too much pressure on you.'

'This isn't your fault,' Allie says, her hands now on his. 'You mustn't blame yourself.'

I want to lunge across the room at her and tell her to keep her grubby mitts off my husband, but I don't want to add fuel to the fire.

'I want you to make an urgent appointment to see the GP first thing,' Brett says next. 'I've spoken to Mum, and we all think it's the best thing for you.'

Trial by jury and they've decided I must be guilty without listening to my defence.

'I'm going to speak to the doctor,' I say, trying to wrestle back some control of the situation. 'I was already planning to, but let's not blow things out of proportion.'

'No?' Brett suddenly snaps, and I shrink back at the explosion. 'You think frightening our children is acceptable, do you? And threatening to push a friend off the roof of a tower block is okay, is it?'

'I didn't—'

'I dread to think how your behaviour is going to escalate next. Are you going to attack me?'

'No, I wouldn't—'

'You made our daughter feel unsafe yesterday, even though Allie was there doing a good thing. A favour to us; taking the kids to the pool so you wouldn't have to worry about the overwhelming noise.'

'But I spoke to Clark, and he said—'

'And there you go again with your conspiracy theories. *He* attacked Allie, don't forget. She was lucky to escape his clutches with her life. Have you forgotten about that?'

'No, but—'

'What, you'd rather believe the words of an abusive ex than the woman who's been nothing but a blessing to this house?'

I stare at Allie, waiting for her to step in and defend me, but she stares back at me blankly.

'I just don't understand how I didn't see the signs sooner,'

Brett says, running a hand through his hair in exasperation, still shaking his head dismissively.

'Brett, please, just listen to me for a second. You're twisting everything.' He opens his mouth to interrupt, but I'm determined to have my say. 'I'm aware that things have been getting on top of me, and I agree that it's time I spoke to the doctor to get some help, but I'm not a danger to anyone, least of all Luke and Caley. I love them more than life itself, and I would never do anything to put them in danger. Deep down, you know that.'

'And what about Monday night?'

I can barely remember the last few days, a cloud in my mind mixing the memories like a soup.

'Throwing the glass against the bedroom wall. Do you have any idea how long it took me to clean up the mess? And even after hoovering it twice, I got up this morning and stood on a shard of glass that cut my heel.'

'I was frustrated and lashed out—'

'And what happens if the next time Luke or Caley are in the way? No, I'm sorry, Jenna, but I'm not prepared to take that chance. I want you to go and find a hotel for the night.'

My mouth drops again.

'No, I'm not doing that.'

'Yes, you will, or I'll be forced to phone the police and report all of these incidents and have you sectioned for your safety as much as ours.'

'Please, Brett, stop overreacting.'

'No, Jenna. I think for tonight you should not be here. You and I can then talk things over in the morning when you've calmed down.'

'No, I want to talk about it now.'

I stand and try to grab his arms to make him listen to me, but Allie also stands and tries to fend off my arms and inadvertently her face catches my elbow and she drops like she's been shot.

'Oh, God, I'm sorry,' I say my hands shooting up to my mouth. 'I didn't mean...'

She looks up and there is blood running from the bottom of her nose.

'Now look what you've done,' Brett says, stooping to help her back up, and pulling a fresh handkerchief from his pocket and pressing it to her nose.

'I'm sorry,' I say again. 'It was an accident.'

'Just go, Jenna. Please? Go before we both say something we might come to regret.'

With that, he takes one of Allie's arms, his hand still pressed to her nose, and he leads her out of the room towards the kitchen; my husband and the cuckoo who's forcing me out of the nest.

42

When I wake, for the briefest moment, I forget that I'm in a family-sized room in the Holiday Inn overlooking the Southampton seafront. It was the only room they had available, a last-minute cancellation.

'Aren't you lucky?' the overenthusiastic duty manager behind the desk quipped when I was checking in last night.

I certainly don't feel lucky right now. I should be at home with my family, not propped up against impossibly soft pillows waiting for the travel-sized kettle to boil while the breakfast news plays on the screen in the background. Sleep, when it eventually came, didn't feel nearly long enough, and I can't stifle the yawn as it erupts from my throat. Tom said he thought I was on the verge of burnout, and I hadn't realised just how right he was. I've been pushing myself harder and harder to balance my pay cheque with family time, and failing at both.

Einstein said the definition of insanity is doing the same thing over and over again and expecting different results. Thanks, Albert, I'll consider that a diagnosis. It was naïve for me to think that I could keep running at full steam without any repercussions. I kept telling myself that I would take a rest when things eased up, but with Marcus constantly badgering me about cost-cutting it's never been the right time. And now with the Gliders account all but secured, the work is only going to ramp up further.

When Allie helped me fix the presentation for Chip, I thought she was an angel sent down to save me, but maybe I shouldn't have been so quick to count my blessings; had we missed the mark, then I wouldn't be feeling this same level of pressure.

I unlock my phone, desperately searching for some kind of message from Brett, apologising for his overreaction last night, and begging me to come home, but there are no messages.

Maybe I should contact him. Is that what he wants? For me to make the first move?

I start typing out a message before quickly deleting the text and starting again. But it still doesn't read right. I want him to know that he was right to raise concerns about my health, and that with his support I will seek out the help I need; if necessary, I'll have to ask Marcus for a few days' leave to get myself together. He won't like it, but I have to start reprioritising; I won't give up my family without a fight.

I delete the text again. I can't get the intonation of the message right, and I'd far rather speak to Brett face to face. It's nearly eight, so he'll be getting Luke and Caley ready for school.

Caley told me you really scared her on Sunday... That's why she's hiding in her room right now.

Hearing Brett say that broke my heart. I hadn't meant to scare Caley at the swimming pool, but I was so convinced Allie was going to steal her away from me, and now because of my reaction, I've pushed the two of them closer together. I remember how frightened I was of Mum's behaviour at times when I was growing up, and I always vowed I would never make my own children feel as I did, and I've let them both down. And I don't doubt Judith has been adding fuel to that particular fire. Even though she wasn't in the room with us last night, I felt her shadow hanging over Brett. It isn't a coincidence that he's suddenly questioning my mental health since Judith showed up uninvited.

I've spoken to Mum, and we all think it's the best thing for you.

Did Brett seek out Judith's view, or was she the one pulling his strings? Ultimately, it doesn't matter as the outcome is the same: me stuck here away from those I cherish most.

I didn't bring my laptop with me, so even if I wanted to log on to work, I'd have to go home and collect it, but I have no desire to work today. My priority has to be to get my family back, and so I dial Marcus's number to report in sick. I'm shocked when he answers the phone, as I was expecting to leave a voicemail.

'Jenna?'

'Um, hi, Marcus. Listen, about yesterday, I just wanted to say that I'm—'

'Listen, Allie explained what happened yesterday. And under the circumstances I think it would probably be best if you don't log in today.'

'Yes, that's exactly why I was phoning. Things outside of work are… difficult, so if I can have today to sort out a few—'

'No, Jenna, I don't think you understand. I don't just mean for today. I think – and I've spent all night reading up on our HR policies – that it's for the best if you don't return until you've sorted out your mental health concerns.'

I almost drop the phone. What has Allie been saying to him?

'You've nothing to worry about as far as my mental health is concerned,' I say quickly. 'I just need a day, two at most. But once I've spoken to Brett—'

'No, Jenna, listen to me, I don't want you working until you're better.'

Although it's out of character, I'm touched by his concern.

'I assure you, I'm fine, Marcus.'

'That's what she said you'd say.'

'Who?'

'Allie. She said you'd phone and say everything is okay when clearly it isn't.'

'Wait, when did she tell you this?'

'After you ran from the roof terrace. She told me everything that's been going on, and I had no idea things were as bad as they are for you. I wish you'd felt comfortable sharing some of that shit with me.'

'What are you talking about, Marcus?'

'She told me in the strictest confidence because she is concerned about you, but I promise I won't breathe a word of this to anyone in the team. I've told Rose you're taking a few days' leave because of a family emergency, and so she can reschedule any meetings you have booked.'

'No, wait, Marcus, I don't need Rose to—'

'Jenna, just calm down. It's okay. If I'd known the pressure you were under at home I never would have agreed to us pitching to Chip and his team. But now that I do know, I won't allow you to work until things are back on a more even keel. I'm sure Allie can cope in your absence.'

What has she been telling him? Things have only got on top of me in the last week because she entered my life. Things weren't perfect before that, but they've certainly nosedived since I approached her on the train.

'Marcus, what has Allie told you?'

'Don't be cross with her. I could see she was really struggling to open up because she didn't want to betray your confidence, but had to relent because she's so worried about you.'

'Worried about me? She barely knows me.'

'Well, that's not true, is it? She told me how you used to mentor her when she was getting her degree.'

'What? That never happened.'

'Um, Jenna, are you feeling okay?'

'She told you I mentored her?'

'Yeah, that's how the two of you met initially. She said you helped her get the job at Acorns Design and that when you decided to pitch for the Gliders account you thought she'd be the perfect sidekick to support you. I mean, I wish you'd let me in on your little plan – I never realised you were so devious – but it all worked out in the end.'

'Marcus, listen to me, none of this is true.'

'It's okay, Jenna. I'm not really mad. As I say, it's the company's gain really and I think things are going to work out well with Allie. And with you vouching for her, I don't see how anything can go wrong.'

'Marcus, I only met her last Tuesday. I didn't know her at university, and I certainly didn't help her get a job at Acorns. Have you spoken to anyone there about her?'

'No, she gave us a copy of her references, remember?'

I think back to her supplying the printed page of references from Acorns, which I thought was unusual and should have challenged. For all we know she could have forged the documents.

'I think we should phone Acorns and check up on her performance history.'

'We don't need to, Jenna, we've hired her, and so far I'm very impressed with her adaptability and resilience. If you have any more candidates like her, let's get them in for an interview ASAP.'

'Marcus, you're not listening to me: Allie is lying to you. I met her on a train last week and I tried to help her out, but you can't trust her.'

There's a pause on the line that has me checking whether I've lost signal.

'Oh, she warned me you might say something like this. It isn't your fault, Jenna. You're not well.'

'No, this isn't about my mental health, Marcus. She's been lying to everyone from the beginning.'

'Oh, Jenna, I hate that you're going through this right now; you're one of my favourite employees – hell, a friend even – but I think the best thing you can do is get the help you need.'

'Marcus, don't hang up. Please, forget whatever she's told you about me. She's the one who's unstable, *not* me.'

'With all due respect, Allie wasn't the one who tried to push her off the roof terrace yesterday.'

'I swear she's lying about that too! Check the security cameras on the roof terrace and you'll see she's lying.'

'Those cameras aren't operational yet, and it's good for you that they aren't or you might be facing criminal charges.'

'For what?'

'Trying to push someone off a roof is attempted murder, Jenna.'

I freeze.

'Listen, I think it's best for everyone that you not try and contact any of the team while you're recovering,' Marcus continues. 'Chip is happy for Allie to take the lead, and I'm sure he'd want what's best for your health as well. I need to go. Take care of yourself, Jenna.'

'No, wait,' but it's too late, he's already hung up.

The phone tumbles to the bed, and my eyes fall on the mirror on the wall across from me. My skin is deathly pale and no matter how hard I try to deny it, I look exactly like my mother right now.

Is this what it was like for her too? Believing her own lies so strongly that they became her reality?

Allie has told two people that I tried to push her off that roof, but I have no recollection of doing that, so either she's lying to set me up, or I'm truly losing my mind. And there's only one person who might be able to shine any light on the truth.

43

I was tempted to ask Tom to accompany me, but I can't keep using him as a shield. And I want to confront Mum, without her putting on her usual mask because Tom is there. I need to speak to the woman I remember, not the drugged-up mirage. I need to know whether I'm suffering as she did, or whether there's a far grander game at play. I could have driven the ten minutes from the hotel back to my house, but I can't speak to Brett while Allie and Judith are there.

The car park to the private hospital is busier than it was when Tom brought me here on Monday afternoon. With the sky a dark shade of grey, the weathered stone gargoyles perched around the edge of the building somehow look more threatening than before. The building itself looks like it could come crashing down with only the mildest breeze, and they really should put some effort in to cleaning it up. A fresh lick of paint would do wonders, but then maybe that's the point; they don't want to give the impression that this place is anything but a last resort.

I know Tom is still keen to have her released and transferred to a warden-controlled flat, but after the way she went for me on Monday, I'm not sure she should ever be allowed out.

I eventually locate a space and walk back to the main entrance, before signing in. I'm asked to wait, and a moment later I am approached by one of the nurses, who says I should have phoned before coming over as Mum hasn't had a good night.

'We've had to sedate her,' she tells me, 'as she became violent with one of the other residents.'

I know it's unkind to think it, but I wish Tom was here to hear this revelation; I'm not sure he'll believe a second-hand rendition.

'She's calmer now, but not quite as cognisant as usual.'

I thank the nurse and allow her to lead me to the room. I knock and enter, but the room is so dark that I don't immediately see her lying on the bed.

'Hi, Mum, it's Jenna,' I say, crossing and opening the curtains a fraction, to brighten some of the gloom.

'Jennifer? Is that you?'

I grind my teeth rather than correcting her. The nurse did warn me she was less with it today.

'That's right, Mum.'

'Where's Tom?'

There's a part of me that wants to say he's just outside talking to Dr Yates so she'll be on her best behaviour, but I resist.

'It's just me today, Mum. I wanted to come and see you because I need to ask you some questions. Is that okay?'

She doesn't acknowledge.

I had a list of subtle questions I'd planned to ask to avoid setting her off, but I think any subtlety will just be lost on her.

'I wanted to ask you some questions about the Easter I turned seven actually,' I continue. 'Do you remember my seventh birthday? It was on Easter Saturday, and the day after you'd arranged an Easter egg hunt in the garden, but it was so wet that we couldn't do it first thing.'

I don't know why I'm waiting for a response, and continue when one isn't forthcoming.

'You and Dad had a heated argument and he stormed out.'

'Good for nothing son of a bitch!'

I inwardly gasp, uncertain whether she's referring to me or him.

'What I want to know, Mum, is whether he ever admitted to having an affair.'

She doesn't respond.

'You always suspected he was cheating on you, but did he ever admit it to you?'

Again, she doesn't respond.

'What I'm trying to understand is whether you were right to suspect him, or whether it was part of your illness.'

Still nothing. I'm wasting my time.

'Did you ever hear voices? Or see apparitions of people that you knew weren't there?'

I study her face, looking for any sign of whether she's heard me or is lost in her own little world.

'The thing is, Mum,' I take a deep breath, 'I'm not sure if I'm losing my mind. People are saying I've done things that I have no memory of, and I don't know whether they're lying or whether my mind is dissociating the bad things, stopping me from remembering. As an example, when I was here the other day, you told Tom that I knocked your things off your dressing table, but I have no memory of doing that. Can you remember?'

When I look across, her eyes are closed, and I think she's dozed off. I'm wasting my time asking her these questions while she's in this state. The nurse is right: I should have phoned first, as I now feel like I've wasted the forty minutes' drive to get here. It feels wrong just to turn around and head all the way back, especially as it looked as though traffic was starting to build up along the M3.

I stand and cross to the small dressing table where the plastic containers of perfume are. I lift one and sniff the end, and it fills my senses with memories of Mum putting on her finest clothes and dragging us along to various school fêtes and jumble sales. She always insisted on wearing perfume if we were going out, but in hindsight I think that was because she wasn't always good at maintaining hygiene and used the scent to mask that as well.

I hear the bed creak and glance back over my shoulder, but her eyes are still closed, so I slide open the drawer of the dresser, curious to know what got her so agitated when I was over here on Monday. There is a square-shaped jewellery box that starts playing music when I open it. I remember being obsessed with the tiny ballerina that spins in time to the music. I instantly picture myself aged eight or nine, being in Mum's room, and spinning just like the ballerina.

The bed creaks again, so I close the lid and return the box to the drawer. Another glance confirms she's still asleep. Beside the jewellery box are a couple of word puzzle books, the corners well-thumbed, and then an upturned photo frame. I carefully lift it out, turning it to face me, but it isn't a picture of Tom and me as I'm expecting, but a picture of Mum and a woman in a pink cardigan. Mum doesn't look much younger than she is now, and I don't understand why she would have the frame hidden away in the drawer rather than on display.

I carry the frame across to the gap in the curtains so I can see it better, but my eyes widen when they fall on the face of the woman in the pink cardigan. The dark hair isn't in keeping with what I'm used to seeing, but otherwise I'd swear that's Allie.

'What have you got there?' I start as I realise Mum is now out of the bed and standing behind me, her arms reaching out at throat level. 'Stay away from my things,' she snaps, reaching for the frame.

'No, Mum, wait, who is this woman?'

I whip the frame out of her grasp as she reaches for it again.

'Mum, I need you to tell me who the woman in that picture is.'

'That's my daughter, Jennifer.'

I'm thrown by her answer.

'No, Mum, *I'm* your daughter. Jenna is my name now, *not* Jennifer.'

'Yes, that's what I said.'

Maybe it's because it's so dark in here that she can't see the photograph properly. I pull the curtains wider, and hold up the frame beside my own face.

'Mum, I want you to look at this picture and then look at me. Who is the woman in the picture with you?'

'I told you: my daughter Jennifer.'

'No, Mum, I'm your daughter. This is not me in the picture.'

She leans in closer, squinting at the picture.

'No, it's not you. It's my daughter, Jennifer.'

She snatches the frame from me and carries it back to the dressing table, this time standing it beside the perfume containers.

'Then who am I?' I say, following her.

She turns and looks at me.

'Dear me, if you don't know who you are then God help us.'

I pull out my phone and dial Tom's number, but it rings out before eventually going to voicemail.

'Hi, Tom, can you phone me back as soon as you hear this? I'm with Mum and she's saying the strangest things.'

I hang up, trying to keep a lid on my emotions, but unable to process why there would be a photo of Allie with my mum. Why did she ask me so many questions about how Mum died if she knew she was alive? Unless she doesn't know that Dawn is my mum?

No, I don't believe in coincidences. Why didn't Allie say anything when I lied about Mum dying?

'Mum, when did you last see the woman in the picture?'

She doesn't answer, returning to the bed, lying back down and closing her eyes. I cross to the side of the bed, and try again.

'Mum, don't go to sleep. When did you last see your daughter Jennifer?'

She doesn't answer, the small rumble of snoring starting. But I'm not prepared to take no for an answer, and so I place my hands on her arms and try to shake her awake.

'Mum, I need to know how you know Allie. Mum, wake up!'

Her head rolls to the side, but her eyes don't open.

I shake her harder, pulling out the pillow from beneath her head in the hope the discomfort will wake her.

'Mum, wake up. I need you to tell me about Allie.'

The door to the room bursts open and when Tom sees me hovering over Mum, his face is ashen.

'What are you doing?' he asks.

'I was trying to wake her up.'

'The nurse said they gave her a sedative.'

'I know, but she was up and talking a minute ago.'

He looks from me to the pillow I'm still holding.

'No, this isn't what it looks like,' I say my voice rising in panic. 'I swear she was awake and talking a few moments ago, and I need some information from her,' I say, but Tom's attention is solely on Mum, and as he presses two fingers to Mum's neck, he quickly hurries out of the room in search of help.

'This isn't funny, Mum,' I say to her. 'Wake up.'

The nurse who showed me to the room comes in and also presses fingers to Mum's neck, putting her ear towards Mum's mouth before slamming her hand against a red button above the bed.

An alarm instantly sounds overhead and it's all I can do to cover my ears, but it barely blocks out the cacophony. Two other nurses hurry into the room, and the first nurse barks orders at them, but I can't stay here any more. I race into the corridor, hands clamped over my ears until I'm outside, and then I hurry to my car. I need to get home. If Mum won't tell me why she has a photograph of Allie, then I'll ask her directly.

44

It's just gone ten when I make it back to our close. Brett's car is on the drive, but I have no idea if Allie is in there with him or whether Marcus will have insisted she go into London today. I don't know which I'd rather: her in London continuing to push me out of a job, or here with Brett, pushing me out of my home. At least the one thing that came from my visit to Graveside is that I know I'm not crazy.

Are you sure about that?

Mum's ghostly apparition stares back at me in the rear-view mirror.

'I know you're not there,' I say firmly, and the apparition slowly fades to nothing.

I've spent too long worrying that I'm mentally unstable and it's become something of a self-fulfilling prophecy. I need to focus on the fact that I've been the pawn in someone else's game. If Allie knew Mum before we met on the train, then she would have known who I was. That means our meeting probably wasn't just a coincidence.

My phone shows three missed calls from Tom, but I don't have time to explain my actions to him. I need to speak to Brett and convince him that I'm not losing my mind and that Allie has been orchestrating my downfall. Once I have Brett back onside, I'll speak to Tom and tell him what Mum told me.

Taking a deep breath, I climb out of the car, leaving my phone on the charger. If I can get Brett into the car, I can drive us somewhere we won't be overheard by Allie or Judith. I just need to remind Brett he knows me, and in his heart, he knows I would never do anything to endanger the children or him. With this thought at the front of my mind, I enter the house, quietly closing the door behind me to avoid attracting attention to my presence.

Luke and Caley will be at school by now, but Brett should be back from the school run. The kitchen is empty, but the kettle is still warm, so I head through to the living room, but there's no sign of Brett here.

Moving to the foot of the stairs, I listen for any sounds indicating who might be up there, but it is deathly silent. I ascend slowly, straining to hear anything to indicate where Brett might be. The door to Caley's room is ajar, but when I poke my head around it, there's no sign of Allie. Luke's room is also empty, as are my bedroom and en suite. The door to the guestroom is also closed, but I don't go in for fear of running into Judith. I'll check the rest of the house first and if I don't find him before, that will be my last resort.

I resist the urge to call out Brett's name, moving now to my office. The door is closed, but Brett could be inside writing. He hates it when I disturb him midchapter, but our future is more important than his damned second book. I open the door, but freeze when I see Allie pacing inside, wearing my favourite dress suit and Bluetooth headset, her laptop open. Her hair is back to the dark colour I saw in the photograph in Mum's room.

Her eyes widen in shock when they fall on me. She looks so professional, and in many ways like a younger version of myself. I hadn't realised just how deeply she'd inserted herself into our lives. I can see now why Mum could have confused her for me.

'Whoa, Jenna, just stay back,' she says loudly, her tone laced with fear.

'Get the hell out of my house!' I yell in response.

'Just calm down, Jenna. Don't do anything stupid.'

'I said get out of my house.'

I march forwards and grab her hand, trying to drag her towards the door, and she yelps, but too late to get out of the way.

'Please don't hurt me,' she shrieks.

'I know what you're doing,' I fire back, still pulling on her arm. 'Did you really think I'd give up my life without a fight?'

I snatch at the headset and it's only then that I see the blue LED and realise she was on a videocall with Marcus and Chip.

'She's an imposter,' I yell at the screen, 'and I'm going to prove it.'

But when I turn back, she's already bolted from the room. I slam the laptop closed and toss the headset onto the desk and find her in Caley's room, shoving her things into her bag.

'Good, you're packing up,' I say, but she stops and straightens, slowly turning and looking at me. 'I found the picture of you and my mum at Graveside.'

All panic and fear disappear from her eyes in an instant, and a grin slowly spreads across her face.

'You saw your mum today, did you? Well, it's about fucking time!'

At least she's not denying the photo exists. I wish I'd brought my phone in with me and set it to record.

'How is Dawn?'

I picture the urgency with which the nurses rushed into the

room as I was leaving, and the look of shock on Tom's face, but suppress the images.

'How do you know my mum?' I ask instead.

'She's a real special lady is Dawn. Took good care of me when I was at Graveside. Showed me the ropes when I first arrived and took me under her wing. She told me how her own children had her committed against her will, and how her daughter had cut off all contact. She had a gaping hole in her heart, and I filled it.'

'You were a patient at Graveside?'

'No, I worked there when I was training to be a nurse. I couldn't believe that anyone could be so cruel to such a wonderful woman. She'd always get excited when her son Tom would visit, but then she'd be down afterwards because she couldn't understand why you'd cut her out of your life.'

'It wasn't like that.'

'Bullshit! Luke and Caley don't even know they have a second grandmother. Do you know how hard it was for me to play along with that lie? They deserve to know she's alive and well, and she deserves to meet her grandchildren.'

'She's not well. I've seen her pretending that the meds are working, but her anger is still there, hidden, but like an itch that needs to be scratched. One mention of my dad and she snaps.'

She scoffs.

'And that's based on what, one visit in years?'

'No, that's based on years of her physical and mental abuse, and as soon as I saw her this week, the mask slipped and the mum who terrified me for so many years was there.'

'If you ask Caley, she'd say the apple didn't fall far from the tree.'

I step forward, wanting to slap her, but stop myself just in time. Now that I'm closer I can see how she's used makeup to cover the bruising to her eyes following last night's accidental elbow.

'Oh, there's the real you,' she crows. 'I wondered how long it would be until you resorted to violence again.'

'I'm not a violent person, and you've been telling everyone that I tried to push you off the roof when we both know I didn't.'

Her smile widens.

'Funny though, isn't it, how easily both Marcus and Brett believed me? The two men you're closest to in your life believing you'd be so capable of such a heinous act. You really aren't a good judge of character, are you? It took hardly any effort to convince Brett that you're mentally ill.'

Mention of him reminds me why I rushed home from Graveside. I need him to hear what she's saying.

'Where is Brett?'

'He's doing a book signing in Salisbury today. Didn't he mention that? Or maybe he did but you were too focused on yourself to understand what support he needs.'

'How dare you? You don't know anything about me. Our marriage is stronger than you realise.'

'Ha! If that's the case, why did he ask you to stay in a hotel last night?'

She's trying to bait me again, but I bite my tongue.

'You have no idea just how lucky you were. A loving husband and incredible writer allowing you to come along on his publishing journey, who gave you two incredibly bright and vivacious children, and you've put your career ahead of both. A nice house in a nice area. An understanding boss at a company that's really going places. And a wonderful mother that you abandoned.'

I can't listen to any more of this preaching. I need to find Brett.

I leave the room and head downstairs, but I hear Allie giving chase.

'Truth hurts, doesn't it?' she calls after me.

'What would you know? Your whole life is a lie. You told Marcus that I mentored you at university. Did you even study graphic design?'

'According to my CV I did.'

I can't believe how willing I was to take things at face value. She approached me in a vulnerable state, making me want to protect her, and then she played a role to keep me on the hook.

'And what about Clark?'

'Don't you mean Charles?' She laughs. 'I genuinely thought I'd killed him, so I was as shocked as you when we got to his flat and he wasn't there. I hadn't expected you to go and meet him, but he's served his purpose now.'

Memories of the last week are now flooding my mind.

'You broke my perfume bottle.'

'Not on purpose.'

'You deleted the Gliders presentation from my laptop when we met with Chip on Monday.'

'Guilty as charged, but I wanted to show Marcus that he could rely on me when you're gone.'

'I'm not going anywhere.'

'You will. The thing is I wanted to meet you to understand how you could abandon Dawn as you did, but now I see how undeserving of this life you are, and that can't continue.'

'You're crazy.'

'Takes one to know one.'

She barges past me into the kitchen and takes a large knife from the block and brandishes it in my direction. I instinctively take a step backwards and put out my hands in case she charges at me.

'Just stop, Allie. You can't just steal someone's life. It isn't right.'

'I'll give you one chance: leave now and don't look back.'

'You really are crazy. I'm not going anywhere without my family.'

'You don't need to worry about them, Jenna. I will take good care of Luke and Caley, and Brett.'

'You'll never get away with this. Brett and the children won't allow me to just leave.'

'Nobody wants you around any more, Jenna. Can't you see that? In time, Brett will learn to love me in the same way Luke and Caley do.'

'I'm not going anywhere without a fight.'

'Then you leave me no choice.'

'They'll never forgive you if you try and kill me.'

She suddenly screams out before headbutting the cupboard door she's standing beside. I am frozen as I watch the blood stream from her nose. But then she takes the knife and plunges the tip of the blade into her side, screaming out again.

'What are you doing?' I ask, catching her as she stumbles forwards and into my arms.

'Help me,' she calls out, and as I turn, I see Judith standing in the doorway, her mouth aghast.

Oh, God, this is what she planned.

Judith reaches for the phone from the charging dock, and hurries away.

'No, Judith, wait, I didn't...'

But she's already gone. I lower Allie to the floor and hurry after my mother-in-law, but she's locked the door to the guestroom, and I hear her say the word *ambulance*.

I race back to the kitchen, whipping a dishtowel from the radiator and press it to the wound.

'Don't die,' I tell Allie. 'Judith is calling for an ambulance.'

'You should run now,' she whispers to me. 'It's your only chance to get away.'

But I don't move. She wants me to run so that I'll look guiltier, but I'm not going to allow her to pull my strings any more.

45

Blood is still escaping the wound in her side, adding to the small puddle slowly spreading across the linoleum.

'Why did you do this?' I say, searching for a fresh towel I can use to stem the bleeding.

Her face is so pale that the bruising around her bloody nose is now more obvious. Where is the ambulance? I wanted her out of my house but didn't want her to kill herself in my kitchen.

'Allie, stay with me,' I say encouragingly.

I wipe the sweat from my forehead with the back of my hand, only now realising that both my hands are covered in her sticky blood. It is so warm in here, and I can feel the inevitable overwhelm clawing at the edges of my vision. I just need to stay calm until the paramedics arrive. They're coming and then they'll take over.

'Help is on the way, Allie,' I say, forcing myself to smile in an effort to reassure her, but my attempts fail.

Her lips part, but I can't hear what she's trying to say. I lean closer so that my ear is just above her face.

'You brought this on yourself,' she whispers.

I straighten and force myself to make eye contact.

'How? I did nothing to you. What gives you the right to judge me and my actions?'

'I never had a mother who cared for me like Dawn,' she says, but again it's difficult to hear. 'She gave you love, security, and freedom, and you turned your back on her. You don't know what it was like having a mother who'd sooner pay for her next fix than buy baby formula. There were times she would leave me at her dealer's house so she could get high. I spent my fourth birthday locked in my bedroom because she was out begging on the street.'

I had no idea she had such a difficult upbringing, but her pain shouldn't invalidate my own lived experience.

'I'm sorry you had to deal with that, but you don't know what Mum was like when I was growing up. She wasn't well, Allie. She still *isn't* well. Graveside is the safest place she can be, for her sake as much as everyone else's. You were a nurse, can't you see that?'

Her eyelids have closed, and so I push the towel harder against the wound, and jolt her awake.

I start as a shadow crosses over me, and I'm half-expecting to see Mum hovering there, but it's Judith, trembling and gripping the phone like it's some kind of weapon.

'The ambulance is on its way,' she says nervously.

'Good,' I say. 'Can you help me? I'm putting pressure on the wound but blood is still escaping.'

Judith looks from me to Allie and then back again, but looks uncertain.

'Judith, please. I don't want Allie to die. Come down here and press this towel against her side while I try and find something better.'

Judith swallows audibly, before getting down on her hands

and knees, slowly shuffling towards us, but her eyes are glued to the discarded knife on the floor. I pick it up and slide it further away.

'It's all going to be fine,' I say, but I'm not sure for whose benefit it is.

And once Judith's ice-cold hand is on the towel, I leap up and hurry upstairs, opening the airing cupboard and pulling out a pile of spare towels and the green first aid box we keep up here. I open the box, but I'm not sure what is going to help, so I bring it with me and head back downstairs as a veil of flashing blue light falls across the frosted glass of the front door.

Opening it, I tell the two women in green that Allie is in the kitchen. They head in, squeezing past Judith, peppering her with questions.

'She's called Allie,' I hear Judith reply. 'She was stabbed in the side by my daughter-in-law.'

My eyes snap open.

'Wait, no, that's not what happened,' I shout from the doorway. 'She did this to herself. She headbutted the cupboard and then stabbed herself.'

One of the paramedics glances up at me, her face masked in doubt, but gives a short, sharp nod.

'You have to believe me,' I announce to the room. 'She did this to herself. I swear on my life.'

And that's when it slowly dawns on me. She's spent the last week sowing seeds of doubt in Brett, Judith and Marcus. Telling them I'm struggling with my mental health and have been lashing out, while also feeding my own paranoia, scratching away until I cracked and threw that bloody glass at the wall. The incident at the pool, lying about me trying to push her off the roof, and now leading Judith to believe that I attacked and stabbed her.

Judith backs out of the kitchen, giving me a withering stare.

'Like mother, like daughter,' she mutters under her breath. 'If I'd known the truth about you I would have warned wee Brett away from you. May God have mercy on your soul.'

And that's the final nail in the coffin. All of this will be tied back to my upbringing and the mental illness they'll all assume I have inherited from Mum.

The front door opens and I see Brett standing there, my knight in shining armour, only he's standing with two police officers and is holding a piece of paper in his hands. He leans towards one of the officers and I hear him say, 'That's her.'

I don't resist as the officer steps forward and introduces himself, telling me that I am under arrest, and cuffing my bloody hands behind my back.

* * *

The rest of the day passes in a blur. I am locked into a cage in the back of a police van, and driven to Southampton police station. I've driven past it so many times before but never been inside until today. The two officers are so courteous, constantly asking if I'm okay, and if I need anything, but I can't speak. Internally, I know my body has shut down, because it no longer believes any of this is real. It is just a nightmare that I can't control and in a few minutes I'll wake filled with huge relief.

Only, I don't wake up. I am processed instead. They ask me to confirm my name, date of birth and home address. They take photographs of me and then they ask me to remove my clothes, which are placed into bags. They take samples of Allie's blood from my hands and also my fingerprints. I consent when they ask for a DNA sample, and then I dress in the jogging trousers and sweatshirt they give me.

This can't be real. It feels real, but I will wake in a minute.

I lie on the firm bed in the cell, staring up at the ceiling, and what feels like minutes later my GP and a psychiatrist enter the room, examine me, and ask a series of questions. He wants to know how I'm feeling, but I can't tell him because my mind hasn't caught up with all of this yet.

The questions keep coming.

'Are you or anyone else in danger of being harmed? How and when did your behaviour change? Are you being aggressive? If so, how? Have you tried to harm yourself or others? If so, how and when did it happen? Have you harmed yourself or others in the past? Have you stopped eating, drinking or bathing? What might realistically happen if you're not detained?'

The two men tell the custody sergeant they're unable to make a diagnosis because I won't answer their questions, and then both say they'll sign the paperwork. My GP tells me they're going to take me to a hospital where I can be properly assessed and treated. He says something about 'Section 2' but I'm not really listening because I'm waiting to wake up and for the nightmare to be over.

Moments later I'm back in the cage in the police van, my hands once again cuffed, but this time my GP is in the van with us. He continues to pepper his questions at me, but my voice won't engage.

I want to scream that none of this is real. I didn't stab Allie. I didn't try to push her off the roof. They've got it wrong and she's been orchestrating this whole mess. When I saw her looking so flustered on the train, I was trying to do the right thing, but I should have known that no good deed goes unpunished.

When the van reaches its destination, I am released from the cage, but when I look up and see the weathered gargoyles staring back down at me, I realise just how much trouble I'm in. I shoulder-barge the officer who is holding my left arm, and then I spin around and try to run back along the extended gravel driveway, but the officer catches me within seconds, and despite my wailing they lead me towards the building where all hope is lost.

46

'How are you feeling this morning, Jenna?' I didn't catch the doctor's name as I was led into the room, or if I did, I've subsequently forgotten it. He must be in his sixties, with a grey nest of hair, and a kind face. His half-rimmed spectacles hang at the end of his long, hook-like nose, but he is painfully thin. The white lab coat hangs off his gaunt frame.

'Are you feeling calmer this morning?' he asks when I don't respond.

I don't know what medication they have me on but it's like there's a blocker between my ability to think and my ability to communicate. I want to shout at him that I can't be calm, knowing I'm still trapped in Graveside, whilst Allie is out there poisoning my loved ones against me and stealing my life. She is the one who should be here, *not* me. It's been three or four days – it's hard keeping track of time with no watch, phone or clock to refer to – since the police officers dragged me inside against my will. It didn't seem to matter how often and loudly I screamed about my innocence, I was led upstairs to the secure wing, and forced into a padded cell. Should they really have been surprised I'd try to get away at the earliest opportunity?

Every hour since I've felt eyes watching me from the reinforced window in my cell. They're observing me and my behaviour, trying to determine if I'm as crazy as Mum, but they won't listen to me when I tell them how Allie has instigated this whole scenario.

'You certainly seem calmer this morning. And that's key to us being able to assess you properly, Jenna. Do you understand? The calmer you are, the easier it will be. At the moment you are here under a Section 2 order, which means we can keep you for up to twenty-eight days, but if we're unable to make a clear diagnosis in that time, we can apply for a Section 3, which will allow us to detain you for up to six months.'

You can't do this to me, I try to say, but my lips won't move. What the hell have they sedated me with?

'We don't want any more of that nasty business from yesterday. Attacking the staff will only make things worse. You understand that, don't you?'

'I... want... to... see... Brett,' I say, but it sounds like I'm talking in slow motion as I struggle to enunciate the words.

'You want to see your husband, Brett, I understand that, and I can allow that to happen, but I want something in return from you. I want you to answer my questions, Jenna. Help me to help you.'

'O... kay.'

'Good. Brett is here today, actually he's waiting to see you, so the sooner you answer my questions, the sooner you can see him.'

Brett is here? Thank God. He must have come to his senses and realised what Allie has been up to. Or maybe Luke and Caley have been badgering him to have me released because they're not as onside as Allie claimed. My sense of self-worth feels boosted, and my mind engages with the doctor's voice.

'I want to know why you attacked Allie.'

'I didn't.'

He frowns at this.

'Would you like to tell me what happened then?'

'She's trying... to steal my family.'

'She's recovering in hospital from a serious injury. An injury you caused, Jenna.'

'No. She... did it to... herself.'

'You think Allie stabbed herself, do you? You don't remember slamming her head into the cupboard and then reaching for the knife?'

'I didn't... She did it.'

'Your mother-in-law witnessed you holding the knife, Jenna.'

I should have known Judith would be involved in this somehow. It would certainly suit her agenda against me to side with the cuckoo.

'No.'

'She also mentioned you waving a knife at her over the weekend. The same knife.'

'I didn't do this,' I say firmly, but the snatches of memory are whizzing through my mind so quickly that I can't focus.

'I'm telling you what the police have told me, Jenna. They say witnesses on a videocall saw you barge into a room, shouting incoherently at Allie, following which you both left the room, and the next witness – your mother-in-law – found Allie on the floor with a damaged face and bleeding from the side, and you standing over her.'

When he puts it like that, I can see why they would reach that conclusion, but that doesn't mean it's true. I've spent the last week questioning my actions, but I know in my heart that I didn't do those things. But I've had days to relive the memories of the last week, and whilst I thought I was losing my mind, I know now I didn't do the things Allie accused me of. I vividly remember the shock of Allie stabbing herself. This is all part of her plan, but I can't let her win.

'She's lying.'

'Who's lying, Jenna?'

'Allie. She's telling lies about me. She is setting me up.'

His brow furrows again.

'But why would Allie do that to you, Jenna? She's your friend.'

'No. She hates me.'

'Nobody hates you, Jenna.'

'Allie does. She told me she wants me to suffer like my mum did.'

His eyes suddenly widen, and I hope I'm finally starting to get through to him.

'You came to see your mum on Wednesday, didn't you? You came to see her here. Can you tell me what happened when you saw her?'

I picture her snatching the photo frame from me, telling me that Allie was her daughter.

'She was confused… She knows Allie.'

'Yes, she did. I know Allie too, and she is a bright, very capable nurse, who is very much missed around here.'

If only he knew how sick and twisted she is.

'No. Allie should be here, not me.'

He sighs.

'You really believe that Allie is your enemy, don't you?'

'Yes.'

'And that's why you attacked her, isn't it?'

'No. I didn't.'

'You attacked your mother as well, didn't you, Jenna?'

I picture the blood draining from Tom's face as his eyes fell on the pillow.

'No.'

'Your mum suffered a heart attack when you were here, Jenna, but she is recovering, you should be pleased to hear.'

I don't like it when people tell me how I should and shouldn't feel. I genuinely don't know how I feel about this news, given how difficult she's made my life. But it hurts that Tom could believe I would be capable of trying to kill her. I see now, I shouldn't have rushed off. I should have stuck around to make sure Mum was well, and should have spoken to Tom about what happened, but I was obsessed with getting to Brett.

'I want to see my husband,' I say next.

'Okay. I'm happy for us to take a break, but I want us to continue our discourse this afternoon. I want what's best for you, Jenna, and I hope you come to accept that sooner rather than later.'

He fixes me with an uncomfortable stare, before nodding and exiting the room, leaving me on my own. I'd love to try and get out but all the doors here are secured and only open with security passes. I can see now my only way out is for Brett to appeal the Section 2 order.

The door opens and two orderlies enter carrying blue restraints.

'I don't need those,' I say, but they ignore me, one moving behind my chair and securing the waist belt I'm wearing to it. They then proceed to fasten restraints around my wrists and to the arms of the chair. At least the sedative seems to be wearing off a bit.

What do they think I'm going to do to my husband?

This is so embarrassing. The way they're treating me is how they rightly treated Mum all those years ago, but I'm not her, and

I haven't done any of the things she did. My eyes are watering at the hopelessness of my situation when Brett is led in by the doctor in the white lab coat.

He waits until the door is closed behind him, before sitting across the table from me. My lips tremble as I finally lay eyes on him. He also looks visibly upset, and it's breaking my heart to see him like this.

'How are you doing?' he asks, the emotion in his voice strained.

'I've been better,' I say, adding a small laugh that he doesn't reciprocate. 'How are you? How are Luke and Caley?'

'They're missing you, that's for sure. They wanted to come with me today, but... I don't want them seeing you like this.'

That they wanted to see me warms my soul, but I'm also annoyed that he's kept them from me, but I agree that I wouldn't want them seeing me restrained in this way, like a common criminal.

An awkward silence descends, with neither of us knowing how to start the conversation.

'I'm not crazy,' I eventually say. 'I know you were worried, and I was too, but I know now what happened. Allie was behind it all.'

He watches me, blinking back his tears, but gives me space to continue.

'She used to work here. Did you know that? I found a photograph of her and my mum here. They were close, according to Allie, and she forced herself into our lives so she could get revenge on me for abandoning Mum. That's what she said to me when we were in the house on Wednesday. I'm guessing she didn't tell you any of that, did she?'

Still he remains silent.

'She said she wanted to make me suffer, so she got close to us, and then started to sow seeds of doubt into everyone's minds, even my own. She lied about what happened between us on the roof at work, and she's lying about me trying to hurt her. I know it sounds crazy, but I swear she stabbed herself.'

He leaps to his feet and turns his back on me, and for a moment I think he's going to ask the orderly to let him out of the room, but instead he throws his arms up into the air, interlocking his fingers and bringing them down slowly, resting them on the back of his head.

'I'm telling the truth, Brett. If you love me, then you'll believe what I'm telling you. She's trying to steal you all away from me.'

'Just stop,' he finally says, a flash of anger in his tone. 'Would you just stop with all this paranoia?' He slowly turns to face me, and I can see the trail of tears on his cheeks. 'Have you listened to yourself?'

I desperately want to reach out to him and wipe away those tears, but I cannot move in this chair.

'I know it sounds crazy, Brett, I can hear how mad it sounds, but I swear it's the truth. Her intention from the start was to see me wind up in here, just like Mum, and for my family to abandon me as I did to Mum.'

'Just stop, Jenna. Please?'

'No, I won't stop until you *listen* to me, Brett.'

'You're breaking my heart, sweetheart. I hate seeing you stuck like this.'

'Then help me get out of here and prove to you that she's causing all of this.'

'Do you want to know why I signed the Section 2 paperwork?'

The question throws me. Brett signed the paperwork that had me sectioned here? I thought it was just the GP and that psychiatrist I met at the police station. He's part of the reason I'm here, and my heart breaks a little more.

'I signed it because the doctor asked whether I thought you

were a danger to yourself or anyone else, and I honestly think that you are.'

'I'm not,' I shout back at him. 'How can you believe her over me?'

'Do you think I want to believe that you tried to kill your mum and Allie in the same day? Do you know how much that is hurting me? I have Luke and Caley constantly asking what's wrong with you and why you attacked Allie, and I don't know how to answer them.'

'Tell them the truth: I didn't do any of this. What Tom saw was me trying to wake Mum, not harm her, and Allie stabbed herself.'

He covers his face with both hands, slowly shaking his head.

'Please, Brett, try and see it from my perspective. Put yourself in my shoes: accused of something you didn't do and knowing the real culprit is still out there living with your family.'

He finally lowers his hands.

'Allie is still in hospital after what you did to her. She almost died, for Christ's sake. You can't keep blaming other people for the mess you've caused.'

'I didn't cause any of this.'

'Listen to me, Jenna, because this is important: you're not well. I don't know how this has happened, but none of us want to see you suffering any longer. You need to accept that, and get the treatment you really need. Please? For all of our sakes. That's the only way you're going to get out of here.'

47

Something must be happening today, because this is the most alert I've felt in I don't know how long. There are fresh flowers on the table by the window, and there is bright sunshine pouring in through the open curtains. One of the nurses knocks gently and asks how I am, and places fresh clothes at the foot of the bed, before asking if I'd like a cup of tea with my medication. I thank her, but ask for a glass of orange juice instead. She says she'll see what she can drum up and closes the door behind her, allowing me to shower and dress.

My hair feels brittle and lifeless between my fingers, but that's the result of using cheap supermarket-branded hair products. But beggars can't be choosers. The navy-blue dress with large white spots feels loose and comfortable on my skin, and so I sit at the table staring out of the window, while I wait for the nurse to return with my juice.

There is a knock at the door a moment later and she enters, placing the glass in front of me, along with the small paper pot containing four pills. I tip them into my mouth and take a swig of the juice, opening my mouth and raising my tongue so she can check I've swallowed them. Satisfied, she takes her leave.

Through the window I can see a bird building a nest, carefully placing the twigs she's collected from the ground by the trunk into place, yet all the time watching for any threats. I know how she feels. It wasn't that long ago that was my life. Working all hours to finance the home that would keep my family safe, all the while waiting for the inevitable catastrophe that would threaten it all.

You mustn't think like that any more, I hear the corrective voice in my head tell me.

I don't hear the knock at the door, but a moment later Brett is beside the table, carrying a small tray with a stainless-steel pot and three cups.

'How are you?' he asks, and I force a smile.

'I'm fine. How are you?'

He looks in good shape, has lost that paunch around his waist, and his skin is shining with vitality, but still as handsome as ever. He asks what I've been up to this week, and I tell him about the small garden I've been tending to each day, how it brings me peace, and huge amounts of dopamine when I see the delicate plants sprouting through the soil. He doesn't mention Allie these days, and I don't ask.

'I've brought someone to see you,' he tells me, crossing back to the bedroom door, and a moment later, he returns, pushing a small pram.

I frown when I look at him. Did I know he was having another child? I can't remember us discussing it, but then I barely remember so many things now.

'Mum, I'd like you to meet your granddaughter,' he says, lifting a precious bundle out of the pram.

I double take on his face.

'Brett?'

'No, Mum, it's Luke, remember?'

I blink several times, the overwhelm clawing at the edges of my vision.

'No, you're not Luke. Luke is my little boy. Stop being silly, Brett.'

He takes an uneasy step backwards, returning the baby to the pram.

'Mum, are you feeling okay? Do you want me to fetch one of the nurses?'

What is happening? How can this be Luke? The man before me is too old to be my son.

'Dad's in California, Mum. Remember?'

I press my hands to my forehead, digging my nails into the flesh, trying to claw at the memories.

'Where's Caley? I want to see Caley.'

'Caley lives in Los Angeles with Dad and...' He catches himself. 'Caley's not around today, but she's doing well. She's working on a new movie at the moment, a part Dad wrote specifically for her. When it comes out I'll bring a copy of it here and we can watch it together. Won't that be nice?'

'I... I don't understand. How can you be Luke?'

A woman enters, beautiful with jet-black hair, and places an arm around his waist.

'She's not having a good day,' I hear him mutter under his breath. 'You should probably take Simone back to the car. We'll try again next week.'

She kisses his cheek, before waving in my direction.

'I hope you're feeling better soon, Jenna,' she says, with a sympathetic smile, before pushing the pram out of the room.

'Who was that woman?' I ask, panic tightening my chest.

'Monique is my wife, Mum. You've met her so many times

before. But listen, don't worry if you can't remember. This happens sometimes. You have good days and not so good days. But I'm here, um, and I'm happy to stay for a bit. Maybe we could play some gin rummy. You always like it when we do.'

This must be a bad dream. This Luke must be in his early thirties at least, but I've only been at Graveside for a few weeks. Haven't I?

I scrape my chair back and stand, needing to see the truth with my own eyes, and so I approach my dressing table, the small plastic bottles of perfume in the size order I like, and stare at the old woman with scraggly grey hair in the mirror. My hand shoots to my mouth.

No, that can't be me. That woman is so old. It's like staring at my own mother.

I feel Luke take my arm and lead me to the edge of the bed.

'Calm down, Mum, stop screaming,' he's saying, but it feels like the walls are closing in around me.

'I'll fetch one of the nurses, Mum,' I hear him say. 'It's going to be okay. Today is just a bad day.'

* * *

MORE FROM M. A. HUNTER

Another book from M. A. Hunter, *The Reunion*, is available to order now here:

https://mybook.to/TheReunionBackAd

ACKNOWLEDGEMENTS

Thank you so much for reading *The Woman on Platform 8*, and for taking the time to read this final word from me.

These last couple of years have been a huge learning curve for me. At forty-three, I thought I was too old to be taught new tricks, but receiving a diagnosis of Autism and ADHD has shown me just how little I know of myself. It is difficult to describe what it feels like to be told that there is a reason why so many things I've experienced have felt so much tougher than for others. There's a sense of relief that I'm not broken, but that my brain processes things in a different way to everybody else. There's also a feeling of disappointment to know that things could have been easier had I known sooner. But the biggest thing I'm struggling with at the moment is trying to understand who I really am, because so much of my life has been spent masking my difficulties and pretending to be someone I'm not that now I don't know who the real me is.

Don't panic, you can put your violin away, I'm not looking for sympathy here. I know how lucky I am and I genuinely wouldn't change a thing about my life as it is today. And actually, these diagnoses have helped to explain the speed with which I am able to develop and write stories. It always panics me when other authors ask how many books I write a year, because when I tell them I write three books a year on average, their faces drop. And when I add that I also have a fulltime job and a young family to support, I quickly become the most hated person in the room.

They can't understand how I achieve it, but I can't understand how their brains can't see the characters and scenes slotting together like a jigsaw puzzle. I know I wouldn't have this creative ability without Autism and ADHD, and I wouldn't swap my brain for anything.

I hope that Jenna's thoughts and observations have helped shine a light on how a neurodivergent brain *can* function. Her views are unique to her and she doesn't represent the experiences of all autistic individuals, but the internal monologue that punctuates her every thought is something I experience all the time. If anything you've read has resonated with you, then I strongly encourage you to dig a little deeper. There are so many resources online, but I can recommend The National Autistic Society (https://www.autism.org.uk) and ADHD UK (https://adhduk.co.uk) as great starting points.

If you enjoyed *The Woman on Platform 8* then please tell all of your friends and family (and any other person who will listen) how great it is. And please do get in touch with me via the usual social channels to let me know what you thought about it (remember to be kind).

I often have too many different ideas for books, and never know which one to choose, which is why it's great to have my agent, Emily Glenister at the DHH Literary Agency, in my corner. She's always ready to share her opinion and remind me that I'm a far better writer than I ever give myself credit for. It means so much having someone to champion my books and I'm indebted to her honesty and support.

Thank you also to my new eagle-eyed editor Victoria Britton at Boldwood Books (and to Emily Yau for all her support with my previous books). The twisted ending to this story was the result of Victoria pushing me, and although it's early days, I already feel like this will be a winning partnership.

The whole team at Boldwood Books deserve huge credit for the work they do in producing my books in the array of formats available. From line and copy editing, proof-reading, cover design, audiobook creation, and marketing. The fact that you're reading these acknowledgements is testament to the brilliant job they do.

My children are an inspiration to me every day, and as they continue to grow so quickly, I am eternally grateful that I get to play such an important role in their development. They continue to show one another affection, patience and kindness, and make being their dad that bit easier. I'd like to thank my own parents and my parents-in-law for continuing to offer words of encouragement when I'm struggling to engage with my muse.

It goes without saying that I wouldn't be the writer I am today without the loving support of my beautiful wife and soulmate Hannah. She keeps everything else in my life ticking over so that I can give what's left to my writing. She never questions my method or the endless hours daydreaming while I'm working through plot holes, and for that I am eternally grateful.

And thanks must also go to YOU for reading *The Woman on Platform 8*. Please do post a review to wherever you purchased the book from so that other readers can be enticed to give it a try. It takes less than two minutes to share your opinion, and I ask you do me this small kindness.

I am active on Facebook, Twitter/X, Instagram, and now TikTok, so please do stop by with any messages, observations, or questions. Hearing from readers of my books truly brightens my days and encourages me to keep writing, so don't be a stranger. I promise I *will* respond to every message and comment I receive.

Stef (a.k.a. M. A. Hunter)

ABOUT THE AUTHOR

M. A. Hunter is the pen name of Stephen Edger, the bestselling author of psychological and crime thrillers, including the Kate Matthews series. Born in the north-east of England, he now lives in Southampton where many of his stories are set.

Sign up to M. A. Hunter's mailing list here for news, competitions and updates on future books.

Visit M. A. Hunter's website: stephenedger.com/m-a-hunter

Follow M. A. Hunter on social media:

- X x.com/AnAutieAuthor
- facebook.com/AnAutieAuthor
- instagram.com/AnAutieAuthor
- tiktok.com/@anautieauthor
- bookbub.com/authors/stephen-edger
- goodreads.com/stephenedger

ALSO BY M. A. HUNTER

The Boat Party

One Wrong Turn

Every Step You Take

Sleepwalker

The Reunion

The Woman on Platform 8

The Tenants

THE *Murder* LIST

THE MURDER LIST IS A NEWSLETTER DEDICATED TO SPINE-CHILLING FICTION AND GRIPPING PAGE-TURNERS!

SIGN UP TO MAKE SURE YOU'RE ON OUR HIT LIST FOR EXCLUSIVE DEALS, AUTHOR CONTENT, AND COMPETITIONS.

SIGN UP TO OUR NEWSLETTER

BIT.LY/THEMURDERLISTNEWS

Boldwood

Boldwood Books is an award-winning fiction publishing company seeking out the best stories from around the world.

Find out more at www.boldwoodbooks.com

Join our reader community for brilliant books, competitions and offers!

Follow us
@BoldwoodBooks
@TheBoldBookClub

Sign up to our weekly deals newsletter

https://bit.ly/BoldwoodBNewsletter